THE DROWNING GOD

THE DROWNING GOD

JAMES KENDLEY

HARPER

VOYAGER
IMPULSE

An Imprint of HarperCollins Publishers

EPub Edition JULY 2015 ISBN: 9780062360656

Print Edition ISBN: 9780062360663

10 9 8 7 6 5 4 3 2 1

To Renée Boudreau Kendley, the love of my life, who believed in this book from the start.

THE DROWNING GOD

CHAPTER 1

The man smiled up at Hanako from the water's edge. He seemed very nice, but something was wrong.

"Come see him," the man said. "Right here on the bank, he has a beautiful present for you."

Hanako wasn't even supposed to leave the sidewalk. Everyone knew the canals were dangerous.

"I'll get in trouble if I get muddy."

"He'll take care of you, heh-heh. He's waiting for you."

The man wore gray Zenkoku Corporation coveralls just like the ones her father wore every day. The man's smile was very wide, and his eyes were very big and bright. He was like a comedian on TV. Hanako stepped off the sidewalk.

Just as she started down the embankment, the wild spring wind brought the stench of rotting fish up from the canal.

"Ugh! What stinks?" She ran back to the sidewalk.

"What, that smell? Just the canal. It only lasted a second. See? Heh-heh. It's already gone." The man beckoned with both hands. He was begging. "Come see him! He'll take you to a magical world."

Hanako was altogether doubtful of magic, but she knew that if magic were real, it wouldn't stink of fish. She also knew the man was lying. He was dangerous in an adult way that she only dimly understood. She couldn't outrun him, and there was nowhere to hide. Empty sidewalk stretched to either side. Somewhere behind her, the fencing that ran along the sidewalk was loose, just in one spot. Beyond that fence, there was nothing, just the back entrances to boarded-up shops, but the loose fencing was her only hope. She had to go somewhere.

She bowed politely as she backed away from the water. "I can't be late for school." She stumbled as she bumped into the fence. "Perhaps we can go to a magical world another day."

The man was still smiling as he charged up the bank.

She turned to the fencing. The loose spot was only a few steps away, and she scooted under. Her satchel strap caught, and she turned to free it.

The strap wasn't caught. The man had it, and then he had her arm. He ripped the satchel away from her. She arched her back and planted her feet so he couldn't pull her under. He still smiled, but his laughter wheezed from behind his bared teeth: "Heh-heh-heh . . ."

Hanako bent forward to bite his hand, but she couldn't reach it. Then he grabbed at her pigtail with the other hand. She could reach that one. She sank her teeth into the webbing between his thumb and his forefinger. The stench of rotting fish filled her nostrils. She closed her eyes and bit down harder.

Her mouth filled with a coppery taste like ten-yen coins. The man yanked her against the chain link, but she wriggled sideways and spread her knees to make herself bigger. The man released her arm to grab her leg, and just as his fingertips touched her ankle, Hanako rolled away. She rolled and rolled until he could not reach her, and then she sat up spitting out his nasty blood.

As she sat up, a boy walked up the bank behind the man. The boy seemed distorted, as if she were looking at him through deep water. The boy's mouth was much too wide, and his hands were much too large for his lanky arms. He looked very, very sick, Hanako thought.

She stared at the boy too long. The man tried to pinch shut his bleeding hand, but the crimson blood continued to flow. "Heh-heh-heh . . ." The man's smile was so wide that it looked painful. He gave up on the hand and let his blood trickle into the weeds. He didn't even look at her as he started up the fence.

She jumped up and ran to the back doors of the abandoned shops. Chain link rattled behind her. She reached the nearest door—locked and rusted shut. She looked up and down the narrow lane. There was no use knocking. No one would answer, and these corroded doors would never open.

She heard the man drop to the asphalt behind her.

By the time she turned, he was almost on her. She dodged right, and he dodged to stop her, but she dug in her heels and ran left. She didn't look back. He was close behind her, closer with each step.

She ran toward a small black gap between buildings. She wouldn't make it, but she ran anyway. As his fingers closed on the back of her neck, she dove headfirst for the gap. His grip kept her upright, just for a second, and then his fingers slipped. She bounced off both walls, but she didn't fall. She ran faster.

The space between the buildings was very tight, crowded with ducting. The rotten-fish man wouldn't fit through it, but she would.

Hanako burst out onto the shopping street between the hardware store and the old bakery. Both were boarded up. It was a good thing she hadn't stopped to knock.

The street was empty except for two old women staring at her in surprise. Her throat burned, and she was still spitting blood, but she held her breath as she peered back between the buildings. Sure enough, the man had stopped at the ducting. He was too big to fit under, and the space was so tight that he couldn't pull himself over. He stared back at her. His smile twisted and his eyes became brighter and wider. "Heh-heh-heh-heh-HEHHH . . ."

Hanako whipped her head back and shrank against

the cool bricks of the bakery. The rotten-fish man had her satchel. It was neatly patterned with stickers from her friend Sachiko, and she would never get it back. It was all too terrible. She burst into tears.

The old greengrocer was first to her side. Within a few seconds, Hanako was surrounded. She had never seen so many people on the shopping street. A high school student ran to the village police station, and he came back with two young patrolmen. A chubby one came up huffing and puffing a few minutes later. He was a sergeant, they said. One young patrolman ran to catch the rotten-fish man, another one took her to the village police station, and the sergeant jogged off to look for the chief.

At the village police station, the young patrolman helped Hanako rinse the blood out of her mouth. He washed her face and smoothed her hair, and then he gave her hot tea and ginger crisps. She said she wasn't sorry for biting the rotten-fish man. She said she would never apologize, not even if she had to go to jail. The patrolman said she would not go to jail. Her mother took forever to get there, and after hugs and kisses, she and the patrolman both asked her questions. She started crying again when she told them about her satchel, and they told her she would get it back. Then her father came, and he was very angry. Hanako started crying harder, but her mother said that he was angry with the rotten-fish man, not with her.

Morning became afternoon, and Hanako met more police and answered the same questions over and over again. She overheard that the police had caught the rotten-fish man quickly. High school students found him first, and by the time the police got there, the students had the man surrounded at the canal bridge. They were fencing at school that week, so most of them had practice sticks. They made the man kneel properly, and they smacked him hard when he tried to stand.

Hanako and her parents stayed in an office crowded with dark furniture. Every surface was covered with yellowed doilies that stank of cigarette smoke. Just outside the door, one policeman told another that the man had a deep wound between the thumb and forefinger of his left hand; Hanako had bitten clean through.

Her father looked at her with an expression she didn't understand. He laid his hand on her head, just for a second, and she didn't know what to say.

Later, an officer told them that the rotten-fish man's name was Hiroyasu Ogawa. His wife had gone somewhere else, he didn't have a job, and he lived alone in an apartment block on the other side of the canal. Before he lost his job, he had worked at Zenkoku Fiber, where her father worked.

Her mother held her close and asked everyone else to leave.

Finally, the chief of the village police station came. He smelled of dandruff and mothballs. He gave her satchel back to her, and she started crying again. Everything made her cry that day, and she was getting tired of it. The old chief told her that the rotten-fish man would not bother her anymore, and she believed him.

By the time she got home, it was already dark. She dropped to her mat and slipped into the dreamless sleep of the innocent pure. For Hanako Kawaguchi, it was finished.

For her village, it was beginning all over again.

CHAPTER 2

Detective Takuda rode in the back of the squad car. On the seat beside him lay two slim folders. One contained the incident report on the attempted abduction of Hanako Kawaguchi. The other contained all that was officially known of Hiroyasu Ogawa, the suspect.

Officer Mori drove. Takuda hadn't really needed a driver; he knew the way to Oku Village very well. Even so, he had requested Mori. The young officer was smart and tough, and he understood that procedure was the heart and soul of police work. Takuda had come to depend on him.

A winding, two-lane road through the forest took them down from the mountain pass and into the Naga River valley's southern end. The trees fell away as the car rounded the last curve and hit the steep straightaway down to the Naga River. The old dam loomed above them to the south, and the narrow, eye-shaped

valley spread out below them in the spring sunlight:
The strangled river wound north past Oku Village,
the irregular net of the old canal system held the village together, and the reservoir formed by the lower
dam glistened at the valley's narrow northern end. On
the reservoir's northwestern shore, the Zenkoku Fiber
plant poured pinkish haze from a neat row of smoke-
stacks. It was just as Takuda remembered it.

Takuda studied the valley as they descended to the
bridge, but when they crossed the river, he didn't look
down into the water.

"Detective, you said you've been here before, didn't
you? Which way should we go?"

"Turn right on the river road, by the Farmers' Co-
op," he said, feigning interest in the folders. There
were other roads they could take, roads that would
keep them far away from the river, but he refused to
avoid it. He was no longer a child. "Follow the river
until the main canal cuts off northwest. Cross the
bridge and keep the main canal to your left and the
river to you right. That will take you directly to the
shopping street."

They drove on in silence. The Farmers' Co-op
building, little more than a thatched barn, appeared
abandoned. The mud-and-lath walls were sloughing
their plaster shell, and the roof straw was black with
fungus. *Father would be pleased.*

The houses grew more numerous as Takuda and
Mori approached Oku Village. Things had changed.
There were traffic lights at the intersections now, and

there were guardrails on most bridges over the main canal. Fallen plum blossoms floated on the current into irrigation channels branching off westward from the main canal, following the current to gates opened to flood the rice paddies for the first planting. The next day, farmers would open the gates on the east side. The rotation was the same every year, as regular as the seasons, as sure as sunrise. The canal slid past the squad car window as if flowing straight from Takuda's memory, as if he had never left.

Slowly, so slowly that he almost didn't notice, his attention was drawn by the Naga River to his right.

Despite the dams, it still ran deep and swift, still carving a new channel in the folds of its older, wider bed. It was tamer now, controlled by engineers at the dams and monitored at every canal gate. It watered fields and filled reservoirs, bringing life to the Naga River valley. *Safe as milk.*

It made Takuda's flesh crawl. He watched the current until he felt Mori's gaze. Their eyes met in the rearview mirror, and Mori quickly looked back at the road.

"What is it, Officer?"

"Nothing, Detective. Nothing at all."

Mori drove on impassively, and he refused to look at Takuda through the mirror again. Takuda sat in the backseat willing him to do so. Why had Mori been watching him? Did Mori sense his unease? Would the young officer be foolish enough to say so if he did? Takuda doubted it. Mori was too precise for idle talk, especially with a detective ten years his senior. Mori's hair was regulation length, his uniform collar was knife-edge sharp, and his hat was at the correct angle. His uniform gloves were spotlessly white, and his hands were at exactly ten o'clock and two o'clock on the steering wheel. Even on this deserted country road, he reflexively checked his side mirrors every few seconds. Avoiding Takuda's gaze made him avoid checking the rearview mirror, breaking his rhythm.

Takuda decided to just let the boy do his job. He spent the rest of the trip pretending to study the skimpy files.

There were no visitors' spots at the Oku Village police station, but it didn't matter. They could have parked on the sidewalk without disturbing foot traffic. They stood for a moment, looking up and down the grubby shopping street. There were more storefronts than people.

"I've never seen so many boarded-up shops. It's like a postwar newsreel."

Takuda turned up his collar. "It's been happening for forty years. The young people run away to the cities as soon as they can."

No one was on duty to greet them at the station. The old squad room hadn't changed. Takuda scanned the tiny offices on the perimeter and found a pale, gray-haired man reading a newspaper. A small sign above the office door gave the man's title. Takuda had heard about the promotion, but he had not truly believed it until this day.

"Chief Nakamura."

The old man looked up from his paper. He showed no sign of recognition as he stood to greet the detective.

Takuda introduced himself and Mori, and he had Mori present the bean-jam cakes they had brought from the city. Nakamura accepted the cakes with three more bows than necessary. Takuda dismissed Mori and asked if Nakamura had time to sit and talk. The old man accepted with a look of surprise.

"Most visitors from the prefectural office are in a hurry to get out of here." He motioned for a young patrolman to bring them tea. "Yes, yes, we can sit and talk about this abduction. Attempted abduction, I mean." He led Takuda into a dingy conference room with stained wallpaper and a reek of stale tobacco. "You'll be taking the suspect with you, I assume."

"No. We have not yet decided whether to take custody. It will depend mostly on the prosecutor."

"Mostly. I see. Well. I wish you would take him. He's stinking up our only holding cell."

A grizzled sergeant brought tea on a tray. He served it delicately, even though the dainty cups almost disappeared in his huge hands. "Excuse me, Detective, but don't I know you? Aren't you Tohru Takuda's son?"

"Yes, I am," Takuda said.

Nakamura went still, and his eyes narrowed.

The sergeant smiled and bowed as he spoke. "I'm Kuma, your senior from the judo club. Remember me? I was away at the academy when you joined the force here."

"Kuma! Yes, I remember." Takuda rose and bowed in return. "You taught me a lot, but you threw me all over the place."

"Oh, I'm sure it wasn't that bad. You were a tough kid," Kuma said. He smiled and shifted from one foot to the other until his chief stared him out of the room. He backed out with another bow to the detective.

"Well, so you're *that* Takuda? I'm embarrassed that I didn't recognize you. And you're a detective with the prefecture now. You were just a skinny kid when you left."

"We were all younger then, weren't we?"

"Your face healed well. Did you have plastic surgery?"

"The scars have just faded. Some of them are hidden in the wrinkles."

"Oh, come on. You look so young. And you keep in shape, too."

Takuda bowed to make him stop. "You're too kind."

"Not judo anymore, right?"

"I teach aikido in private life, and I help out with basic training for the prefecture."

"Aikido. Yes, I could tell it wasn't judo. You don't move like a judo man at all." Nakamura sat back and crossed his hands. The cuffs were worn threadbare on his bony wrists. "It seems strange that we never saw you. None of us ever heard anything more about you. It's as if you were on another planet."

"I was mainly working in the central region of the prefecture and on the coast."

"So you haven't been back to Naga River valley, not even once?"

"Not since my wife and I left."

"Ah, yes. And your wife, she's well?"

Takuda willed himself to bow. "Very well, thank you."

"I assume you didn't have any more children."

Takuda searched Nakamura's face for malice and found none. Nakamura might simply be as stupid as he had always seemed.

"No. We chose not to have more children."

"Well, that's understandable. What happened to your son really was a tragedy." The chief pretended to be at a loss for words. "Still, it's surprising that you haven't been back for so many years."

Takuda drank his tea.

Nakamura shifted in his seat. "Yes, it might be hard to recognize the place. Zenkoku Fiber has really helped things pick up around here. It's really something. We keep on losing the young people to the cities, just like every other country town, but Zenkoku Fiber keeps the Naga River valley alive. We still have the pottery, of course. Despite the mountain shadow, green tea and rice still do well, thanks to the old canal system. But Zenkoku Fiber is our savior."

"The suspect Ogawa worked for Zenkoku, didn't he?"

"Umm—yes, yes he did. However, I think it's important to mention that he was fired well before the incident. They tried to reassign him. Zenkoku is like that, a healthy mix of old-fashioned loyalty and progressive resourcing. He refused to leave the valley, so there was nothing they could do."

"This is a small matter. There's no reason to bring Zenkoku's name into it."

"Well, you go straight to the point, don't you? Honestly, it's a relief. I mean, the reputation of a fine company shouldn't suffer because of the actions of one lunatic. And as officers of the law, we protect the innocent in any way we can."

Protect the innocent. From Nakamura's mouth, the words were poison. Takuda couldn't even look at the man.

"The thing is, it's all Ogawa's fault. You see, he's like a glue sniffer. The fumes have affected him. It's really the worst case I've ever seen. We had a boy in here a few years ago, a glue sniffer. He had been sniffing paint thinner and gasoline and anything else he could get his hands on. That boy was a genius compared to Ogawa. The fumes have destroyed whatever mind Ogawa had."

Takuda frowned despite himself. "How was Ogawa exposed to harmful fumes?"

"Ah, well, he's obviously been in parts of the plant where employees need breathing equipment, but he didn't follow protocol. It's completely his own fault."

"How do you know that fumes from the plant affected him?"

Nakamura raised his skinny hands in a gesture of mock defeat. "Exactly. That's an excellent point. There has been no medical examination. I imagine it would take a great deal of medical evidence to link his idiocy to the plant. Perhaps it's better if you ignore my guesswork. I'm just a village constable at heart, after all."

Takuda sat forward. "If the court needs information about Ogawa's health or mental aptitude, appropriate measures will be taken."

"Just so, just so. Let's all just do our own jobs. Personally, I'm not sure it could have anything to do with the plant. My son-in-law works there. As part of the safety crew, he knows all the procedures. It's lock-and-tag all the way."

Kuma came to tell them that the suspect was ready. Nakamura led them to a cluttered room that had been a small armory when Takuda had worked there. It was cluttered with public safety posters, pamphlet racks, and a man-sized eagle suit. Kuma patted the suit.

"Our mascot. We wear it to the schools."

Nakamura waved him out. "We usually store all this in the interrogation room, but we thought someone might come to question the prisoner."

Nakamura grunted and strained against a standing rack of yellowed safety pamphlets. It finally slid aside to reveal a grimy one-way mirror.

There was a pleasing symmetry to the scene in the interrogation room. Two patrolmen, their lines clean and crisp, flanked the twitching, drooling suspect. It was perfect. The young patrolmen protected the entire country from this man. They were the first circle of protection. The walls were the second. Takuda himself was the third. Through the court system and the prison system, Japan would wrap this man tighter and tighter, in layer upon layer. The system would bind this man so tightly that he could never hurt anyone, not even himself.

Spittle ran down the prisoner's chin as he raised his face and grinned at Takuda.

Nakamura laughed. "Look, Ogawa the idiot can't tie his own shoes, but he can see through one-way glass, huh? He seems alert right now. Perhaps you would like to question him."

Nakamura opened the door and stood aside, waiting for Takuda to enter.

Something is very wrong here. The grinning prisoner didn't fit the rest of the picture. Takuda bowed to the chief and stepped into the interrogation room.

"There you are," the prisoner said. "How nice. Heh-heh. How very, very nice."

CHAPTER 3

The interrogation room smelled of lemons. The shackled prisoner couldn't bow from the waist as the guards did, so he bobbed his head several times, slowing until he simply nodded at Takuda with a slack-jawed grin.

Takuda knew the look, and it didn't belong on this suspect's face. The glazed eyes told the story of a hopelessly hardened criminal, a man to whom interrogation was a game. There should have been an arrest record going back to junior high school, a record as thick as a phone book. Instead, the report in Takuda's hand told Hiroyasu Ogawa's quiet life on three pages. There was nothing in the slim folder to explain the sly creature who awaited him.

He took the chair across the table from the suspect. The smell of lemons was stronger, undercut with a faint stink he couldn't quite place.

"Are you Hiroyasu Ogawa?"

"Ogawa? Hiroyasu Ogawa? Heh-heh. He's gone."

So he is, and whatever took him away isn't in this report. "You are Hiroyasu Ogawa, born on February 7, 1960, in Osaka. So you just turned thirty last month."

"Heh-heh."

"You attended public schools, studied civil engineering at Tsukuba, and then you went to work for a prestigious engineering firm."

Ogawa leaned forward as if to peek at the folder. "Where did he go?"

"Who?"

"The engineer. The bright boy." The suspect looked down at the folder. "Is he in there?"

"The real Ogawa isn't in this report. We all know that."

With manacled hands, Ogawa swept the folder off the table. The young patrolmen almost ran to retrieve it. At a look from Takuda, they slowly straightened back to attention.

Ogawa raised his eyes from the folder on the floor back to the detective's face. "Heh-heh."

"There's not much in the folder, is there? You married a fellow employee. You took a job with Zenkoku Fiber and moved to this quiet little valley. A year later, your wife moved out. She lives down in the city, and you're alone."

"Ogawa is never alone."

"Who is with you?"

"Ogawa is never alone."

"Come now. First, you tell me that Ogawa is gone.

Then, you tell me that Ogawa is never alone. If Ogawa is gone, how can you know he isn't alone? If you are not Ogawa, then who are you?"

"Oh, yes." The suspect smiled shyly. "I'm Ogawa. I forget sometimes." The oily intelligence behind Ogawa's eyes peeked out to see if it was fooling anyone. When it saw Takuda waiting, it retreated, leaving gooseflesh prickling on Takuda's forearms.

Takuda sat back in his chair and lowered his eyes. "Someday, we would like to find the Hiroyasu Ogawa from the folder. Maybe he's gone for good. But let's leave that Ogawa out of this for now."

"No, no! Let's talk about him now! What will happen to him? Will he go to the big city? A better jail?"

Takuda smiled despite himself. "If you're smart, you'll try to stay where you are. In the city, jail life would be much more difficult. For one thing, I'm sure the food is much better here."

"Oh, fresh and hot! Fresh and hot! Not really what I've been craving, but beggars can't be choosers, as they say." Ogawa nodded with his eyes half-closed. "How long do you think I should stay here, Detective?"

"You don't have much say in the matter. You could be facing the prosecutor this afternoon. Then again, it could take ten days to decide whether to prosecute you, if the station chief petitions for an extension. On the other hand, you could have a quiet little hearing and be released on probation without ever having to enter a formal plea. No prosecution, no conviction, no black mark on your record. But none of that really matters to you, does it?"

"Oh, Detective, I beg of you. Please get me out of here. They beat me mercilessly." Ogawa lolled in his chair, slapping his jail sandal against his heel. "These men are desperate. They'll do anything to get a confession out of me. I fear for my life." He concluded with an elaborate yawn.

"I'm sure it's awful here. Let's just pretend you're going to cooperate to some degree."

Ogawa snorted. "Me, cooperate? You should cooperate! Eventually, I'm going to call my lawyer friend. You should be afraid of that. He's very, very scary. He could get the Buddha's mother sent to Hell."

"Let's talk about Hanako Kawaguchi. Her father works at Zenkoku. Was that how you chose her?"

"Chose her? For what?"

"To take her down to the water."

Ogawa shook his head. "I didn't choose her."

"That was the first time you ever saw her?"

"Me? Yes, that was the first time for me."

Takuda kept his face immobile. "You told her someone wanted to meet her."

"I don't remember saying that."

"Someone magical. Someone was going to take her to a magical world."

Ogawa made a show of straining his memory. "Oh, that. Maybe I said that."

"Then you chased her. You laid hands on her, and you tried to pull her back under a fence. Why did you chase her?"

Ogawa's gaze wandered. "She ran. Boys chase pretty girls. It's an old story."

"That's an old story, but this magical world, this is a new story. What happens in your magical world?"

After a few seconds of silence, Ogawa leaned forward to examine Takuda's face. Ogawa's lips were slack, but his eyes were bright and hard. His gaze stopped at Takuda's left eyebrow. Takuda willed himself to sit still under the scrutiny. The suspect's head bobbed slightly, as if he were counting the gaps in the eyebrow. Then his eyes traced the faint scars down Takuda's face, across the jawline, down the throat, all the way to the starched white collar.

The suspect fell back in his chair as if exhausted by the effort.

"You'll never know about a magical world. You had your chance."

"What?" Takuda pressed his palms to the table. "What did you say?"

With the clinking of manacles, Ogawa raised his right hand in a claw. He turned it toward himself and drew it down the left side of his face.

Mockery of a detective's scars was too much for the patrolmen. One pulled the prisoner's hand away from his face while the other slapped him in the back of the head. As the slapping continued, Ogawa grinned with real pleasure.

"Heh-heh-heh!"

It was probably the first human touch Ogawa had felt all day.

While the young men badgered the prisoner into an apology, Takuda kept his own palms against the stainless steel tabletop. When he raised them, they shook very slightly. His palms, suddenly sweaty, had left small clouds of condensation.

Ogawa finally stood to apologize. His whole upper body seemed to undulate. The patrolmen released his arms; this sloppy, fishlike bow would have to do.

When Ogawa finally came to rest, all three men stood looking at Takuda.

It was a moment of decision.

One choice was to act offended and leave the ratty little interrogation room and the prisoner who was not what he seemed. Nakamura would be at the door, bowing a little too deeply. They could agree that the prisoner was a brain-damaged idiot. On his way out, Takuda could clap Kuma on the shoulder. They could talk briefly about the old days in the judo club, and perhaps Takuda could put Kuma in a wristlock to demonstrate his grip strength and superior aikido technique. That would give Kuma something to talk about when he stopped by the neighborhood pub on his way home. Meanwhile, Takuda and Mori could be back to the city just after lunchtime. Takuda could report that the attempted kidnapping of Hanako Kawaguchi was an isolated incident. Really, that was what everyone wanted to hear.

Or I could do my job like a man and continue the interview.

Ogawa and his captors still waited for him to accept the apology. He sat looking at his hands. They no longer trembled. The trembling had moved down into his belly.

"So I can't go to the magical world. I've had my chance."

"Detective, why won't you accept my apology? I have no excuse. Please forgive my . . ."

"Sit down. Don't act stupid."

"I've caused you so much trouble."

"How many have you killed?"

"I've killed spiders, cockroaches, the odd mosquito, lightning bugs, and a hamster." Ogawa collapsed into his chair. "The hamster was an accident."

"We're boring you."

"All this talk about a magical world is boring me. It's stupid. It was a line. Haven't you ever used a line on a girl?"

"Not on a girl her age. Why Hanako Kawaguchi?"

Ogawa looked at the ceiling. "Probably because she looked—*tender.*"

Yowarakai. "That word could mean a lot of things. Do you mean she was impressionable? Weak-willed? Flexible? Soft to the touch?"

"Tender like sea bream. Tender like steamed crab."

The patrolman on Ogawa's left swayed where he stood. His face had gone gray, and his brow glistened with sweat. Takuda decided to wrap things up.

"Ogawa, did you plan to eat Hanako Kawaguchi?"

"Me? No."

"Not just a little?"

"Maybe just a little."

The patrolman exhaled loudly, trying to keep down his breakfast.

Takuda stood. "You men get some fresh air. I'll be done in a few minutes."

Ogawa bounced in his chair. "A real beating! Finally!"

The patrolmen hesitated, then bowed and left. When the door clicked shut, Ogawa said, "I'll never sign a confession. You know I won't."

"I don't want a confession." He sat.

Ogawa cocked his head at him.

"Let's just sit here a few minutes so they think I'm doing my job."

"Are you paid by the hour? A private security firm would probably pay better for a big boy like you."

"Let's just sit."

"You're trying to bore me into a confession. This is the worst party game ever."

Takuda leaned across the table toward Ogawa. The smell was worse. "You'll stay in that cell as long as I can keep you there."

Ogawa's smile wavered.

"You are unique. Did you know that? You're the first one ever caught."

"The first? The first *what*?"

"Most detectives would want to study you like a

rare plant. Not me. I don't care how you became what you are."

"What am I?"

"To me, you're nothing but bait."

Ogawa froze.

"Why act surprised? You can't keep saying you're not alone without someone believing it."

"You don't know anything."

"I know you're just the latest in a long line of accomplices."

Ogawa stared.

"We'll see who shows up to keep you quiet. All we have to do is wait for them."

Ogawa blinked, and then his face fell back into the heavy, loose-lipped grin. "Wait for *them? Them*, you say? You know nothing. I'll be in here, behind steel doors. You'll be out there in the valley with your ignorance and your notebook. You want to keep me here ten days?" He brayed sudden and sincere laughter. "You'll be begging to trade places with me before the week is out."

"Are you finished?"

"Quite finished. Heh-heh."

"Behind the bars and mesh, you have a window on the shopping street and a window on the canal. I'll have the glass left open on one of them tonight. Which one do you want open?"

Ogawa closed his eyes. "I'll sleep like a baby either way."

"Even after I tell everyone I meet on the way out how cooperative you've been?"

"Tell them what you will. Can you call the patrolmen, please? I'm missing my morning beating."

As he left the interrogation room, the sickly patrolman stepped forward. "Detective, I'm really sorry. Maybe it's the stink. We rubbed him down with lemons, but the stink is in his hair and his skin. I want to do my job correctly, but my stomach is weak."

"Patrolman, what's your name?"

"Kikuchi, sir."

"Kikuchi, it's not just the stink, is it?"

Patrolman Kikuchi gave him a guarded look.

"We vomit up poison. It's natural. It shows you have a bit of a sixth sense for dangerous criminals."

The young man bowed. "Thank you. The chief says Ogawa is an idiot, but something doesn't add up."

Takuda nodded. "You'll never understand people like Ogawa. No matter how many you meet." *I understand them less every day.* "Sometimes our bellies know better than our brains. Listen to your belly, Kikuchi. It might help you save a citizen's life someday."

"Yes, sir. Thank you, sir."

Takuda exchanged bows with the boy and turned to the chief's office. *The belly always knows.* His own belly hadn't squirmed like this for years, but he ignored it. There was work to be done. He had already decided to start with Ogawa's apartment.

CHAPTER 4

"**C**anals were the veins and arteries of Naga River valley. We lived and died by them. Detective, do you remember feasting in the flat-bottomed boats? We ate broiled eel with cold beer in summer, and we ate roasted sweet potatoes with hot saké in the winter. Do you remember that, Detective?"

"Yes, Chief. The boats passed our dock," Takuda said. They walked along the main canal. The water ran smooth and dark.

Nakamura sighed loudly. "No one's made a living as a boatman for decades. It's very sad, of course."

The suspect's apartment complex was across the canal from the public services building. Nakamura had insisted that he and Sergeant Kuma accompany Takuda and Officer Mori.

"See, here's where the suspect attacked the Kawa-guchi girl. That's the fence she slipped under, right there. You know, Detective, I used to go to school by boat. That was before your time. The canal used to come up behind the athletic field, but there were problems, so they filled in that section . . ."

"Chief Nakamura," Mori said, "did your men search this area?"

Nakamura blinked at the interruption as if startled that Mori could speak. "Yes, of course they did. As you can see, there is very little to search."

Mori pointed to a concrete cube at the water's edge. "Chief, what is that structure?"

"It's something to do with the canal, Officer. There are pairs of them at regular intervals. See, there is one on the other side."

Another concrete cube squatted on the far bank. Water lapped at the thick steel grate in its face.

"It's a storm drain," Kuma said. "It lets the runoff from the main canal into the spillway."

"Quite right," Nakamura said. "The spillway."

Takuda walked carefully down the slope.

"Detective, don't fall in," Nakamura called from the pathway. "The bank is slippery."

"Oh, he's fine," Kuma said. "When he was a kid, he could walk on top of the wall all the way around the school, even the gates. We called him 'cat' . . ." Kuma trailed off under the chief's gaze.

Takuda stepped up onto the concrete cube. He knelt on the far edge. If he leaned out just a little farther, he could check the grate. All of a sudden, leaning over the opening was the last thing he wanted to do.

"Detective, what are you doing?"

In his mind's eye, the water itself rose faceless from the canal and dragged him down into the storm drain. *You're no longer a child.* He took a deep breath and leaned out to look at the opening.

As Takuda had expected, the steel grate was missing. A torrent roared down into darkness. It triggered a memory of black current rushing, tumbling him among the river rocks, his brother's sleeve slipping from his fingertips, his son's anguished little face slipping beneath the dock, the pain raking downward across his face—*gone.*

Takuda stood.

"Detective? Is something wrong?"

He turned to face them. "Why was Ogawa down here? Do you think Ogawa planned to take the girl down into the storm drain?"

Kuma shook his head. He hitched up his pants and took a step away from the chief. "The river is high from snowmelt, so the canal current is still too strong. No one could stand up in that spillway, not until the irrigation really gets going."

"Where does the spillway lead?"

"Down to the runoff pond by the Zenkoku plant and then through gates to the north reservoir."

The water rushed into the spillway. Takuda could feel it beneath his feet, through the concrete slab. He needed a wet suit, a stout rope, and spiked fishing boots. With Kuma and Mori at the other end of the rope, he could find out what was down there.

"Detective, the apartment is this way," Nakamura said.

There was nothing down there right now, nothing but the sound of water.

"Let's have a look at that apartment then," he said.

They crossed the narrow pedestrian bridge single file. Mori ended up behind Nakamura.

"Chief, you said students no longer take boats to school. Why is that?"

"Why? Well, it was dangerous. Kids used to get in trouble down there, smoking and all." Nakamura turned his attention to Takuda. "But kids were tougher then. We could handle it. Later, there were too many drownings. It's as if kids forgot how to swim. Kids got soft from postwar liberalism and television."

Takuda tried to keep his tone casual. "So you never lost classmates in your day? None ever disappeared?"

"Well, a couple did. But not as many as later. If they didn't show up back in those days, we assumed they had run off to the city. That was where my classmates went. Sometimes they sent us postcards, but they never came back."

As they left the bridge, Mori moved up to Takuda's side. If the officer was curious about Takuda's history in the Naga River valley, he had yet to show it.

They turned down the winding path to the apartment complex. The complex followed a pattern common to public housing from the 1980s: identical buildings set at varying angles on park-like grounds. The curved walks and roadways had been designed to produce a relaxed, pastoral effect. Now the grounds were overgrown with trash-choked weeds, and several of the buildings nearest the canal appeared abandoned.

"Talks are under way with Zenkoku Fiber," Nakamura said. "If they buy this complex, they'll clean up the grounds and turn the empty buildings into free housing for their workers."

At that moment, Mori casually handed Takuda an evidence bag. He had produced the crinkly plastic sleeve silently, from nowhere, as if he were a carnival conjurer. Mori looked straight ahead and picked up the pace, leaving Takuda to read the evidence bag's handwritten label:

HIROYASU OGAWA, left hip pocket.

"What do you have there, Detective?"

"I'm not sure, Chief." The bag contained a clipping from a magazine: a cartoonish image of a smiling Kappa, a mythical water sprite.

"That's one of our evidence bags," the chief said. Takuda handed it over, and the chief shoved it into his hip pocket without looking at it. "How did you get this?"

"I'm more interested in the picture." He turned back toward the apartment buildings. "Why was Ogawa carrying a picture of a Kappa?"

"Well, it's obvious," Nakamura said. "He's a pedophile, and he studies cute, cartoonish images in order to lure children."

The sergeant hurried off as if to catch up to Mori. Neither Takuda nor the chief spoke for a few seconds.

"Chief, is there any indication that Ogawa lured Hanako Kawaguchi with images of any kind?"

"Well, no, not images as such. It was more of a picture in words, if you understand me."

Takuda held his tongue. It made no sense for Ogawa, a grown man, to be interested in the Kappa. The Kappa was a ridiculous figure: the shell of a tortoise, greenish skin, webbed feet and hands, a simian skull with a raptor's beak, a ring of long black hair, and in some renderings a bowl-shaped depression in the crown of its head. It had once been drawn as a lean and evil creature. Now it was cute and rounded, usually smiling, an ancient monster demoted to mascot for candies, toys, magazines, and other nonessential consumer goods.

Takuda stuck his hands in his pockets. If he stayed quiet long enough, Nakamura might say something useful.

"Ogawa did paint a picture in words, and he was talking about the Kappa," Nakamura said. His voice was insistent. "Ogawa told Hanako that there was a god. That's the first thing he said to her before he tried to lead her off the pavement."

After a few seconds of silence, Nakamura sighed loudly.

"So it makes sense," Nakamura said. "Technically, a Kappa is a water god from the old faith."

"There was nothing about a god in the final incident report," Takuda said. "Chief, why did you leave that out?"

Chief Nakamura looked around as if for support. Mori and Kuma were still a few yards ahead. "Well, there was no way to include everything, was there? It was a single comment from an initial report. It hardly seemed important except that it showed how crazy Ogawa is."

They reached Mori and Kuma.

The chief threw his hands in the air. "The girl Hanako even mentioned a boy at the water's edge, a boy following Ogawa, but there was no boy. We're sure of it. There's no report of a boy missing anywhere. That's not in the report, either. Ha!"

Officer Mori said, "Excuse me, but I've read the initial reports, and I think there may be a misinterpretation here. Ogawa can't have meant 'Kappa' when he said 'god.' All children know that Kappa near water mean danger, don't they? There are Kappa signs all over Japan to warn children of drowning danger."

Nakamura shook his head. "Not in the Naga River valley."

"There must be."

Kuma shook his head. "The chief's right. Not around here. The only Kappa I ever saw were the ones I painted myself. And someone always took those down or painted them over. They looked more like ducks, anyway. Green ducks. I'm not an artist. I gave up."

Takuda said, "Well, anyway, Ogawa didn't have that clipping for Hanako Kawaguchi's benefit. An advertisement for toilet wipes certainly wouldn't be an effective lure for a little girl."

The other three stared.

"Kappa Kleen Wipes. You don't recognize the mascot? Mothers use them when little boys piddle on the rim."

"Ah." The chief nodded. "Your wife uses them at home?"

Mori and Kuma went still.

"She did when my boy was alive," Takuda said.

"Ah, yes, of course. That's what I meant." The chief turned away from the apartments. "You know, it's funny, but the Kappa was still very popular here when I was a boy. There was an old shrine to the Kappa somewhere below the south dam, and there was a big Kappa festival every year until the war. By the time I was old enough to go, it was just a few old farmers dancing. They finally had to quit. It's still everywhere in the language, though. They call the railing on a dock a 'Kappa fence,' and they call stillbirths and drowned infants 'Kappa babies.'" Nakamura gasped. "I'm so stupid, Detective. I have such a big mouth."

"My son was hardly an infant, Chief. He was three years old."

"Yes, yes, I remember now. Like old times, but not very pleasant memories. Speaking of your family, it's odd that you don't know more about the Kappa. Didn't your father ever mention it to you?"

"No, not once." *My father mentioned very little to me.*

"Really? Your father was almost fanatical about destroying the old faith, if I may say so. When I was a boy, he was head of the Eagle Peak Temple lay organization. He was the one who got Oku Village to stop the Kappa dance, and he got the village symbol changed from a Kappa to an eagle. Postwar secularism, you know."

After a few seconds of silence, Takuda said, "Let's find keys to Ogawa's apartment, shall we?"

Kuma exhaled as if he hadn't breathed properly for several minutes. Then he turned and ran toward the office. Takuda hadn't imagined the man could move so fast.

The manager was a sad-eyed youth who balked at opening Ogawa's apartment. After Nakamura threatened the boy with arrest, he faxed a copy of the search warrant to the prefectural housing office and reluctantly handed the key to Kuma. He refused to look at Nakamura.

They smelled rotten fish as they approached the apartment door. They braced for the stench as Kuma turned the key, and Nakamura backed down the stairs with his handkerchief to his nose. When the door swung open, the smell seemed no worse. It was as if the stink had penetrated the concrete walls and spread itself evenly through the plaster and paint.

At the darkened doorway, Takuda finally recognized the smell.

He also realized why it had taken him so long to place it: Memories buried so deeply could only emerge to protect him from danger.

That stench had clung to his younger brother's corpse. That stench had wafted from below the dock just before his little son had been snatched away into the dark water. That stench had leaked from his own tattered face as he recovered from the attempt to save his son. That stench had filled his house as he struggled with his wife's violent grief and his own craving for oblivion.

It set off phantom pains in his scarred flesh, and it set off waves of panic in his gut. The worst thing that could happen was happening. As he approached the threshold, part of his mind watched as if from outside his body. That part of his mind was relaxed and ready, as if it had been waiting for this day. That made sense. Takuda had rehearsed for this day in his nightmares since he was nine years old.

As if in a dream, his nightmares come true, Detective Takuda entered darkness.

CHAPTER 5

The air was dense and foul. Takuda stepped up from the entranceway into the kitchenette without taking off his shoes. The others followed.

"Officer Mori, check the closets and cabinets," Takuda said.

"What a stink," Nakamura said. "Is it from the garbage or the refrigerator?"

Kuma turned on lights. The apartment was grimy, but there was no garbage in sight. There was nothing unusual—a kitchenette, a tiny dining area, a living room, two bedrooms, a bath, and a toilet. It was perfect for a married couple without children. Except for the stink and the northern exposure, it was very much like the apartment Takuda shared with Yumi, his wife.

"Detective," Mori called from the back bedroom. "This may be important."

The smell was a little stronger in the bedroom. Mori, Kuma, and Nakamura stood facing the back wall, and they moved aside so he could see.

The wall was plastered with hundreds of scraps cut from magazines, comic books, and food packaging. Almost all were representations of the Kappa, but a few were photos of the Naga River and the surrounding mountains. In the center of the wall was a bulletin board covered with pages ripped from a dictionary. The entries were nearly illegible due to scribbled notes and corrections.

"That looks like the gibberish the kids send each other on their cell phones," the chief said.

Stacks of papers slouched against each other beneath the bizarre collage.

Mori knelt to go through the papers. "They're all the same. It's some sort of grammatical study in a modified phonetic alphabet, I think."

"It's all gibberish," Nakamura said.

Mori frowned as he held one sheet up to the light. "I don't recognize the language, but it sounds like this: *Sineani sineni wakka keera'an kuru kewe ku-ro—*"

As Mori intoned the foreign words, the room suddenly began to feel smaller. Kuma stepped back against the wall.

Mori's voice faltered, and he came to a sudden stop. "That might be just words thrown together. It doesn't flow, does it?"

"Well, he's an idiot and a madman," Nakamura said. "What did we expect? I'm just glad there's not a body in here. The only surprise is that he had the attention span to make a collage." He picked with his fingernail at a smiling Kappa that hadn't been glued down completely. "On top of everything else, Ogawa will lose his damage deposit."

Kuma seemed agitated. He stepped away from the wall and poked at a soiled futon in the corner. "That's what smells," Kuma said. "That black slime, that's what was on his clothes when we caught him."

Mori prepared to photograph the bed.

"Hey, that's a tiny little camera." The sergeant stepped forward and blocked what little light Mori had. "That's something. We use a first-generation instant camera the size of a brick."

"If this were a crime scene, we would call out a photographer," Mori said. "Please step back."

"Oh, sorry."

"Officer, there's no need for pictures," Nakamura said. "He slept in his clothes, and he soiled his sheets. That's all we need to know."

"Officer, let's take the chief's advice," Takuda said. "If the prefecture decides to press charges, we'll search the apartment properly."

"I understand, Detective," Mori said. He had already pocketed his camera. The chief grimaced at him.

"Officer Mori, I think we're done here," Takuda said. "Our main concern was that Ogawa had harmed someone else."

Nakamura rubbed his palms together. "Well, no

bodies in the cabinets although we'll probably find a drawer full of little girls' underwear later on. Ogawa seems more like a glue-sniffing panty thief than a serial kidnapper. It looks like our fine village police force caught him on his first outing."

Takuda walked toward the door, and Nakamura fell in step behind him. "Say, are you and your driver in a hurry? Are you going back to the city early? We should go sing some songs, have a drink, and talk about old times."

"It's not even noon yet."

"No, I meant if you were staying till supper. You must be looking forward to the local cuisine after—how many years?"

"Seventeen."

"Seventeen years! We have some great little restaurants, and I'll bet the clubs haven't changed at all."

I'll bet they haven't. The seedy little pubs with their careworn matrons and antiquated karaoke rigs would sadden Takuda as much as anything else he had seen that day.

"Chief, it's kind of you to offer. However, the sooner I get back to the city, the sooner my superiors will decide whether to recommend that Ogawa be charged."

"Well, I won't stand in your way. We're all waiting to hear when the prefecture will take the suspect off our hands. It will really help us allocate our meager resources."

"Chief, if you'll excuse me, I must make a call."

"Of course. I'll wait for you at the office."

The chief sauntered toward the bridge. He sang an old country song in a thin, reedy voice.

It was a day for singing, a beautiful spring day, but Takuda felt no joy in it. If it were simply a question of family honor and personal vengeance, he could easily drive away and never see the Naga River valley again. For Yumi's sake, he could let it all go. Unfortunately, there was more at stake.

The prefectural police force used a powerful little hybrid cell phone that performed well on either of Japan's competing wireless telephone systems. Even so, Takuda had to walk right up to the edge of the canal to find a signal.

She answered on the fifth ring.

"I just wanted to hear your voice," he said.

"Well, here it is," Yumi said. "What are you doing? Where are you?"

"Working. I'm out on the job now, but I should be home early."

"You should go home now. Really, you should pull over somewhere and get a nap."

"I've got a uniform to drive me today."

"Did you get any sleep at all?"

He smiled even though she couldn't see it. "A little. I got up just before dawn."

"I know when you got up. You think you're silent as a cat, but you aren't."

"You're the only one who can hear me. You've got ears like a fox."

She sighed. "Is that supposed to be flattery? It would be better if you didn't try at all."

"As you wish," he said. "I'm just lucky to have a woman like you."

"Don't be such a fool," she said. "Everyone is busy. Finish your work and come home to me."

"All right. I'm teaching this afternoon."

"If you get there first, take a nap. I'll broil mackerel, and you'll tell me what's bothering you."

He broke the connection just as Mori and Kuma came out of the apartment. Mori carried a plastic garbage bag in each hand. Kuma followed him with a pained expression.

"Tell him," Mori said.

"Detective," Kuma said, "I'm sorry about all this, but the chief . . ."

". . . wants to know the real reason why I came. Why now, after all these years."

The sergeant looked shocked.

"I saw him pull you aside back at the station."

"Oh, right." Kuma grinned. "He does that kind of thing. It's not that he's suspicious. He just gets nervous if he's not sure what people want."

"Tell him I was homesick. Tell him I wanted to clean the family tomb."

"Hey, that's good. It's close to the vernal equinox, so it's perfect timing. Do you mind?"

"Not if you keep Officer Mori company for the rest of the morning."

Kuma's face fell into lines of worry. Mori showed no expression at all.

"The officer is a good man, Sergeant Kuma. You don't have to be on your guard with him."

"I don't know about that." Kuma pointed to the garbage bags in Mori's hands. "He's already taking stuff away."

"Sergeant, you can trust him. At this point, Ogawa's apartment is not a crime scene. If the officer learns anything interesting, he will share it."

The sergeant scratched his chest. He still looked worried.

"We won't let you get in trouble with the chief. If anyone ever asks, we'll say the officer gathered the material while you weren't looking."

Mori didn't even blink.

Kuma shrugged. "All right. But we can't go back to the station, or there will be a lot of questions."

"You don't have to go to the station. The officer will tell you where he wants to go."

Kuma bowed dejectedly. "Well, it was good to see you again, anyway. I hope you have a good trip back." He turned and stumped off toward the bridge. He kicked trash as he went.

Takuda turned to Mori. "And you. Do you want to ask why I have come back after so many years?"

Mori bowed as if he had been waiting for the question. "I trust that you'll tell me what I need to know. When and where should I meet you after I finish with Kuma?"

The young officer's blind, unquestioning loyalty was suddenly sickening. The garbage bags in Mori's hand were evidence of his willingness to please. He had started to follow Takuda around almost from the day he had arrived from the academy, and now he had begun to stray from procedure even before Takuda asked him to. If Takuda allowed it, the young fool would follow him into disgrace.

It would be better for everyone if Takuda broke him then and there. It would be violent and ugly and humiliating, but taking the bus home in a dirty uniform would teach Mori to be more careful in his loyalties. It would save his career, maybe his life.

Mori had no idea. He looked Takuda in the eye. "Sergeant Kuma may have important information. I'll take him to lunch and put him at ease. He doesn't seem like a baseball fan, so I'll play sumo trivia with him. I follow the tournaments, and I know a lot of the wrestlers' stats."

Spring wind whisked through young trees lining the canal bank. Takuda fought to keep his face immobile. "You're not surprised that I was born and raised in this valley? You're not curious why I didn't tell you that before I brought you here?"

"I'm not surprised, Detective. Again, I'm only curious about what you think I need to know."

"You're not concerned that I may have some personal interest in this case? Some personal interest that could compromise my objectivity?"

"Detective, you have no objectivity. You are rather dangerous, actually. You may be the tip of the lever that pries open this whole rotten mess."

"What mess is that, Officer?"

"I believe the local officials refer to it as the water safety question. They seem to do so without any sense of irony."

The water safety question. That bland, innocuous little phrase represented a nightmare of grief for the people of the Naga River valley, untold generations of mothers' tears. Those words coming from Officer Mori's lips unsettled Takuda. He looked into Mori's eyes. There was no belligerence, no fear.

"Officer Mori," he said, "what do you know about the water safety question?"

"I gather that the extent of the water safety question has been downplayed in official correspondence. There may be procedural irregularities in the Oku Village police station's handling of drownings and disappearances."

Takuda stood very still. There was little to say in response to such an understatement. "Officer Mori, there may be procedural irregularities on our end, as well."

Mori hefted the garbage bags in reply: *There already are.*

"It could cost you your job, Officer."

"I make my own choices." Mori lowered his gaze and spoke so quietly Takuda had to take a step forward to hear him. "The situation may not respond to standard procedure. However, your paperwork doesn't have to reflect irregularities. Leave all that to me. I'm quite good at smoothing out irregularities. No one will suspect me of it even if they become suspicious of you."

Suddenly, strangely, chills rippled down Takuda's spine. *This is too easy.*

He stepped back and rubbed his eyes as if he were simply tired. "Perhaps you're right. Perhaps your training better prepares you for a situation like this. I wouldn't be surprised."

Mori bowed.

They turned toward the bridge. Kuma was leaning against the railing. He straightened when they started walking in his direction.

Takuda took a deep breath. "Don't let the chief see you with the sergeant. Take the car and get out of here. At noon, I'll be waiting at the west end of the shopping street. There's a cemetery."

Mori glanced at him and then looked down quickly. "I'll pick you up."

They caught up with Kuma, and they all crossed the bridge together. Mori had Kuma talking about sumo before they reached the other side. On the path by the canal, the same path on which Hanako Kawaguchi had met Hiroyasu Ogawa, they split up. Mori took Kuma west for gentle interrogation.

Takuda went east to visit ghosts.

CHAPTER 6

Miyoko Gotoh lived at the dead end of the shopping street, down the hill from the cemetery. It was a bad spot. Trash blown in from livelier parts of Oku Village covered the cracked pavement at her doorstep. Behind her house, flotsam choked the last bend of the main canal. In the vacant lot across the street, a tangled, man-high mound of rusting bicycles and stripped scooters rose from the weeds.

Gotoh herself stood in the middle of the dead end stirring the trash in a childlike imitation of sweeping. As Takuda approached, her clouded gaze locked on him. When he was almost close enough to touch her, she suddenly recognized him.

"Detective! Welcome home!" She bowed again and again, as if to a benefactor. "I knew you'd be back someday." Her seamed face split with a grin of pleasure, but the smile stopped just short of her eyes. It was the second time that morning the eyes didn't match the story. Gotoh was a simple village matron, but she had the dead, expressionless stare of a prison guard left on the job too long.

What happened to her?

"I'm sorry about my house. The kids now, they all just drop trash. The wind blows it right to my door-step."

"Your house looks just the same, always welcoming." Thick moss erupted through cracked roof tiles, and the faded cedar siding was more green than gray. The house was rotting where it stood. He looked away from it. "I came to thank you for taking care of the tomb."

"It's no problem. I tell your ancestors that you'll come back to see them someday. It was just too hard, everything happening all at once like that."

All at once. It had taken agonizing years for the Naga River valley to destroy his family, but he hadn't come back to argue with an old woman.

"You know, you send too much money," she said. "I tried to send back the extra, but the bank refused it, so I started putting it aside. Last winter, I bought a new kerosene heater, a nice one with a fan and filters and a thermostat, and I bought the old man a new TV."

"Ah. Your husband is well, I trust."

She made a dismissive gesture. "We're old. We keep on living for some reason."

Takuda bowed. "My wife and I appreciate your looking after the tomb."

Gotoh leaned on her broom. "Well, I take care of my family at the same time, so it's no problem." She hadn't put any special emphasis on *family*, but it rang in Takuda's ears just the same. "You're too late for the vernal equinox cleaning. I did it yesterday, and I swept this morning. Still, you can go sprinkle some water and wipe off the stones. You can never be too tidy. You're here about the little girl?"

Takuda bowed in reply: *At your service.*

"It's scandalous, isn't it?" She leaned over to peer at his shoes. She didn't seem to approve. "A shocking thing for our little village."

"Gotoh-*san*, what has happened to you?"

She looked up at him sharply.

"You're not the same woman I knew. What is it? What has happened?"

She studied him with filmy eyes. It was the first real interest she had shown. "Do you pray, Detective? Do you go to the temple?"

The question surprised him, and he faltered. "Sometimes."

She nodded to herself. The hesitation had told her all she needed to know. Takuda was useless to her. She didn't give herself easily to hope, nor did she waste energy on disappointment. She simply looked over her shoulder toward the cemetery on the hill above her house. "Your father was a good man. He was the last good Buddhist in all of the Naga River valley. You should pray for him."

She started stirring the trash again. Takuda was dismissed. He headed toward his family's tomb, his face burning with a sudden and surprising shame. Stammering because he didn't practice his father's faith, then lying transparently to save face? It wasn't like him. He was a decorated detective and a martial arts expert, one of the top in his style, but one question from an old woman had reduced him to a bashful child.

Coming home was full of nasty surprises.

The gravel path to the cemetery started at the end of the pavement beside the Gotohs' house and snaked up into the foothills of Eagle Peak. At the end of the path, two stone pillars marked the entrance to a cemetery nestled among the towering cedars. Stepping between the pillars, Takuda entered a silent, windless world.

As his eyes adjusted to the shadowed stillness beneath the trees, Takuda was disoriented. The last time he had come, the cemetery had been full, a dark forest of pristine stone obelisks. Now there were just a few neglected tombs standing in different parts of the cemetery. To his right stood stacks of toppled stones. Needles and cones from the cedars above obscured the gravel between the tombs, all but a straight line toward the far end, a cleared path leading to the Takuda family tomb.

He walked toward it slowly, reading the names on abandoned tombs along the way. Some tombstones were so blackened with age and neglect that the incised characters were barely legible. On others, the names were completely covered with moss. One inscription stopped him: *Gotoh.* The tomb had not been touched for years. Blackened, moldy debris from the cedars above had piled up on the offering platform as if in a deliberate and shocking parody of familial piety. The old woman simply ignored her own family tomb.

The Takuda tomb stood spotless in the place of honor, farthest from the entrance and facing south. It was an irregular obelisk of black granite artfully carved and polished to appear like a naturally occurring boulder and set atop a four-tiered pedestal. It still looked new even though it had been erected in his grandfather's time.

He pulled out a cigarette. There was no reason to pretend to clean an immaculate tomb.

On the obelisk's face were inscribed the names of his distant ancestors, then his grandparents, his parents, his brother, Shunsuke, and his son, Kenji. The inner surfaces of the incised characters shone with gold leaf. There had been no gold when his son's ashes had gone into the base of the tomb. Had Takuda really sent that much money, or had Gotoh used some of her own meager income?

Takuda sat on the pedestal of a ruined tomb. *A tombstone is still only a stone.* He had been a fool to come.

He flicked ashes into the gravel and gazed at the gilt characters. Just long enough to finish his cigarette, then he'd be off. But off to where? The only thing he owned in that valley was the tomb right in front of him.

There was his father's name lined with gold: *Tohru*

Takuda. His father's only lasting legacy, the name they shared. He pictured himself in the Eagle Peak Temple, at his father's side with the old Reverend Suzuki leading the chanting congregation. There was a feeling of security there, a sense of strength that he had seldom felt since. In many ways, worship at the temple had been the happiest time in his life. It always helped that the temple was high up above the southwest corner of the Naga River valley, so much brighter and sunnier than any place down in the valley itself. He always felt as if he were stepping out of the shadows when he went to temple.

Those days were long gone. He had no business there. He could just walk away right now. He and Yumi had escaped, and they had a good life in the city. If he tried to solve the water safety question, he could lose his career, his reputation, everything.

The valley is someone else's problem. The thought turned over and over in his mind, formless, soundless, just empty and unspoken words in search of a voice.

He tried to speak it aloud, and he could not. The words stuck in his throat.

Hundreds of people, maybe thousands, had pulled their covers over their heads as killers prowled the canals, as innocent lives were destroyed, as women wept for their lost children. They had told themselves it was someone else's problem.

He took a deep breath and ground his cigarette into the dirt, burying the butt with his heel. He loosened his tie and stretched his arms wide, easing his bunched shoulders. He had slept poorly the night before, tortured by the illusion that he could decide whether to walk away. The illusion was gone. He would sleep like a baby.

Just like Ogawa the predator.

He recited the second chapter of the *Lotus Sutra*, just as he had up at Eagle Peak Temple for so many years. It was soothing, as always, but he was distracted the whole time. *The decision is made, but I'm too scared to do my job properly.*

Returning to the Naga River Valley had awakened fear. Not nerves or worry but *fear*, primal, bone-chilling, gut-quickening fear. Something he didn't understand was at work here in the valley, and the stink of it was working its way into his heart.

What am I so afraid of?

Patricia Hunt hated the Naga River valley, and she was afraid of it. She had been there less than an hour.

"I heard this was the place," said her husband, Lee. "It's supposed to be a great swimming hole." He looked down at the river, chuckling and burbling in its narrow, rocky bed. "It's still pretty swift with snowmelt, I guess."

Patricia sat on the bank. She had picked her way among the slick, mossy stones that paved the river's older, wider bed, but she had turned back before getting close to the water. She had never been to this remote valley where her husband worked on Wednesdays and

Fridays, and she wouldn't have come for a swim if she had known the southwest corner, this supposed swimming hole, would already be partly in shadow by early afternoon.

"Lee, you've been had." She threw a stone in his general direction. "When have Japanese people ever told you about some fun, touristy thing without at least meeting you there? Hmm? Never happens. Where is this student who told you about this place?" She looked back farther southwest, where the river crept out of a darkened cleft at the base of Eagle Peak. Far above, the sun shone on a tiny dam, a dam that looked like a miniature set from an old movie. Wisps of water sprayed out of spillways at the top. On the way into the valley, she had seen a building at the western edge of the dam, a bright, white building. It was a temple. She was sure of it.

He was down among the rocks at the water's edge, frowning at the dark, gurgling water.

"Lee, let's go back up and find the road across the dam. I just saw a car cross it." That was a lie, but she thought she could make out a guardrail and streetlamps. "Let's get out of here. This place is a hole."

"Do you hear that?" he said.

"I hear my afternoon flushing down the toilet. Let's go, Lee."

"Shhh," he said, staring downstream. "What is that? Is that a little boy?"

"What?" She stood. She stared downstream as well. There were rocks and dark water.

"Jesus," he said. He straightened and backed upstream, but he didn't step away from the water. "Jesus, it dove so quick, like a water snake or something. Too fast."

She stepped down to the rocks and reached out to him. "What is it? Come up here, Lee."

"I can't . . ." He looked down. "Oh God, it's—"

Lee's legs shot out from under him, and he disappeared among the rocks.

"LEE!" Patricia ran down among the rocks. "LEE!"

She leapt over stones to reach the river, but he was already gone. Then he was bobbing up to grab at the rocks at the next bend, so far away, so far away.

His hair was slicked over his face. He was pawing at a rounded boulder, trying to pull himself out. He was gasping like a fish out of water.

She didn't call his name again. She just ran, and Lee slipped backward into the water before she had taken the third step.

She ran along the river all the way to the main canal. She ran until her breath was ragged in her lungs and her feet were blistered in her tennis shoes, but she found no sign of her husband. She never saw him alive again.

CHAPTER 7

Gotoh rose wearily from her front stoop as Takuda approached. "So, you prayed for your family?"

He bowed. "It's been a long time, but one never forgets the sutras."

"Oh, people forget," she said. "People in this valley have forgotten truth and piety." She shook her head violently, as if she were being attacked by insects. "Awful, awful place. You asked me earlier what happened to me. I'll tell you what happened. I watched all the good people die. The good people like your father all died. The Naga River valley sucked their lives away. Your father lost one son to the river, then he lost his grandson to the canal, and then he lost his mind." She bared brown teeth at Takuda. It might have been a smile, but it looked painful. "Even your father's faith wasn't enough in the end. The Naga River valley kills the strong outright. The weak just move away."

Takuda nodded. He was relieved that someone had finally said it aloud. "It's true. I was a weak and cowardly young man. I could have stayed to help make things better here."

The grimace faded, and her face fell back into lines of worry. She eased herself back down to her stoop. "Oh, I'm a stupid old woman." She sighed. "No, no, of course you couldn't have stayed here. Your wife would have died of grief, just as your mother did. Wait, your wife is the old-fashioned girl—" Gotoh made jabbing motions at her own throat.

Inwardly, Takuda winced. "Yes, she tried to take her own life."

Gotoh nodded. "You see, I know these things happened to someone, but it's all getting more and more confused. Sometimes I don't remember your father's face, or your mother's. When tragedy comes after tragedy for so many years, it all runs together."

He sat on the stoop beside her. "What about your family? What happened to them?"

She made a dismissive gesture. "They moved away, and I never heard from them again. That happens, you know. People who move away from here never come back, and they hardly even write. When you try to find them, they've already moved again, as if memories of this awful place keep driving them farther away. The old man is my only family now. When he dies, I'll sell this house and get an apartment down in the city. I'll move while I can still walk. Maybe I'll only be able to live on my own for a month, but I'll be out of the Naga

River valley. Maybe they'll put me in a home in the city. At least I won't die here."

Takuda didn't know what to say. No one would buy her house. It was a rotting hulk on a dead-end street of a dying village in a dismal valley.

Perhaps she had the same thought. "You were right to leave. I should have left, too. I was a fool to stay."

Takuda pitied the woman. She had been one of the bright and energetic middle-aged worshippers who had made up the core of the temple lay organization. She had always been in the center of volunteer activities, celebrations, and annual cleanings. Takuda's father had said of her, "She works harder than anyone else at the temple." Then Takuda remembered overhearing his mother's reply: "Of course she works harder than anyone else at the temple. She has to make up for her husband."

Her life was blighted just because her husband didn't go to temple? It didn't make sense.

"Life was good here once, despite everything. You know, right here at the last bend of the canal, that's where everybody used to tie up to make out." She grinned like a backward child, her mind decades in the past. "More babies were conceived in those flat-bottomed boats than under the blankets, I assure you. And at the end of the summer, during the festival for the dead, the canal would take our ancestors away on their little paper boats, and the candles would all go out as the boats went over the spillway into the river. That's before they built the northern dam. Now, I suppose the paper boats would just collect down at the drainage pond by the plant. It's all gone now, all those days are gone, and all that's left is a canal full of rusted bicycles."

Rusted bicycles? "Doesn't it get dredged?"

"What, the canal? Sure. Sometimes."

"Who does it?"

"The Farmers' Co-op used to do it, but they're all old men now. They used it as an excuse to get drunk, and they did a poor job. Now the village does it, barely. In a dry winter, the water level drops so much that you see things sticking out of the water. Bicycles, umbrellas, furniture, anything. When I was still strong, I pulled out a scooter. The registration number was scratched right off, but the sticker was from the city, downriver. I could tell by the color. Who would throw a whole scooter into the canal? I took it to the village police, and nobody claimed it. Now they don't even bother to take them away. See those bicycles and scooters?" She made a vague motion toward the mound of bikes and scooters across from her house. "The village workers pull them out of the canal and just leave them right there."

"This morning, when I was coming in, I saw that the boat docks were all rotting."

"Of course they are. Nobody uses them anymore. Some city people were building summer houses here a few years ago. Summer houses, here! Can you imagine? They all built new docks, and they tried to get the canals dredged properly. One summer here, and they never came back. In a few years, those new decks will be rotten, too."

"How long ago did you stop getting around by boat?"

"Me? I stuck to the shopping street. The old man took the boat everywhere until he got smart."

"Why did he stop taking the boat?"

She shook her head. "Maybe he didn't swim so well anymore. You should be careful of the water, too. Only people who understand the canals very well travel freely by water."

"Who travels freely?"

She struggled to her feet. "There are people in Oku Village who've always traveled freely in the canals. Find out who they are."

"Why? What do you know?"

"I don't know anything. I never wanted to know. If I knew something, what would I do about it? Who would I tell?" She turned to go into her house. "Talk to Reverend Suzuki up at Eagle Peak Temple. He might know something that will help you."

Takuda met Officer Mori coming up the shopping street, and he slid into the backseat without a word. There was only one road out, the same hard straight-away that had brought them into the Naga River valley that morning.

Near the top of the straightaway, Takuda had Mori pull over. He got out and looked back down the grade. Mori joined him.

"No lights here, just reflectors on the guardrails," Takuda said. "Can you imagine riding a bicycle down this road after a night on the town?"

Mori folded his hands behind him. "It would be suicide. Is that the explanation for all the abandoned bicycles and scooters? Stolen by drunken farmers and ridden back into the valley?"

"I don't know how they explain it away. The bikes and scooters started showing up after I left."

Mori pointed back up the hill. "Around the bend lies the real problem with that explanation. It would take Olympic athletes to pedal those rickety old bikes up those winding roads."

Takuda looked over the valley, already partially shadowed in the early afternoon. "Let's get out of here."

Mori drove in silence, as if they had agreed not to speak. They crested the last of the foothills, and they were out of the Naga River valley and into the mountains. They both breathed more deeply. Mori cracked the windows, and the car filled with a fresh, wild breeze. Takuda bowed his head from side to side to crack his neck, and Mori loosened his grip on the wheel.

The breeze swayed the cedars on the mountainsides. It stirred stands of bamboo at the roadside and sent showers of falling plum blossoms across the windshield.

When they left the mountains and began to descend toward the city, Mori closed the windows so he didn't have to shout over the wind whipping through the car.

"So, Kuma is as simple as he looks. He doesn't know anything. He doesn't see anything strange because he's never been anywhere else."

Takuda frowned. "What happened when you mentioned the water safety question?"

Mori glanced at him in the rearview mirror. "He mentioned a boy you both used to know, a boy nicknamed Little Bear."

Takuda slapped the back of the seat. *Little Bear.* Sergeant Kuma had been the biggest in the club, so the boys had joked that he was a bear, *kuma,* even though the characters of his family name did not mean "bear." When the new Kuma had shown up, the nickname "Little Bear" had been inevitable.

"You knew the boy?"

"Yes, the other Kuma. Tadanori was his given name. He was tiny, with arms like chopsticks. His mother pushed him into judo, and he cried every day. About the time he disappeared, we also stopped seeing his father heading to the fields. Someone said they were living with an uncle in the city."

"This attempted abduction makes you think otherwise?"

"It sounds like the sergeant thinks otherwise, doesn't it?"

Mori didn't reply.

Takuda closed his eyes. Spring sunshine warmed the car, and shadows played blue and orange across the insides of his eyelids. The hum of the car was soothing, almost hypnotic. Soon he dreamt of sunlight flashing on the brownish water of the canal branch beside his parents' house. Something moved beneath the surface, and then he was underwater, face-to-face with his brother. His brother was suddenly yanked away, but he dragged Takuda along behind. As they sped deeper and deeper toward the riverbed, his brother became his son. His son screamed soundlessly. Takuda could not see what force dragged his son down into the rocks and murk, but it was relentless. His heart died inside him as his son's tiny hand slowly slipped out of his grasp, again, again, again, always just out of reach. As his son disappeared in the greenish water, the river stilled around Takuda. He could not breathe. He was trapped, spinning in darkness.

Then the river tore his face from his skull.

He woke screaming, but he could not open his mouth. It took a moment to remember where he was.

In the rearview mirror, he caught Officer Mori returning his eyes to the road.

CHAPTER 8

At headquarters, Detective Takuda filed a perfunctory report while Officer Mori returned the car to the motor pool. Takuda presented a copy at the desk of Superintendent Yamada.

"I'd like to stick around this case. I know the area very well," Takuda said.

Yamada sat in the center of the office so subordinates could reach him. The detectives at desks that surrounded his didn't bother to hide their interest in the conversation.

"Takuda, it's a good thing someone knows that area. Some people think it's the ass crack of the prefecture, and other people think it's the armpit. As with ass cracks and armpits, no one ever gets a good look. I forget it's even there. Every time I meet someone who's actually been, I'm surprised."

"Oku Village is my hometown, Superintendent."

Yamada raised his eyebrows as he put aside Takuda's report. "I think I knew that, but I forgot. Did anyone else remember that?"

The other detectives had drifted off from the conversation. A few appeared busy, but others stared off into space as if lost in thought.

Yamada looked Takuda in the eye. "Don't let this confuse you. One attempted kidnapping doesn't mean anything. Chief Nakamura is a fool, but he might be right this time."

Why is he dressing me down? "I'm not confused," Takuda said. "I'm trying to do my job."

"Telling the station chief you make recommendations about prisoners' custody? Not your job. Nobody asked you to decide anything."

Takuda felt the blood rise to his face.

"The chief was on the phone with me while you interviewed the suspect. Now, I don't care what you tell the village police, and you have your reasons for what you're saying up there, but it's really not like you. Don't get confused. Sometimes discipline and process are all we have."

Takuda said, "The fact is, there's something strange in the Naga River valley. Do you remember that Yamaguchi-gumi enforcer we had in here last fall? The kneecap-cracker?"

Yamada studied his fingernails.

Takuda pressed on. "Nobody wanted to be in the same room with that guy. Even when he was shackled, the attorneys had a hard time talking to him."

"I remember, Detective. I'll never lend you to the Organized Crime Division again, okay? Is that what you want?"

"Superintendent, five minutes with that thug made us want a weekend at a hot spring to scrub off the filth."

"What's your point?"

"It's the same thing here, repellent evil, but it's not from a hardened criminal. He's a hydrological engineer."

Yamada slouched forward to read Takuda's report. "It says here that he emits a foul odor—possible neurological damage—nothing about repellent evil."

"Of course not. Look at the bottom."

"Ah—'Suspect may have criminal background not documented by village police personnel,' and—" Yamada read on, then looked up with a deep frown. "You're making recommendations in your dailies now? Recommending that we keep him in Oku Village while you burn man-hours investigating a failed abduction? When will you recommend to the prosecutor that this suspect be charged? What is your threshold for prosecution of a suspected pedophile and failed kidnapper, Detective Takuda?"

Takuda put his hands on his knees. He stopped himself from bowing. It wasn't over yet.

"Well? What do you say for yourself?"

"If the suspect stays in the village holding cell long enough, accomplices might surface. If he is charged, he'll be brought to the city, and we'll never know about local contacts who might have shown up."

Yamada leaned back in his chair. "You think he had accomplices."

"He's told us as much. He said he is never alone, as if he were a madman. I think he's hoping to cover a lie with a thin blanket of truth."

"But he laid it on too thick."

"I don't think he expected anyone to take him seriously."

"Why did you take him seriously? Are you hearing what you want to hear?"

Takuda stood.

"Detective, we're not finished here." Yamada made to stand, but he looked around and decided to remain seated. "Look, Takuda, I just need to hear you say you'll know when to walk away. No detectives in Japan get more freedom than this crew. That's how we keep this prefecture clean. But that means we have to produce results. Do you understand? It's not playtime."

As he walked down the hall, Takuda wondered why the superintendent was chewing him out for pursuing the case but still giving him the freedom to continue. *Maybe just giving me enough rope to hang myself.*

He spent the afternoon looking through case files related to drownings in the Naga River valley. They were useless, a shambles. The cross-referencing was nonexistent, so he had to hunt down individual folders. Many of the folders were misfiled in obviously sloppy ways, some were dumped in a hand-labeled "miscellaneous" section, and most were missing basic documentation. It was as if the prefecture itself avoided knowing anything about the Naga River valley.

The files on his brother and his son looked pristine, exactly where he expected them. He didn't read them.

That evening, he left the office to oversee an aikido class at the local community center. The class practically ran itself thanks to a few dedicated young men and women, but casual students complained if no senior black belt showed up. It was absurd. Many of them didn't practice between classes. They wanted to absorb the art just by being in the same room with advanced black belts. This kind of foolishness was the last thing he needed after a morning in the Naga River valley and a strange afternoon at headquarters.

He was preoccupied. During the freestyle drill, the entire class lined up to attack him, one by one. After the first few throws, the hobbyists approached him very slowly, even timidly. He barked at them to keep up the pace. It took him several more throws to realize that his practice partners were ending up very far behind him. They were taking a long time getting back to the end of the line, and some were missing. He turned to see a few students sitting at the edge of the mats rubbing their limbs and checking each other's teeth. He had tossed them all the way to the back wall. He had tossed them like laundry.

He rushed over to help the seated students back

into line. Luckily, they at least knew how to fall, and no one was injured. Takuda was ashamed and confused, but he managed a quick, impromptu speech about demonstrating the power of aikido. He hoped they didn't think he was bullying them. He merely wanted to show them where they were going if they kept on the path.

They bought it. The relief shone in their faces, and most of them even seemed inspired. Takuda calmly restarted the drill, but he was in turmoil. Only with the advanced black belts did he ever use more than a fraction of his true power, and usually just to demonstrate the martial application of the techniques. Tonight, the flow was more powerful than usual, more powerful than it had ever been. As the drill continued, he barely touched the hobbyists. He was rooted deep into the ground by an invisible axis of energy, and that energy *pulled* the students toward him. He simply took away their support, and they fell as he wished.

When the young black belts got to the front of the line, he eased into a little more power. When he applied a full technique, even with very little of his newfound power, the strongest of the young black belts flew away from him and bowled over the next three students in line.

While they picked themselves up, Takuda stood on the mats, flexing his hands. They looked normal, but he could have crushed a man's forearm with grip strength alone, and that was just the beginning. His whole body was charged with power beyond physical strength. He was *connected*. He flexed his feet on the mats, and he felt the tough straw stretch and snap. He could have pulled the flooring to bits with his toes.

Only the blindest, most foolish vanity would let him believe that his years of practice had suddenly paid off with superhuman power. This was new. He simply hadn't been this strong in the morning.

Where did this come from?

He looked up at his next partner, a young office worker named Matsuo. She had received her first-degree black belt in the winter test. Her chin was high and her expression was calm, but she was ready to burst into tears. She was not ready to practice with him.

He stopped the drill and had students practice in pairs. This strange new strength was easy enough to control, but it was seductive. Even after endangering his students, he still wanted to experiment with it.

The class continued without incident, but the students seemed more interested in talking about him than in practicing their techniques. They seemed impressed and excited. That was the most humiliating part. Not only had he abused his students, not only had he been tempted by the power so that he continued the experiment when he knew it was dangerous, but now his students admired him for it. Showing off like that was a perversion of the art, an abuse of the trust placed in him by his own teachers.

Humiliation made Takuda laugh at himself: He was now in agony over his own betrayal of the hobbyists, students whom he had held in complete contempt at the beginning of the class.

I don't know what I'll think ten minutes from now.

It helped to make small talk after practice. The camaraderie of fellow martial artists and a hot shower made him feel like a member of the human race again.

Matsuo fell into step with him as he left the showers, and they left the building together.

"I wasn't afraid back there, Teacher."

"I could see that."

"I'll fight you now, if you want."

"You're a fool, Matsuo. Go home."

She laughed and tousled her hair. It was still damp from the showers, and it smelled of—lemons? He gave an involuntary shudder.

"You were really tossing us around back there. A very powerful man, aren't you?"

"Aikido is about discipline and control. I'm embarrassed about that display."

"Yeah, it was a little much. Still, I'll bet people will work harder. That is, if anyone comes back."

He laughed for her sake, but it was a poor effort.

"Teacher, a few of us go to a pub at the next station after practice. You should join us. Some of the guys you tossed would probably like to buy you a beer. It would cheer us all up."

He wondered if there was an ulterior motive. He mentally reached for his intuition as a carpenter might reach for a saw, but he found nothing. It was strange. Maybe Matsuo was just a modern girl trying to get laid.

Maybe she was attracted by the strength he had shown in practice. Maybe, like the hobbyists, she thought she could just absorb Aikido technique by being around him. Or maybe she was just trying to be polite. He didn't know. The day before, he would have known to a near certainty what she wanted. For some reason, he suddenly had no clue to his own intentions, much less anyone else's.

He turned to her and bowed. "Listen, please tell them that I'm sorry, Matsuo. Tell them that drinks are on me after the spring testing, okay? For right now, ah—I've got to go."

He left her standing there bowing and confused. It was awkward, but Matsuo could take care of herself. Right now, he had bigger problems, problems that made his unexpected power seem insignificant.

He had to tell his wife he had been to the Naga River valley.

CHAPTER 9

Yumi scolded him at dinner. "You should text me," she said. "When you call, I have to leave the office. They don't care that you're a detective."

"I just wanted to hear your voice," Detective Takuda said. *Always true.* She spoke in a husky whisper due to her damaged larynx. The scar on her throat had faded, but it was still so deep that it had its own shadow.

Yumi licked broiled mackerel off her thumb. "You make me stand out on the sidewalk with the smokers."

"I was in the valley."

She stopped with rice halfway to her mouth. "Our valley? The Naga River valley?"

"The Naga River valley," he said.

She dropped the rice back into the bowl and tossed her chopsticks on the table.

"One of us had to go back eventually," he said. "The Gotoh family has been so kind . . ."

"You should have told me." The color had drained from her cheeks.

"It was time to go back."

"Did you go about that little girl? The one who was almost kidnapped?"

"That was the excuse."

Her eyes flashed at him, but she held her tongue.

"Not much has changed. The Zenkoku plant keeps the valley alive. Everything is older and dirtier, and more storefronts are boarded up on the shopping street. The docks are rotting away, and the satellite dishes have sprouted like mushrooms. That's about it."

She rubbed the edge of the table. "The Gotohs?"

"I didn't see him. She's turned strange and bitter. She won't tell me what's happening."

"Is something happening?"

"I don't know. It—it smells like it." With that, he had told her as much as he dared tell anyone. "The suspect is not what he seems. At first, I thought it might be a case of identity theft, but it's not. It's as if some insane drifter moved into an engineer's body."

"What did they think you were doing there?"

"I told them I was sent there to gather information. I told them I would recommend whether the prefecture would prosecute."

"Recommend? Do you do that?"

"I've never been asked, really."

"So you lied to them?"

He put down his chopsticks and picked up his beer. "Well, I don't mind lying to the Oku Village police force. Nakamura is the chief."

She stilled, and her eyes narrowed.

Takuda continued, just to get it out of the way: "He didn't recognize me at first. He asked how you were."

She snatched up her chopsticks and tore into her fish. "I would have scratched his eyes out. I don't think I could have helped myself."

"Maybe it's best that I was the first one to go back," he said.

"Seventeen years ago, only half the village police were fools. If Nakamura is chief, then they all must be fools. Someone should test the water." Her eyes welled with tears, and her hands shook. "Nakamura. It's unbelievable. It just goes to show that anyone can succeed in Japan. It's true. If you're too stupid to move on, too cowardly to die, and too poor to retire, they'll eventually put you in charge of something."

They ate in silence while Yumi regained her composure. Takuda flexed his hands under the table. His newfound strength wasn't hard to control, but he wanted to keep it in mind.

When Yumi spoke again, she sounded more sad than angry. She asked if he visited the tomb, and he told her that he had, of course he had. He told her it was beautiful and peaceful, which was true, as far as it went.

Later, they lay under the covers watching the curtains move in the cool spring breeze.

"It was selfish of you to tell me about Nakamura," she said. "You're the one who decided to go back. You're the one who decided to dig up all that pain. If you made that decision on your own, you should have kept it all to yourself."

"It's not the past. It's not over."

"I know it's not over. Every time I look at the bankbook, I see the payments to the Gotohs. It breaks my heart just thinking of my little Kenji's tomb." She turned toward him. "Let's save the money we send to the Gotohs and move the tomb up here."

He turned toward her. "I mean that it's not over for the valley. There's something wrong there."

"There's always been something wrong there."

"All day today, people were trying to tell me something, but they wouldn't come out and say it. They were trying to tell me about the canals."

"The canals are dangerous. Who knows that better than we do? Who's lost more to the canals than we have?"

He rolled over. *Maybe someone has lost more to the canals, but I don't know who.* He drifted into dreams of dark water.

Sergeant Kuma woke with a start and struggled to his feet. He had dozed off at Chief Nakamura's desk again, and he hated being caught sleeping on the job.

The office was empty. The lights were dim, and the kerosene stove was nice and warm. Kuma heaved a sigh of relief. It would be just like the chief to pop in unexpectedly even though Kuma had taken an extra shift to watch the prisoner. The chief had been difficult all day because of the prisoner and because of visitors from the prefectural police. Seeing the detective again had just made the chief worse. When the chief had realized he was sitting knee-to-knee with Detective Tohru Takuda in his little conference room, he looked as if he'd swallowed a toothpick. The memory made Kuma grin as he eased his bulk back into the chief's chair.

It was good to Takuda again, but he wasn't so sure of Officer Mori. He had known someone would come to him when questions started building up. It always happened that way because everyone thought he was simple-minded. Maybe it was true. Sergeant Kuma couldn't make sensible answers unless the questions were right, and Officer Mori was an intellectual. He couldn't feel around the edges and ask the right questions. No one in the Naga River valley could tell the detective anything unless he asked directly, at the right time, and in the right way.

The water safety question. That was as close as anyone could come to talking about it. The more directly anyone spoke about it, the vaguer the conversation became. Kuma could make hints about it, though. He had told Officer Mori about Little Bear because he knew Takuda would remember, and he knew Takuda would care.

Whatever happened to Little Bear? Kuma was brooding, and he didn't like it.

Just then, he heard the murmuring. It was a voice, but it was strange and whispery. He wasn't even sure he heard it through his ears. The hair suddenly stood up on his neck. Was he hearing voices in his head? He listened carefully. There was just the constant rushing of the canal down below the station, the clang of the pachinko parlor up the street, and the far-off sound of a scooter. He did hear a voice, but it was a different voice. Ogawa's voice, coming from the holding cell. The suspect was not alone.

The sergeant vaulted to his feet, and his knees were shaking. The blood rushed to his head, and he had to bend over and hold on to his knees to keep from fainting. By the time he got to the holding-cell door, the voices had stopped. Kuma listened for a second, and then he quietly opened the door.

Ogawa stood on his cot. He stared at the toilet. The stench of rotting fish was overwhelming.

Kuma almost retched from the smell. "What are you doing?"

Ogawa shifted his gaze from the toilet. His eyes were wide with fright.

Kuma hit the switch outside the door, and the fluorescent overheads stuttered into life, casting stark, greenish shadows over the whole room.

Ogawa stepped backward on his bunk to lean against the wall.

Kuma opened the door all the way, just to be sure there was no room for anyone to hide behind it. He stood in the doorway picturing that space behind the door, a very narrow space between the door and the wall even when it was all the way open, space for something smaller than a child . . .

He thought he should peek into that space behind the door, through the gaps between the secured, sealed hinges. He couldn't bring himself to do it.

Behind the door, under the cot, behind the toilet, too many spaces to hide. . .

"If only it were a Japanese-style holding cell," Ogawa moaned. "No steel cot, no plumbing, no hinged door . . . this wasn't a holding cell at all to start with, was it? Who would design a holding cell with a hinged door that swings inward?"

"Shut up, fool!" Kuma edged forward, covering his mouth and nose with his handkerchief.

Ogawa slid down the wall as if suddenly boneless. He lay in a heap, staring blankly at the toilet. "Stupid, stupid, stupid . . ."

The open door was at Kuma's back. He was too fat to bend down and look under the cot. He was too afraid to do anything but shuffle toward the reeking toilet.

Ogawa went silent. Kuma looked over his shoulder to see Ogawa huddled on the cot staring at him, eyes glittering in the harsh fluorescent light. It was the first time the suspect had more than glanced at Kuma, and Kuma didn't like it at all.

He reached the toilet. There was no water in the trough, nothing but black, stinking slime. The suspect had turned off the water and flushed the toilet dry before doing his business. Kuma bent, groaning, to turn the water back on, one eye on Ogawa the whole time. As the fish stench began to fade, he suddenly felt much braver, brave enough to chastise the suspect.

"You're disgusting. What have you been eating? Can't you even use a toilet?"

"I am not the one."

Kuma felt a chill pass up his spine, like cold water being poured into his body. "What do you mean?"

Ogawa stared. "The trouble has just started."

"What trouble? What are you talking about?"

Finally, the suspect lowered his feet to the floor. "I am not the one you are looking for, but I know who is. If you want to find him, I can help. I need to talk to that detective again."

Kuma found himself nodding in agreement. He didn't have the authority to call the detective back into this case, but he wanted to get out of the cell quickly. Something was terribly wrong in there.

"Also, you have to keep me in jail. My life is in danger."

Kuma nodded as he backed out of the cell. When the door was locked and bolted, he leaned against the wall to catch his breath. He knew as much as he wanted to know, and he was determined not to know any more. If the detective or the officer wanted to ask questions, he would steer them toward the suspect. Ogawa seemed ready to talk, but Sergeant Kuma was more committed than ever to keeping his own mouth shut.

CHAPTER 10

It was Thursday afternoon, two days since the attempted abduction of Hanako Kawaguchi. For his interview with the suspect's estranged wife, Detective Takuda had chosen a Japanese-style pub, a dark place with an interior of red paper lanterns, painted screens, and polished cedar. Customers sat cross-legged at the low, lacquered tables. It was perfect for informal interviews. The pub always emptied quickly after the lunchtime rush, so they would have the back room to themselves. Takuda drank cold barley tea and waited.

Ogawa's wife walked in with a wary expression, but her face went smooth and bland when she saw him. She nodded to the bowing waiter and wound her way among the tables. She was beautiful in a high-strung, overbred way. She wore a designer suit with the perfect accents of jewelry, probably also from the correct designers. The silk handkerchief held lightly in her left hand was colorful enough but not garish. Everything was just right, the perfect picture of a young woman overcompensating for marrying a psychotic would-be kidnapper.

Takuda stood and bowed as she reached the table. As he presented his card, he felt a strange mixture of sympathy and satisfaction. She hadn't slept properly in a long, long time, and she had been crying, drinking steadily, or both. It was too bad she had to suffer so, but he was glad to finally meet someone whose eyes matched the situation.

She said, "The divorce isn't final yet, but you should call me Okamoto, my maiden name."

He nodded. "I appreciate your coming to see me. This has been very difficult, I'm sure."

She looked at him steadily. "The most difficult part is that this is all a mistake. Hiroyasu Ogawa is not a criminal. I wouldn't have married such a man."

"Of course not," Takuda said. "Whoever he was, he is no longer the man you married. Frankly, I don't know what he is."

The waiter glided to her side. Okamoto fidgeted for a second before sending him away. Takuda could see her deciding whether to defend her estranged husband or to distance herself from him.

When the waiter left, she turned to Takuda. "You have experience in such things. What do you think happened to my husband, Detective?"

"I don't know. Tell me everything, and I may find out." He looked at the tabletop. "There's no reason to defend him, by the way. There's no point in pretending to love him anymore, either. You may think society expects the pretense, but it's absurd. You know he's gone, and you know he's never coming back, and you want to cut yourself loose."

Her cheeks flushed crimson, and the grayish, puffy flesh around her eyes stood out like a mask. "You mistake me. Cutting myself loose is not my goal, Detective."

"You left him before he snapped, and you've agreed to meet with me," Takuda said. "Keep doing things correctly, and you'll be on the road to freedom."

She gathered herself to leave. "I'm sorry, Detective. I thought this was to be a professional conversation. I have your card, so I'll . . ."

He raised a hand to silence her. "Answer every question I ask, tell me everything about your time in the Naga River valley, tell me what you saw and heard and smelled. Everything. I'll help you disappear."

She sat frozen, staring at him.

"I can misplace every document that ties you to Hiroyasu Ogawa. The only solid link to your husband will be in Osaka, where you were married."

She blinked several times. Finally, she said, "The family register at the Oku Village office . . ."

"His family register could disappear. Such things happen."

She glanced down at his business card on the table. "May I see your identification, please?"

He handed over his ID. She studied it. She compared his face to his photograph. She apologized and bowed as she handed it back. "It's just that I don't know if . . ."

"You have no assurance that I'll keep my part of the bargain," he said. "Even worse than that, you'll have to trust a policeman who offers to break the rules."

"Yes. Yes, that is worse."

When the waiter returned, she ordered a beer. They were silent until the waiter departed.

"I've been thinking about the newspapers," she said. "I've been dreading reporters at the door."

He shook his head. "They probably wouldn't find you until the trial, and he may never be tried at all. Zenkoku Fiber has that valley gagged and bound."

Music from Takuda's youth played in the background. He sat still as she talked herself into telling the whole truth.

"Detective, what would you do if I didn't help you?"

"Either way, your name probably wouldn't become public until your husband's trial, as I've said. Whether you help me or not, I'll help you disappear."

She stared. "How did you know I would be so reluctant to talk?"

He didn't know whether to smile or frown, so he shrugged. "Our country is still just one big fishing village, no matter how rich we are. A woman in your position, with a husband who's insane, or evil, probably homicidal—you can't really afford to tell the truth out loud, can you? If you tell anyone what's happening in that valley, they'll think you're crazier than your husband."

She covered her face with both hands and sobbed freely. After a few moments, she stood and strode to the restroom. Every woman in the restaurant watched her go, and when she was out of sight, they turned reproachful stares on him.

He drained his tea and waited.

She was gone longer than he expected. He gripped the table leg, thinking to test his extraordinary strength. He squeezed to a normal degree. No problem, a grip slightly stronger than normal, but no problem. Then he engaged the *extra*, and the wood began to crack quietly. He was still amazed that it was so easy to control. Somewhat horrifying, but easy to control.

When he released the table leg, small fissures of split lacquer radiated from his cooling handprint. His palm was smooth and pale, not even red despite the wood-splitting pressure he had exerted.

Weird.

"I hate pubs like this," Okamoto said when she returned to the table. "They seem so old and dirty." She turned up her glass and drank half her beer in one go. "The whole valley is old and dirty like this." Her voice was steady and full of hatred. "And it all stinks. There's a stench of dead fish everywhere you go. Everything from the nasty little beauty parlor to the roach-hole karaoke clubs. It happens to the people, too. Nasty."

"I was there yesterday," he said. "Not everything in the valley smells like that."

She frowned at him. "No, of course not. My husband brought that stink home, and I can't get it out of my nose."

He paused with the cigarette in his mouth. He sucked in smoke until it burned the insides of his cheeks, but he still couldn't think of anything to cover his interest. He tried to act casual as she continued.

"He brought the stink home to Osaka. He was designing a system to keep plant runoff from the main spillway system. He didn't really do much. He was just representing the family."

"Representing *your* family, wasn't he?"

"My family, yes. Okamoto Hydrological Systems. You've heard of it? It's not a huge company, but it gets big contracts. The board members are all retired bigwig politicians."

Takuda shook his head. "He threw it all away, didn't he? If he had only shown up to work for a few more years, he would have had Okamoto Hydrological Systems in his pocket, but he quit to join Zenkoku?"

"As a new employee, at a new employee's salary. A lot of the other new employees were fresh out of high school. And he was proud about it, happy about it."

"You left Osaka to join him. Didn't you visit the Naga River valley before moving there?"

"He made it sound wonderful. When I got there, it was a nightmare." She leaned forward. "Zenkoku keeps employees like slaves."

Takuda frowned. "The corporate culture of a company like Zenkoku is a pretty powerful force. I'm sure some salaried workers feel their lives are limited . . ."

"They disappear from the apartments by the main canal in the middle of the night. Whole families. Just gone."

Chills traveled up Takuda's spine. "Give me names. Give me names of families that disappeared."

"Tanaka. And *Yo*-something. Yoshida, maybe. The Yoshidas had a boy named Junichiro."

"Are you serious? Is that all you have? Do you even know in which units they lived?"

"I'm sorry. I didn't feel very chummy if you know what I mean."

Useless. Utterly useless. He sat back against the polished wooden railing. She couldn't help him solve the mysteries of the Naga River valley, but maybe he could still help her.

Okamoto motioned for the waiter. "I'm hungry for the first time in a week," she told Takuda. I lose half a kilo every time the phone rings."

She wanted one order of grilled chicken livers and two orders of asparagus spears grilled in bacon. It was a hearty lunch. Takuda ordered rice in hot tea with pickled plums.

She switched from her sidesaddle pose to stretch her legs out under the table. Her face was flushed from the beer, and she looked happier and more relaxed already. *You can't fake that.* "This place isn't so bad," she said. "It's actually cozy. Are you buying lunch?"

He smiled and motioned the waiter to bring Okamoto another beer.

"Getting me drunk won't help. I've already decided to tell you everything."

"Getting people drunk doesn't yield useful information. Anyway, one more glass of beer won't hurt you. You've had a hard time."

She asked for one of his cigarettes. "You've read me pretty well, Detective. Are detectives trained to know whom they can trust? I mean, can that be taught?"

"Can I tell you something sad?"

She blew smoke toward the rafters. "Feel free."

"There's a science of observation. It can be taught, but smart liars can beat it. There's another way, though, an intuitive sense, a second sight that can't be taught. It's a gift, and it's never wrong. Two days ago, I could look into people's eyes and see straight into their hearts. Since I met your husband, I've completely lost that second sight." He remembered his confusion about young Matsuo's intentions after the aikido lesson the night before. "Now I have no idea what you're thinking. You could stab me in the throat with a chopstick, and no one would be more surprised than I."

"Maybe the stink clouds people's minds. I felt that way. Once my husband came out of the canals with that stink, everything started going dark. That's why I left."

"He worked deep in the plant. Why was he in the canals?"

Her brow furrowed. "His job didn't involve the canals?"

"He worked in a wastewater management control room."

She sighed. "Ah, my lying, stinking Ogawa. Everything was a lie after we got to that valley. He was studying Ainu. He told me he was thinking of going back to work for the family and expanding our operations into Hokkaido. He said that speaking the aboriginal language of the north might help. I knew better."

"What about the Kappa pictures?"

"What about them? Another bizarre obsession. I thought he was clipping pictures of women. He was ignoring me, so to see what kind of women he wanted, I looked in his folder. All these stupid cartoon Kappa pictures came spilling out. Ridiculous."

Takuda shook his head. "Career suicide, obsession with the canals, obsession with his Kappa, studying a language useless in this part of the country—I didn't bother to ask, but he's a complete loner, right?"

She rolled her eyes.

He continued: "Attacking a little girl—but you don't think he's insane, and you don't think he's a child molester."

"I still wonder what he is." She looked up at Takuda. "I wouldn't have left him for simple insanity. I would have pulled him out of that valley, drugged him and carried his limp body if I had to, and I would have gotten him help. But that wasn't the problem. He wasn't insane."

His phone rang. It was Officer Mori. Takuda got up and stepped away from the table to take the call. He kept his face impassive as Mori told him what had happened.

As Takuda paid the bill, Okamoto said, "Detective, do you mind if I ask what's happening? Is it related to my husband's case?"

"Indirectly," he said. "It seems that there was some sort of accident in the valley yesterday afternoon, and someone is missing. An American. Apparently a sports-related accident."

"A sports-related incident that left someone missing? How strange."

He left her as she started to tear chicken livers from the skewer with her teeth. *It's not so strange,* he thought as he walked away. *Not so strange at all if the sport is swimming. If the canals can't have a little girl, then the river will take someone. Anyone. No matter what else happens, the valley must be fed.*

CHAPTER 11

Sergeant Kuma was leaving the village police station just as Detective Takuda arrived. Kuma blocked the doorway, and he didn't seem to know which way to go. He bowed as stiffly as his belly allowed, and he wouldn't look Takuda in the eye.

As Takuda squeezed in past Kuma, Chief Nakamura shouted for the sergeant via the antiquated intercom. Kuma had escaped just in time. The two young patrolmen scurried around the building to find Kuma in a vain attempt to make the chief happy. Nothing was going to make the village police chief happy on a drowning day.

Nakamura answered Takuda's questions in a cold, halfhearted manner. When Takuda asked him what progress they had made with Lee Hunt's disappearance, the chief grimaced. "That's our business. We can handle the foreigner's disappearance. As to the matter

that brought you here yesterday, I talked to your office."
Nakamura shook his head sadly. "Your superintendent
says you didn't come here to decide whether to recommend prosecution in Ogawa's case. He says it's strange
that I would think so." He looked Takuda in the eye.
"He says there is some sort of—misunderstanding."

The first real lie I tell in years, and I get caught. He
pulled out his cell phone. *But if I get caught, I won't be
caught by this old scarecrow.*

Nakamura's gaze wavered even though he didn't
know who Takuda was calling. Superintendent
Yamada answered on the third ring. "Takuda, where
are you?"

"I'm in the valley, the police station in Oku Village,"
he said. "I don't think our office should exercise jurisdiction in Lee Hunt's disappearance, but I would like
to lend logistical support."

Nakamura blinked. His eyes were watering, and
his nose seemed to twitch on its own.

Takuda's boss snorted. "You're doing my job now?
Glad you're doing someone's job, since you don't seem
to be doing your own. Anyway, I was going to send
you up there if you ever checked in today."

"Of course. When I heard about the missing man, I
came straight here to find out what I could."

"Sometimes, all we have is discipline and procedure. If we don't have discipline and procedure, we're
nothing. We're no better than gangsters who live by
their own rules."

"I understand," Takuda said. There was no way he

would apologize for not going to the office, not in front of Nakamura.

Yamada sighed heavily into his ear. "I don't know what's happening with you, but if you can't control yourself, you won't be able to control the situation in that valley, and control is what we need right now. Do you understand? Control. I'm already getting pressure to keep this small."

"I see. From whom?"

"Don't worry about that."

"I hear you, Superintendent. I promised Chief Nakamura nothing yesterday in terms of recommending prosecution or exercising jurisdiction in the attempted kidnapping of Hanako Kawaguchi."

"I don't care," the superintendent said.

"Yes, that's right. No promise at all. There was obviously some sort of—misunderstanding."

Nakamura turned scarlet.

Takuda suddenly found the chief grotesque. He averted his eyes. "As far as the search for the missing man goes, I'll call for Officer Mori. No divers yet. The village police can start their search of the places where bodies always wash up. They know how to find drowning victims here. They call it the water safety question. Finding corpses is what they do best."

Chief Nakamura's eyes burned.

Yamada growled into Takuda's ear: "Enough! Takuda, don't find any bodies. Don't find anything. Just make sure they're going in the right direction and get out of that valley till you hear from me. Do you understand?"

"I understand," Takuda said slowly, but his mind was racing.

"And don't bother calling for Mori. I'll have him sent to you by lunchtime. Just stick to procedure, keep it clean, keep the details clear, and document what you see."

"Thank you, Superintendent."

"And Takuda—oh, never mind. Document everything on your end, but don't sign off on their reports. Just be smart. Don't find anything, don't sign off on anything."

"Yes, sir. Thank you." He hung up. Chief Nakamura stared in stony silence as Takuda explained that he would simply make sure the village had all angles covered. Then the chief bowed stiffly and left without any acknowledgment that Takuda had spoken at all.

Takuda was free of the chief, but he had to be careful of his own superintendent. Someone had reached out to Yamada. It was probably a well-placed friend of Zenkoku Fiber, probably no one from the company itself. At any rate, the call had been made, and the superintendent had been put on notice that the case was being watched.

Am I being watched as well?

He found the two young patrolmen studying a map of the canals. Takuda remembered it well. Their newer copy was laminated, and certain bends and gates had been highlighted red so many times that the washable marker residue bled a pink haze into the surrounding fields.

He said to the taller one, "You're Kikuchi, right?"

The boy bowed, pleased the detective had remembered. He introduced the shorter one as Inoue.

Takuda took the map from them. "With the spring runoff, nothing is likely to catch higher up." Takuda pointed to a bend in the Naga River he knew too well. "Here is the lowest point on the river where a body is going to show up. Start there, and then work your way upstream toward the site where Hunt was last seen. That eliminates the river. After that, check the choke points in the main canals."

The patrolmen glanced at each other. "The chief has us starting at the far end of the north reservoir and working our way all around the shore."

To give someone else time to find the body? It didn't mean the chief was part of some specific plot. It had always been standard operating procedure with the water safety question. The longer you waited to look in the right place, the more likely the corpse would disappear.

"Look," Takuda said. "The water is cold, but the sun is warm. It's been more than twelve hours already. If the body washes up in the sunshine, the warmth will make your job more—unpleasant."

The patrolmen looked troubled.

Good.

"So, to save yourself trouble and cut traumatic waiting time for the family, do as I say. If you still don't find the body, look right at the end of the shopping street, at the last bend of the main canal." He laid a finger on a pink cloud of marker residue behind the Gotoh house, right down the hill from his family tomb. "More than one corpse has shown up there."

"Detective," Inoue said, "we've been busy this afternoon with the family . . ."

"Where are they?"

"Just his wife. She's in the interrogation room."

Takuda swore. "Put her in the chief's office. Get her some food and close the shades to give her some privacy."

They jumped to obey, but he stopped them. "In a second, in a second. First, tell me if you're going to have any problems doing this right."

Kikuchi said, "No, no one will stop us. Sergeant Kuma slipped out to search the cooling pond . . ."

"You were pretending to look for him a few minutes ago." Takuda looked at the map to avoid embarrassing them. "Right, then let him look busy, just to keep the chief happy. Go find that body and don't let my name come into it. It's all on you. If someone asks why you were looking in the right place, it's not because I countermanded the chief's orders. You were stopping for a bowl of noodles or a soda from a vending machine, or you thought you saw a badger-dog acting strangely. Understand?"

Kikuchi blinked. "So, you aren't coming with us?"

"No, I'm not. I have other business this afternoon."

From the parking lot of Eagle Peak Temple, Takuda watched darkness devour the Naga River valley below. The eastern side of the valley floor still glowed in the yellow rays of the afternoon sun, but the sunset shadows of the western mountains took the valley house by house and farm by farm. Despite the advances of science, despite the electrification of rural Japan almost fifty years before, farmers scurried to finish their work in the half-lit fields. Everyone wanted to be home before nightfall. It had always been so.

As far as Takuda was concerned, the shadows could have it. The whole day. He crushed his cigarette into a concrete urn. *Perhaps tomorrow will be better.* He continued to grind the butt even after he was sure it was dead. He was tired of waiting for better tomorrows.

"It hasn't changed that much, has it?"

Takuda whipped around. The priest, the younger Reverend Suzuki, smiled and bowed. "I'm sorry, I didn't mean to startle you."

Takuda bowed in return, eyeing Suzuki as he did so. Suzuki was very thin and very tall, a full head taller than Takuda. He wore a white kimono with an embroidered sash of cream-colored silk slung casually over his shoulder. He carried his prayer beads in his right hand and a lit cigarette in his left. He held the cigarette far from his body to keep ashes and smoke away from the sacred sash.

"You move very softly for such a big fellow, Reverend Suzuki."

Suzuki grinned and bowed. He was obviously delighted that Takuda had come.

"Your father, was he the head priest before you?"

Suzuki bowed in reply. "He disappeared seven years ago, apparently drowned. I have the honor to serve as head priest."

"He was a good man. You seem to know me, Priest. Do I know you?"

Suzuki grinned again. He seemed on the verge of bursting into laughter. "I'm Ryutaro, the boy who stole your brother Shunsuke's toy airplane. Don't you remember me?"

Takuda flushed crimson. He remembered thrashing one of the old priest's sons, but he hadn't remembered which one.

The airplane thief still grinned. "Detective, I'm very glad to see you again. You showed me a direct expression of karma in human life."

A parable for the afternoon. Suzuki's lighthearted approach was all a patronizing front, a sugarcoating for the pill. "Ah, I see," Takuda said.

Suzuki took the last drag of the cigarette. "I can tell by your expression that you don't." He flicked the butt expertly into the concrete urn. "Maybe I'll explain it to you sometime. You didn't come here today for a lesson in practical karma." He winked like an actor in a Hollywood movie. "Let's go inside."

They ascended the stairs from the parking lot. With each step upward, more of the temple came into view: the great peaked temple roof piercing the heavens, the eaves turning up at the corners like wings to reveal the bright white stucco of the outside walls, then the dark cedar trim dividing white walls into perfect rectangles. The yellowed bamboo fencing marched on either side of the worn paving stones straight up to the main gate.

At the top of the steps, Takuda stood once again on the wide, sparse approach to Eagle Peak Temple.

"No," Takuda said. "Nothing has changed much."

Suzuki slapped him on the back, startling him again. "Let's go in the side door. It's cozier that way."

Takuda followed Suzuki toward his own childhood.

CHAPTER 12

Smells of incense and wax brought back childhood memories, but the worship hall was even dingier than Takuda expected. The walls, once white, were a mottled cream. The ancient floor matting was faded paler than winter straw. Near the altar, the mat bindings were threadbare, worn away by a very small congregation of old people who sat close to the priest so they could hear.

"When I was a boy, this room was full three times a week." Takuda said.

"That hasn't happened since my father's funeral. I tried door prizes, but I think it was already too late."

"You have a pretty breezy attitude for a priest."

"Acting holy is pointless for a country priest. Don't you ever step out of your role as a detective to do your job better?" He slid open the door to his quarters and bowed. "For example, do you ever pretend to break rules in order to encourage a witness to cooperate?"

Takuda stopped on the threshold and turned to face Suzuki. Suzuki couldn't know about his promise to keep Okamoto's name out of the investigation of her husband. He wasn't psychic.

Suzuki was still bowing. Their faces were centimeters from each other, and Suzuki didn't blink. "Please enter my home," he said.

The kitchen smelled of fried potatoes and dish detergent. Takuda sat at the table while Suzuki prepared the tea.

"So you've been away from the valley, too." Suzuki was far too tall for the low kitchen counters. "I went away for school, you know, after your brother died, and since I came back, I've mostly stayed up here."

"All your brothers went away to school too, didn't they?"

"All of them. I was the only one to come back."

"Why did your father send you away?"

Suzuki poured Takuda's tea. "Here in the Naga River valley, they call it the water safety question."

Suzuki's face was bland and unconcerned. He dumped a bag of ginger crisps onto a plate.

Takuda took a deep breath. "The water safety question is what brings me up here. One of your congregants seems to know something about it. Her name is Gotoh."

Suzuki paused with a ginger crisp halfway to his

mouth. "I know the Gotoh family. I hope you're not asking me for personal information."

"I didn't say that. She said you know how some people in the valley travel safely by water. What did she mean by that?"

"Ah. Well, that's okay." Suzuki didn't mind talking with his mouth full. "First, you should understand that most of my knowledge is historical. I've had little direct experience with the water safety question, and almost no contact with the Kappa worshippers."

Takuda snorted. "Worshippers? Now you're confusing superstition with religion."

"Not at all. The Kappa was an object of worship, and it still is, for some. You see, this temple has not been completely successful. The cult is no longer in open practice, as it was after the war. Your father and my father together finally broke the practice. They went door to door to stop the Kappa festival, and they got the city symbol changed from the Kappa to the eagle. But vestiges of the Kappa worship remain under the surface. Do you remember the eagle suit, the one the police have now?"

Takuda nodded.

"Well, if you peeled the fabric off the top and the wings, you'd find an old Kappa costume underneath. The clacking wooden beak has been wired shut and painted yellow, but otherwise, the costume is complete. The street was filled with them, my father said, clacking their beaks to represent the Kappa tearing the internal organs from its victims."

"They were still doing that dance when I was a kid."

"Yes, in the old Farmers' Co-op hall, but not out in streets. From what I understand, the dances stopped altogether eight or nine years ago, before my father's disappearance. So the dance is ended. However, that doesn't mean the cult is dead. I know of only one surviving member who has completely renounced the cult. For all I know, the others still hobble on up to the old shrine."

"So there really is a shrine."

"Oh, yes. The Kappa dance was just the tip of the iceberg. Yes, the shrine is right below us, in the southwest corner of the valley. The dark corner. It's called the Shrine of the Returning Apprentice."

Takuda described a photo Mori had found in Ogawa's apartment, a place on a river where two stones formed the uprights of a shrine gate. He sketched it for Suzuki.

"Yes, that might be the approach from the valley floor. I've never been there. The uprights formed a natural rock formation that the cult venerated. The shrine itself is on a rocky outcropping above those stones."

Suzuki had spent half his life living directly above the shrine, but he had never climbed down to see it. It didn't make sense. Takuda said so.

"Ah, but there are specific reasons I've never been." Suzuki stood to get more crisps. "Eagle Peak Temple was built high above the Naga River valley so that recitations of the sutras would float downstream and protect the valley. Powerful prayers were supposed to keep the old water spirits in check." He smiled at the look on Takuda's face. "You want to laugh, but the priest's job here is to counteract superstition and evil on behalf of the whole community. The constant presence of a priest is important here. That's why I came back."

Takuda took a ginger crisp just to fill the silence.

Suzuki joined him. "There was a very active cult here before the war, and it was important to stave off any modern resurgence. You see, when we refer to cults these days, we mean deadly gas attacks on the Tokyo subways. This was different. The cult here didn't have a charismatic leader. They had a living god."

"What?"

"A living god." Suzuki bowed his head as if in silent thought. After a moment, he asked Takuda to wait, and he left the room. He returned quickly with a large wooden box. It was very old. Gold leaf still glinted in the ornate relief carving.

"These treasures explain why the temple was built in the first place." Suzuki removed the lid and set it aside. He laid a silken scarf on the table and pulled on white cotton gloves. He then removed two scrolls from the box and laid each on the silk.

He unrolled the first scroll. "This is a grant of land from the chief of the Kuroda clan, the Kuroda clan that ended up in Chikuzen. The year is illegible, but we know it is before the clan moved to Harima Province during the Warring States period. My father believed this was from the early fifteenth century."

The scroll was weathered and water-damaged. Much was illegible, and the remainder was in an old-fashioned cursive that Takuda couldn't read. "And what else does it say, Priest?"

"From what we can read of this, it grants the land for three main purposes. The first is to spread the light of Buddhism. The second is to promote the wisdom and practice of the three sutras for the protection of the state." Suzuki's face was drawn and expressionless. "The third purpose is to end the worship of the Drowning God."

The Drowning God, *Dekishi-no-kami*. It was a disgusting phrase, a nonsensical title aping ancient names of gods from Japanese animistic religions. *A pet name for the make-believe mascot of a murderous cult.*

"You're saying that the Kappa was an ancient god, the Drowning God referred to in the scroll, and that Eagle Peak Temple was built just to end the worship of the Kappa."

"The Kappa and other spawn of ignorance and superstition."

"I see. For a second, I thought you meant that the Kappa was real."

Suzuki put the scroll back into the box without responding.

"The Kappa is a myth, a story to scare children

away from the water. Why were our fathers so opposed to the folklore?"

Suzuki said, "It was not simply folklore. The Kappa is ancient Japanese animism, pure pagan superstition, and it doesn't fit with any version of the truth."

"When you say 'truth,' do you mean objective reality, or do you mean Buddhist law?"

Suzuki smiled. Takuda was beginning to see that priest's smile might have nothing to do with happiness or amusement. "The Kappa was originally a water god, of course. Not a very powerful one, more of a deadly prankster, but the Kappa is tenacious. It was never absorbed into Buddhism, not like so many others."

"Like the flesh-eating demons."

"Exactly. As the light of Buddhism dispels the darkness, we adopt the old gods and devils. Here in Japan, some sects claim the sun goddess and other deities from the old religion as devotees, protectors of the sutras. My sect, however, avoids revering the gods of the old religions. It's difficult, of course, because our Buddhism is deeply intertwined with Hinduism and Taoism. We keep some of those traditions, but we've rejected the animistic Japanese gods. It's not that we're so pure. We just don't want to confuse ourselves."

He unrolled the second scroll. "This is one priest's history of the cult. Most people thought he was mad. He lived before my family married into the priesthood, but we were already distant cousins. His account has more of the oral tradition from the local people. It actually indicated that the Kappa was shackled underground, beneath the shrine. The Kappa apparently weakens when bound by metal, especially iron."

"Just as Ultraman's strength fades in earth's atmosphere."

"Or silver kills werewolves in Europe." Suzuki smiled as he pulled a clanking silken bag from the box. "These are supposedly left over from those days." He let two sets of shackles slide out of the bag. "Please examine them."

Suzuki hovered over him. Takuda used the bag to pick up the shackles. It was actually just one pair of shackles: two flat iron bars, each with oblong bracelets on each end. There were holes along each iron bar. If a prisoner put his hands through both sets of bracelets, then the jailer could pull the hands away from each other so that the oblong rings on each side would close on the wrists, and the jailer could secure the shackles by passing a small rope through the holes along the flat bars. Securing the two bars with iron rings or links of a chain would be better. The prisoner would not get far, even today.

"These are apparently designed to capture the Kappa," Suzuki said. "They are a gift to you."

"What? I can't accept these." *And why would I want to?*

"These are my personal property, not the temple's. They aren't a huge gift, but they're appropriate for a detective of the prefectural police. It's a fitting souvenir from this valley."

Takuda turned the shackles over in his hand. The

iron was almost jet-black. Suzuki pointed out characters forged in the oblong rings.

"Chinese characters in very old forms, along with
Pali script. They are names of Buddhist protectors,
sworn votaries of the sutras." Suzuki sat. "That's one
of the reasons I think it is a good gift for you. You have
become a policeman, a protector of the people, but I
think you may be something more."

"I'm not much of a protector."

Suzuki nodded. "There was little you could do for
your brother or your son. You didn't have enough information. Now, you're ready."

"Ready for what, Priest?"

"Take a walk with me tomorrow."

Takuda's cell phone buzzed in his pocket. It was Officer Mori.

"Detective, where are you?"

"I'm just above the valley."

"Well, please hurry. They found Lee Hunt's body
at the first gate. The chief made them pull it out and
bring it back to the station."

Takuda wasn't sure it mattered where they took the
corpse. What he was looking for couldn't be hidden,
no matter where they took it. "Keep them there. Don't
let the victim out of your sight."

Suzuki followed Takuda out the door. He picked up
books and bits of vestment along the way. "Can I ride
with you? It's easy for me to get a ride back. Besides, I
would like to tell you a little more."

The mountain peaks still held a bit of sunset glow, but the valley below was black. The lights from Oku Village and scattered farms twinkled like stars reflected dimly from the surface of an inky pool. Takuda and Suzuki descended into the night.

CHAPTER 13

Patricia Hunt was sick with grief. Her red-rimmed eyes moved dully from Detective Takuda's face to Suzuki's. "You want to pray for him? But he's agnostic—was agnostic," she said. "I don't know if that's a problem."

"No problem for me," Reverend Suzuki said. Suzuki's English pronunciation was good. Takuda thought it was good, at any rate. "I pray for everyone, everywhere, every time."

She slid back into the chair across from Chief Nakamura's desk. It was the only decent room in the building, but it afforded her no privacy. Takuda and Suzuki bowed low, and they held the position to acknowledge her grief. After a few seconds, she turned away from them.

Suzuki tugged on Takuda's sleeve, and they walked slowly out of Nakamura's office toward the interrogation room, where the corpse was laid out on the steel-topped table.

"The poor woman just wants to be left alone," Suzuki said, "but I didn't want to pray over her husband's body without her permission. Thank you for taking me to see her."

Kuma shuffled aside and tried to melt into the wall as they neared the door of the interrogation room. They had to squeeze past his belly.

The smell hit them as they opened the door.

There is a cloying sweetness to the corruption of a human corpse, a sickening odor that clings to the palate and ruins the next few meals. It's not unlike the reek of spoiled pork. Takuda knew the smell, unfortunately, and he also knew the sharper, fishy undertone. Lee Hunt had not died a natural death.

The village doctor, Fujimoto, looked up at Takuda. The doctor had not aged well. "You again," he said.

"Me again, Doctor." He stepped toward the table with a nod to the patrolmen who flanked the door on the inside. "You knew it was only a matter of time."

Suzuki crossed behind Takuda and took up a station at the far end of the room. He unrolled a thin cushion, knelt, and began reciting the sutras.

"Hey, Priest," the doctor called out. "Did you bring any incense? It would help with the perfume." He was obviously drunk. He looked around as if seeking approval from the patrolmen. He should have known better. Kikuchi and Inoue stared straight ahead, showing their embarrassment only in the stiffness of their necks.

Fujimoto gave an exaggerated shrug. "Useless. You see, it's just like that fool Nakamura to leave three men guarding a corpse, if you count Kuma as a man." He reached under the sheet and lifted the corpse's arm by the wrist and dropped it on the table. "This one won't try to escape."

"Doctor Fujimoto, you're drunk on the job, and you should go home," Takuda said quietly.

"I had a couple before they called me," he said, offering Takuda a jar of mentholated gel. "I'm not performing surgery tonight. Not on him, anyway."

Meeting the doctor's challenging stare, Takuda declined the gel. A dab under his own nostrils would help cut the stench. This time, though, Takuda didn't need it. He was getting used to awful smells.

The doctor shrugged and put the gel away. Then he whipped the cover off the corpse's face.

The victim's battered features were twisted in an expression of torturous pain. The sightless blue eyes were wide with terror.

Takuda almost looked away. It was shocking, especially with the whiteness of the skin. Aside from the patches of lividity and bits scrubbed raw by river rocks, much of the skin was ridiculously white, white as a fish's belly, white as if it had been bleached. As a child, Takuda thought "white" was a political euphemism for Europeans, much as "yellow" was used to describe

Asians even though they were actually anything between the color of cream and the color of bricks. He had believed this until he saw a television program that featured British schoolchildren playing on a lawn. They were as white as paper. That had disgusted him, but this pale corpse was simply pathetic, a broken bit of another family tragedy, stiff and cold on the interrogation room table.

Takuda pulled the sheet down farther. Aside from abrasions and scraping, the corpse appeared whole. There were five parallel slices down the calf and a gaping wound just under the ribs on the right side. Just as he had expected. Takuda felt his fists flex and tighten of their own accord.

The man had been lured to his death. He and his wife had planned to swim in the upper reaches of the Naga River. The current was dangerous at this time of year, and only ignorant strangers or truant children would be foolish enough to swim in such a flow. He had heard something, his wife said, a whispering voice that she had been unable to hear. He had seen something, perhaps a child. He had suddenly disappeared as if pulled beneath the surface. He had surfaced once but slipped into the river again. His corpse was dragged from the first gate almost eighteen hours later.

The wounds were familiar. The murderer of his brother and his son was still killing. If Takuda had to destroy the whole cult, household by household, he would do it. He would start that very night.

The doctor motioned to the patrolmen. "Pick him

up and take him to my office. We'll do a proper autopsy in the morning." He leered at Takuda. "That will give everyone time to be more professional."

Suzuki chanted in the background. The patrolmen didn't move.

Takuda said, "Doctor, the body will undergo autopsy down in the city, and there will be an official inquest."

The doctor smirked. "I understand. I do need to take some samples. When they autopsy this poor foreigner, they'll find a hole where his liver used to be. Half his intestines will have been sucked out his anus as if they were noodles, and the slices in his leg will be full of unidentifiable toxins. They'll call it death due to drowning, even without water in his lungs. They'll write that they found postmortem soft tissue loss due to freshwater eels. Eels! They'll say those five parallel cuts on his leg were from rocks."

Takuda felt his heart slowing in his chest as blood rushed to his head. The doctor swabbed the cuts in silence.

"Doctor, I'll need to talk to you about all this when you're sober."

"You'd better catch me before noon, then. Right, patrolmen?" He cackled at Kikuchi and Inoue, who stood a little straighter and stared straight ahead.

"You've seen wounds like these before."

The doctor sighed. "I've seen your son. I've seen others. Now I've seen this one."

"Sober up and tell me what you know."

"Look, Detective, I don't really know anything. Every time I had a chance to learn something, I drank instead, just to be sure I never really knew what was happening. The chief chooses to be blind and deaf, the sergeant chooses to be fat and stupid, and I choose to be drunk." He grinned. "You chose to leave."

"I'm back."

The doctor's grin faltered. He packed away his swabs with the exaggerated care of the profoundly inebriated. "I don't really know anything, but if—I'll help if I can."

He covered the corpse with an almost reverential delicacy. He bowed to Takuda, ignored the young patrolmen, and walked unsteadily out of the interrogation room. There was the sound of his soft collision with Sergeant Kuma, then muffled curses. The door closed with a soft click.

Suzuki chanted on. One of the young patrolmen swallowed loudly.

"You've done a good job here. You looked where I told you?"

They bowed. They seemed to want to speak.

"You don't have to choose sides. You've done your jobs. Leave now," Takuda said. "It's about to get worse."

Kikuchi and Inoue walked quickly, but they didn't quite make it. They almost ran into Nakamura on the way out.

The chief stepped in with his chin held high, perhaps to reduce the wattles on his wrinkled neck. He regarded Takuda with cold, expressionless eyes.

"You've dismissed our doctor, Detective Takuda."

"He says he doesn't know anything about this victim's wounds even though he's seen them before." Takuda pulled off the sheet and pointed to the cuts on the corpse's leg. "Don't tell me you've never seen these before."

"I may have seen a familiar pattern. Tragically, some people unfamiliar with the water safety question cut themselves on river rocks."

"The rocks in this river were already smooth in the days of the woolly mammoth."

"I don't have your grasp of geology. I cut myself on a rock just last summer. The pattern was similar."

"Where, Chief? Show me the scar."

"I don't have time for this."

"How do drowning victims get the same cuts time and again? Exactly the same cuts, with no sharp rocks in sight. Measure the scars on my face against the ones on this corpse's leg."

"Grief has driven you mad. You should go back to the city."

"Not until the water safety question is solved, Chief. Not until it's solved once and for all."

Nakamura's eyes narrowed to slits. He turned as if to storm out, but he decided in mid-turn to walk out slowly, in a stately manner. He was silent until he opened the door to find Kuma blocking his exit. "Get out of the way, you fool."

Takuda and Reverend Suzuki were alone. "Hey, Priest. You wanted to take a walk tomorrow? You wanted to show me something upriver? Well, I'm ready. Officer Mori has taken over my paperwork, so I'm ready to listen to anyone who'll tell me something useful."

Suzuki didn't answer. He didn't even open his eyes. He just continued to chant.

Takuda didn't really care. He reached for the sheet to cover the body, but he noticed something strange. The victim's face had relaxed, and the eyes were clear. It was not the slackness that comes with the lessening of rigor mortis. It was the relaxation that comes with the cessation of suffering.

He turned to look at Suzuki. *Can the chanting ease the pain of the tortured dead?*

He covered the corpse. *It did nothing to help me keep my tongue with the chief. No chanting is powerful enough to keep me from making a fool of myself.*

Then again, perhaps it gave me the strength to finally say what must be said.

He bowed his head as Suzuki chanted on. *No matter how the chanting works, we're going to need it. Things will only get worse from here on out.*

CHAPTER 14

"This is where Lee Hunt disappeared," Detective Takuda said.

He and Reverend Suzuki stood on the riverbank. It was Friday, only three days since the attempted abduction of Hanako Kawaguchi. The morning sun sparkled on the Naga River, churning and roiling in its narrow bed. The river had carved a course meandering over the centerline of the older bed, a wide trough of ruts and boulders. The flow was much reduced by the construction of the southern dam, but the river apparently still had the power to carry off a full-grown man.

Especially with a little help.

"The current dragged him north," Takuda said. "His wife said he kept going under, even though he seemed to get handholds. She said he caught a boulder and almost made it to the bank."

"He probably caught a handhold there," Suzuki

said, pointing to a boulder just before a bend in the river. "Maybe again down there." He started downstream with long, rock-to-rock leaps. At each landing, his long, skinny arms sank slowly as his trailing shirttail caught up with him. He seemed to float down like a crane choosing its roost.

"Where are you going, Priest?"

Suzuki turned, teetering on a boulder. "I thought we would see where he tried to get out."

"There's nothing to see downstream. There's nothing more to know about the victim. He's cooling in a locker in the city, and they won't find anything to change anyone's mind about the water safety question. They never do." Takuda pointed upstream, southwest. "We're going in there. That's where we might find something new."

Suzuki nodded slowly, almost sadly. When he reached Takuda's side, they turned together and faced the next bend, the mouth of the darkest corner of the Naga River valley.

The southwest corner of the valley was in perpetual twilight. It was a place of moss and stagnant pools. No one lived there. In that corner of the valley, the struggle between light and darkness had been lost millennia before. Hundreds of meters below Eagle Peak Temple, the river had carved its own hollows and caverns, places that had never seen full sunlight. Takuda peered ahead into the dim ravine. He could see nothing. He had never been there himself, and he didn't think he had ever met anyone who had. It was so far from the daily life of Oku Village that he felt somehow surprised it really existed.

The stunted trees drew closer as they followed the bend of the river south and left the sunlit world behind.

The ravine continued to narrow and deepen. The river ran swift and sullen in its older channel, trapped in the stony roots of the mountains. The river had dug deep, and soon the west bank was too steep for walking, so Takuda and Suzuki climbed the slippery, leaf-covered clay to the foot of the mountain. Even ten meters above the surface of the water, they were still in shadows.

"There was a trail here once," Takuda said. "The footing is still pretty good. A lot of people walked into darkness here."

"This is an old, old trail. When people first came here, this was probably the riverbank. See, there are the old stone lanterns."

At the inside edge of the path lay toppled stone lanterns, black and green with slime and moss. Takuda saw that they were not hollow, and they had never actually produced light.

"Eagle Peak Temple originally set these up as a reminder to Buddhists that this was a path to evil," Suzuki said. These lanterns were placed along the path to represent the light of *dharma*." He stopped and pulled the underbrush aside to reveal a toppled stone lantern. Its base had crumbled, and the top had split. "These were erected in the fifteenth century. This is the power of the light of faith. The cultists kept the path clear all these years, but they never had the heart to throw the lanterns into the river. There, you can see where they lead." He pointed upstream.

Around the next bend, they looked down upon two irregular stone pillars standing side by side in the river-bed. Hundreds, perhaps thousands of years before, the current had undercut the foot of the mountain, sending a flood of soil and stone into the river. The soil had washed away, leaving a jumble of stones supporting two upright splinters, each twice the height of a man. Before the dam was built, the columns would have appeared to stand alone above the water. Now that the flow was reduced, the river burbled madly over the blackened stones that shored the pillars in place. The pillars themselves were brown below the old waterline.

"The gate to the Shrine of the Returning Apprentice," Suzuki said.

Takuda frowned. The photo from Ogawa's apartment had been taken from a lower angle, and the waterline had been higher. "I've seen a photo of this place taken from the water," he said.

Suzuki turned to him. "A photo with a group of men on the stones?"

"No, no one, just the stones. Why?"

"I once saw a group photo of the Farmers' Co-op taken down there. Everyone in it is dead now."

"What were they doing out here?"

"The Co-op was a cover for the cult after the war, but I don't know if the men in the photo were here on cult business. It probably wasn't a ceremony. Ceremonies were not held so openly. They were seldom held in daylight." Suzuki looked around. "If you call this daylight."

As they drew closer, Takuda spotted the dark lines near the tops of the pillars, probably the rotted remains of rice-straw rope.

"Someone must have cut it," Takuda said. "It's not so old that it would have rotted through in the middle, and there's nothing hanging down at the sides."

"No," Suzuki said. "I'll bet there was never a length hanging between the pillars. You see that at more modern shrines. This is a much, much older form of superstitious animism. They tied offerings directly to the object of worship. If you wanted good fortune from the earth, you bound your offering and buried it in the earth. If you wanted good hunting from the forest, you hung your offering from the tree branches."

"If you wanted mercy from the Naga River . . ."

". . . you tied your offering to the stones in the water. Maybe we can get down there later," Suzuki said. He squatted on the path and opened his backpack. "Let's stop and eat lunch."

Eat here? Takuda scanned the river below and the mountainside above. He wasn't hungry.

"I have to eat every couple of hours," Suzuki said. "It's my metabolism. I'm hungry all the time these days. Please join me." He handed Takuda a homemade rice ball and a can of tea. "I don't want to eat in a place like this either, but I can't hike on an empty stomach. I get nauseated and cranky."

They squatted on the trail because the ground was too damp and nasty. There were no birds, no frogs, no buzzing flies. There was only the rushing of the river below and the sound of their eating.

Into that stillness, Suzuki said, "I almost died when your little brother drowned."

There wasn't even a polite noise appropriate to such a statement. Takuda continued to eat.

"I loved your brother like my own brother, and I had been miserable ever since I stole his toy airplane. I hated going to school because I had to see him. He sat a few seats ahead of me, and he never turned around anymore, no matter what I said or did. I was ashamed of myself, and nothing was fun anymore. One day, I wished he would die so I wouldn't have to see him anymore.

"Then all of a sudden, he was dead. I was there when they pulled him out of the canal with his leg all cut up and with bloody water gushing from the wound in his side. I knew it wasn't my fault, of course. Even at that age, I could tell magic from direct causality. But I had stolen from my best friend, and all I had gotten for it was a little shove. Even after I wished him dead, that's all that happened. It didn't make sense. There was no balance and no justice and no mercy in the world, your brother was gone forever, and there was no way for me to make it up to him.

"Then I ran into you, and you beat me badly. That beating made more sense than anything before or since. You cracked one of my ribs, you know, along with the bloody nose and the black eye. It didn't matter. I slept like a baby that night. It's difficult to describe what a relief it was."

Takuda stood up. "I said I was sorry for that. We were just boys. It was stupid of me. Please accept my apology."

Suzuki leapt to his feet. He towered over Takuda. "No, it was an important lesson."

Takuda turned and headed up the trail, but Suzuki was suddenly ahead, facing him. Suzuki was quiet and fast, when he wanted to be.

"That beating was an indirect result of my incorrect thoughts, incorrect words, and incorrect deeds. It was a perfect and shining application of practical karma. It taught me to take responsibility for my thoughts and my actions. It taught me how to be a man."

"Well, let's be men and go see this shrine of yours." Takuda skirted Suzuki and followed the trail up toward the overhanging stone.

Suzuki said, "Do you know how your little brother idolized you?"

Takuda stopped on the trail with his back to Suzuki. "We were close."

"He wanted to be just like you."

We're on the job. We need to get up to that shrine. Instead, he turned to face Suzuki. "He was a good boy. He was a gentle boy. He wasn't like me at all."

"I was jealous of him. I wanted a big brother like you. None of my brothers were so athletic and strong."

"You still think you caused his death."

"No, don't be stupid. I just miss him. I miss Shunsuke Takuda."

Well, now he's done it. Takuda looked at the leaf-covered clay at their feet. "Okay, Priest. You miss Shunsuke? I miss him, too."

"We both lost our innocence when he . . ."

"Wait, please. Have you attached yourself to this business because you feel guilty about stealing a toy from my brother? Because you miss him?"

"No, I have forsworn revenge, but I want to spare others that kind of pain, if possible. I attached myself because it's a man's job. I don't know what else to do. I don't know how to stop the evil in this valley. Neither do you. But maybe I can help, if a way presents itself. Does that make sense? Is that good enough?"

Takuda laughed. The sound was ugly in his own ears. "Of course that's good enough. Everyone is content to let me cut off my own head these days, so I'm glad at least one person will be with me when the sword falls."

"Detective, I understand."

"You understand? That's good, because I don't. I have a country priest and a green officer on my side, Chief Nakamura and his doctor probably want me dead, and my boss is slowly forgetting I exist. I've already started lying and breaking rules, and I still don't know what I'm fighting here. Now you bring up Shunsuke . . ."

"Hey, speaking of green officers, I wanted to ask

you about Officer Mori. Is he a swordsman? Does he fence at all?"

Takuda looked at Suzuki for a few seconds, but he couldn't tell just by looking if Suzuki was truly mad. Suzuki had brought up Takuda's dead brother and pledged himself to a cause neither of them understood. Now he changed subjects as casually as a small child would discard one toy for another.

"I don't know, Priest. Officer Mori is handy with a standard-issue staff. He's probably done a bit of fencing along the way." He turned and walked up the embankment toward the shrine above them.

Suzuki followed him, muttering the sutras as they walked.

Takuda felt a little uneasy with this odd priest, and the chanting that had seemed so soothing the night before seemed out of place and unnerving in this dark ravine.

Now it feels like a bad idea to enter the darkest corner of Japan with a stranger.

CHAPTER 15

The shrine was a plain cedar box perched on a lip of rock overhanging the Naga River. Detective Takuda and Reverend Suzuki dug into the clay with their boots as the ascent steepened, and then they hit the last three meters: an almost vertical climb to the stone lip. Wooden posts jutted from holes in the exposed stone, but the posts were rotten, spongy and wet to the touch. Takuda broke the posts off with his bare hands, Suzuki dug out the blackened pulp with a spoon from his backpack, and they used the empty postholes to climb the face. At the top, Takuda pulled himself over the stone lip and then pulled Suzuki up after him.

The shrine lay above the shadow of the river's passage. It was sun-splintered, dry as kindling. The door rattled in its stone track and finally refused to slide at all, so Takuda lifted it aside.

"It's been rebuilt in the last century or so, but no telling how long it's been since anyone came here," Suzuki said as he ducked inside. Takuda stayed at the door, playing his pocket flashlight over the faded red walls. The building was basically a cubical hut, but the corners had been filled in at seemingly random angles to make an irregular octagon with a square altar in the center.

Takuda stepped into the octagon. The painted panels were lurid and amateurish, impossible to ignore. On the wall opposite the door, a thin and vicious Kappa glared into the distance past Takuda's shoulder as it wrestled an improbably large horse into a stream. On the next panel, the Kappa feasted on the entrails of a drowning man. On other panels were sooty scenes apparently unrelated to the Kappa: a monk approaching a temple in a dark valley, the same monk praying at an altar half-submerged in a black pool, a demon swimming with fantastic sea creatures, a demon in ragged robes approaching a village, the same demon set aflame by villagers with torches.

Takuda turned away from the painted walls. The floor was unfinished wood, bare save for windblown leaves, dust, and a length of yellowed nylon rope. The altar in the center of the floor was a plain cubical box with a stone lid. The lid was a flattish trapezoidal boulder bound with crude iron straps, straps perhaps designed to attach a chain to the stone.

"We need a winch up here," Suzuki whispered.

They stood quietly. Takuda was considering the

wisdom of removing the stone, winch or no winch, when he realized they were being watched.

On shelves placed near the ceiling in the eight angles of the room stood ancient terra-cotta statuettes, the kind that had guarded the giant tombs of princes. Those statuettes were from the beginnings of their culture, before Buddhism had come to the islands, before the territories were united, before Japan even had a single name.

Takuda nudged Suzuki to indicate the statuettes. Suzuki shook his head as if to say he didn't know why they were there, either.

These were the most primitive type of such statuettes, like bowling pins with holes for eyes and mouths. Takuda had always considered them simplistic parodies of human figures, comically inept in terms of sculpture. Seeing them in this place, he realized that they had never been meant to represent humans. They were terrified ghosts, eyes wide in alarm, mouths agape in everlasting screams.

The strangest part was that the statuettes did not face outward to protect the stone altar from the outside world. They faced inward to protect the world from whatever waited beneath the stone lid.

Suzuki stepped forward, and the wooden floor whined and popped beneath his feet. As he approached the stone slab in the center, his footsteps resonated more deeply. The wooden floor covered a hole or fissure in the rock. Takuda stepped back at the alarming give beneath their feet, but Suzuki inched forward. He bent as if to lift the slab.

"What are you doing?"

Suzuki straightened, but he didn't step away from the slab. "Why are we whispering?"

Takuda didn't laugh at himself, and he surprised himself by continuing to whisper. "Stop playing with the slab. This floor is weak."

"This old cedar lasts forever, and no one has been wearing out this flooring. I don't think anyone has been up here in a long time. I don't see what it could hurt." Suzuki spoke at a normal volume. His voice was painfully loud inside the shrine. "Besides, why have pulleys to lift it if there's nothing to see underneath?"

"Pulleys?"

Suzuki pointed to the ceiling. There, in the shadows, old oaken pulleys were lashed to the rafters.

"That wouldn't lift this stone. Even if it did, that ceiling beam wouldn't hold up."

Suzuki slid his backpack onto the floor and grasped the iron bands on the stone. "That was part of their ritual, you see? They lifted the stone, but why? What could be under there? Don't you want to see what's under there?"

Takuda wasn't as concerned about what lay beneath the stone as what lay under the floor. "Step away from it now. It's going to give."

Suzuki slid his hands under the iron straps. "See? This one goes here, and this one—wait a minute—

ouch—there!" He stood back, shaking his pinched finger. "Now, help me, and we'll just guide it to the floor over there."

"No," Takuda said. "This isn't . . ."

The floor began to buckle beneath Suzuki. Nails squealed and ancient cedar popped as the box leaned like a capsized ship awash in the ancient wooden floor. Suzuki made to jump, but one hand was still in the iron strap. He would go with the stone when the floor gave out.

Takuda leapt forward, grabbed Suzuki by the back of the trousers, and squatted.

"Get your hand free of that thing!"

Takuda pulled for all he was worth, but it seemed to take forever for Suzuki's center of gravity to shift backward. Out of the corner of his eye, he saw wood slowly splinter and rend beside the altar. The floor was giving way in the center, and Takuda couldn't pull Suzuki backward faster than the floor collapsed.

The altar and the stone disappeared, and Suzuki began to sink feet-first, screaming, into the buckling floor. Takuda splayed out his own legs and elbows to make himself too big to fit through the gap. The buckling of the floor warped the flimsy cedar walls to bring the clay guardians crashing down from their perches.

The stone lid crashed in the echoing darkness below, and the falling cedar chattered down on top of it.

At least it's not bottomless—

There was a faint, meaty stink in the cool, damp air rushing up from beneath.

Suzuki's long legs flailed as he slid forward into the priest-wide hole, and Takuda was going with him. First Suzuki's belt loops entered the darkness, then Takuda's own hands, then his wrists, then his forearms, and then his own head . . .

Takuda's mass stopped them. He lay with his arms hanging into the hole in the floor. Blood trickled down his right arm, but it was only a scrape. The real problem was Suzuki's squirming. As Suzuki swung in Takuda's grasp, the creaking wood slowly splintered.

"Hey, Priest, stop moving around so much."

"I'm caught on something!" The echo from below was immense.

"Yes, I have you by the back of the pants."

Suzuki went still. "Can you please pull me up?"

"I could, but I'm flat on my belly here, so it wouldn't help you," Takuda said. "I could try to swing you up so you can catch the edge."

"No, no, no swinging. Just don't drop me. Are you okay? Can you hold me?"

"I could hold you here all day," he said, and he felt as if he could. "What do you see down there?"

"Nothing. It's pitch-black."

The nylon rope from the old block and tackle was barely within reach. When Takuda let go with one hand to reach for the rope, Suzuki shrieked in the darkness.

"Sorry. Here, rope coming down," Takuda said.

"Warn me if you do something like that again, okay?"

When Suzuki had tied the rope under his arms, Takuda rose to his knees and began hauling him up.

"Hey, just lower me," Suzuki shouted.

"Lower you? Don't be a fool. We don't know what's down there."

"Can you reach my pack? Hand it down here."

Takuda passed it down. In a few seconds, a flare exploded into blinding red light, and a cloud of sulfurous smoke singed Takuda's eyebrows and burned his nose. It was Suzuki's turn to apologize.

As Takuda lowered Suzuki into the darkness, the detective felt as if he were an adventurous child in a story from a grammar school reader. He and Suzuki were searching for treasure hidden by mountain bandits. It was ridiculous.

"I see light coming in down there," Suzuki said. "Wow, that's a long way down! This is about fifteen meters, don't you think? There's an opening just at the waterline. Just a little daylight at the bottom. That fall would have broken my leg, I'll bet! Okay, the flare is helping. There's a little water down there, some pools from the river water leaking in, I guess, and the stones—Oh, no. Oh, no."

Takuda felt the rope go slack as Suzuki found the bottom.

"What's going on down there?"

"Oh, oh, oh. There are iron shackles on the

wall—oh, look down here, Detective." Suzuki stood in a reddish circle. "Can you see?"

"Priest, what's going on down there?" Takuda stretched out farther over the ragged gap in the wooden floor.

Suzuki lowered the flare. There were bright round-ish stones and ordered sticks like baskets all over the cavern floor.

They weren't baskets. They were rib cages.

"These are skulls, Detective. Oh, oh, oh. The floor here—it's covered with human bones."

The floor popped and lurched under Takuda's belly. He reached for the rope, but it slid down into darkness. He had nothing to hold on to but the tilting floor itself, and it was giving way beneath him.

I hope Suzuki has the sense to move aside.

As the cedar splintered and folded all around him, he looked into the eyes of one of the toppled clay guardians. The silent sideways scream of frozen terror would fall with him into the cavern below.

The floor went silent as it finally released him. He fell free of the splintered wood into red-lit darkness, an echoing void. He prepared himself for the cavern floor rushing up to meet him.

CHAPTER 16

Detective Takuda didn't have time to tuck as he fell into the cavern beneath the Shrine of the Returning Apprentice, but he tried to relax and bend his knees. He felt oddly serene.

His feet hit first. He heard bones snap, but not his own. His legs bent properly, but his weight was so far forward that the impact drove his knees into his chest. His head whipped forward, and his chin hit his sternum so hard that his jaw rattled. His body briefly compressed into a ball, and when nothing more could compress, he bounced. As his body sprang forward, he hit Suzuki, and they somersaulted through the darkness together.

Takuda protected Suzuki's head on the first roll. He let go, and they separated. Takuda rolled to his feet, sliding among the skittering ribs until his boots bit in. After such a hard landing, he expected to see stars, the blue-and-orange sparks of a knockout punch, but he saw only the darting red glow of Reverend Suzuki's flare.

Suzuki landed flat on his backpack with his head pointed toward Takuda, the sputtering flare still grasped tightly in his hand. Takuda winced at Suzuki's impact, but Suzuki stopped his slide and swung himself around on the bones as if he had planned the whole thing. "Detective, are you okay?"

He said he was. He felt himself for breaks and punctures. His jaw ached from the impact with his own breastbone, but one hard little part of his mind noted without passion that the damage was more than acceptable for a fifteen-meter fall into darkness.

"This is horrible," Suzuki said as he clambered back up among the bones. He was covered with muck and shards of shattered rib. His eyes were wild in the last glimmerings of that flare. He pulled another from his backpack. His hands trembled as he struck it alight. "I counted seventeen skulls, Detective. There are probably many more in the shadows, all covered with mold and slime."

Overhead, Takuda saw the dim outline of the broken floor. Even the shrine was brighter than the cave. His eyes adjusted to the flare light. At his feet were jumbled bones, shattered stone, and splintered cedar. He and Suzuki had managed to ruin the most important crime scene in Japanese history.

"I've got one more flare after this one," Suzuki said. "I don't know about gases down here . . ."

"If it were flammable, we would already be dead."
He grasped Suzuki's wrist and held the priest's trembling hand aloft to get a steady light from the spitting flare.

The reddish light made a scene from hell. The narrow cave cut ten meters into the roots of the mountain. The floor of the cave was black, silty mud, and in that darkness were gray and cream and brownish skulls half-sunk among jackstraw ribs. All but hidden by the long bones and newer skulls were older bones blackened with slime and moss.

They stood speechless.

"There must be—there must be thirty skulls here," Suzuki said.

Takuda nodded. "At least thirty," he said, "but that's only in the top layer."

Suzuki looked at him in astonishment as the little flare sputtered out.

Takuda and Suzuki stood silent in the darkness. Takuda released Suzuki's wrist and waited for him to speak or to light another flare, but Suzuki was silent as well.

"Priest, what are you doing?"

"I'm waiting."

"For what?"

"To see what will come."

Ridiculous. In some ways, Suzuki was a great and clumsy fool, and he tried to make up for it by aping wisdom, which only made it worse. Standing silent in the darkness when there was work to be done? A vain pretense.

"Priest, light your flare. I haven't found my flashlight yet."

"Soon, Detective. Soon."

Takuda had to restrain himself from reaching out and shaking the man till a lit flare fell out of him. Instead, he listened to his own heart pounding in his chest and waited for Suzuki to finish his game.

He was truly in the mouth of evil, the sacrifice pit of the Kappa cult. The water safety question wasn't a question anymore. This was murder. If he could not bring the killers to justice, he would stop them by any means possible. He would clean up this wretched little valley for good.

There was a slight rustling sound, a grinding of bones underfoot, the sound of Suzuki shifting from one foot to the other, bracing himself, reaching carefully into his bag.

The hair stood up on Takuda's neck. *What a fool I've been.*

It had been Suzuki all along. Suzuki had played innocent to lure him into this cave, this burial pit, and Suzuki meant to crawl out alone. Suzuki had even invoked the name of Takuda's murdered brother to lull him into a state of trusting stupidity. Now Suzuki was drawing out a poisoned blade, or five poisoned blades, the same blades that had killed Takuda's brother and his son and Lee Hunt. Takuda raised his left arm to defend himself and raised his right hand high to deal Suzuki an invisible, open-handed blow from above, a blow that would shift Suzuki's head a palm's width to the left before the first cervical vertebra could catch up, severing the spine and killing him instantly. If Takuda used some of his newfound power, the blow would pulp Suzuki's brains as well, but that was incidental. *It's too bad. I liked him.* He stood frozen in the dark, waiting for the bite of a blade.

"I've got it," Suzuki said.

"What do you have?"

The flashlight clicked on in Suzuki's hand. It lit his puzzled expression from below. "What are you doing? Warding off bats? There are no bats here. The exit is too low and too watery."

Takuda slowly lowered his hand.

"I was standing on your flashlight." He handed it to Takuda. "Before that, I was just praying for the truth about this place. I know why we're not afraid."

"Priest, I am afraid of this place. Very afraid." *You'll never know, Priest.* He was so afraid that he had almost slapped the man's head off his neck.

"No, that's just nerves. Stay still for another minute. Feel for it. There's no evil here. It's just a hole full of bones. This place is deserted. This is all old sacrifice. Years old."

Takuda stilled himself and listened to his heart. Suzuki was right. *There's no meat on these old bones, and the trail from here is cold. Stone cold.*

Forensic evidence in the cave wouldn't give them a living suspect. The murderers had their own process, their own discipline, and they would never, ever deviate. That was how the monstrous sacrifice had survived for so long with multiple murderers, generations of murderers covering for each other. As far as corroborating clues from the outside, there was less than nothing. There might be pictures linking dead members of the Farmers' Co-op to the stone pillars on the river, but nothing linking anyone, living or dead, to the shrine itself or the narrow cavern beneath. Unless one of the worshippers had dropped his wallet into the chasm, there would be no way to prove that anyone from the cult had even lifted the stone, much less committed murder.

"Priest, do you think news of this will flush out the killers? Do you think someone will crack?"

Suzuki sighed as he rummaged for a flare. "That happens in the movies, doesn't it? Some brave widow steps forward, or some old man wracked with guilt. But here? In this valley? Don't bet on it."

Suzuki was already crouching as if to crawl out though the low fissure to the river. He picked his way through the bones.

"Take off your pack," Takuda said. "You'll get stuck."

"Then hold it for me," Suzuki said. "No, wait, I'll tie it to the rope so it follows me. Now you take the end. Hold it tight!" He crawled down among the bones to look out through the fissure.

Takuda swore and grabbed Suzuki's legs. He was ready to jerk Suzuki out if anything went wrong.

"I see light coming in here," Suzuki said. "Wow, that's a long way out! There's an opening just at the waterline! I'm going through!"

Takuda released Suzuki's legs. The priest's grunting diminished as he crawled, then there was silence, and then there was just Takuda and the rope passing though his fingers. The bones clunked and rattled with the rope's passage.

Finally, two sharp tugs, and it was Takuda's turn to follow. As he crawled through the muck and jumbled bones toward the fissure in the rock, his nostrils flared. He thought he caught a whiff of rotting fish, but it was hard to pick out from the mud-bloody smell of the moldering bones. Still, he was tensed in every muscle as he belly-crawled on the wet sand. He had never felt claustrophobic, but he was in a very, very tight spot.

It's not going to be the last time I'm in a tight spot if I follow this mad priest.

He came out squinting in the perpetual twilight at the river's edge. Suzuki was nearly naked, perched on a stone washing his pale, bony body in the cold river water.

"I need your help, Detective."

Takuda pulled himself out of the fissure, dragging his back pack behind him. The rope trailed down the sandy slope to Suzuki's feet.

"You didn't even bother to tie off the rope? I'm glad *I* didn't need *your* help with anything. What do you need?"

"My vestments. And I need you to check the opening."

"What opening?"

"The other entrance to the cave. There."

Takuda turned. A few yards upstream, parallel to the stone columns, a man-high cleft hid in the roots of the mountain. The pillars obscured it from the higher bank, but it was visible down by the new waterline. Before the dam was completed, the cleft would have been completely underwater. At the mouth of the cleft were piles of toppled stones. Stacks of them still stood at the mouth of the cleft, as if there had been a wall.

Gooseflesh stood on Takuda's neck.

There had been a wall to keep something trapped inside the cave, just as there were ancient statuettes to keep it contained from above, just as there was a shrine for sacrifices to keep it quiet, just as there was a secret cult to make sure it got its fill.

Suzuki pointed upward. "Did you see the sacrifices? Up on the pillars?"

Fish and birds, including cranes and cormorants, had been tied to the pillars with rice-straw ropes. They were blackened husks, dried and leathery despite the moisture in the air. Takuda looked away. "If you want mercy and benevolence from the Naga River, you make your offerings directly, right, Priest?"

"This is nasty, Detective. It's old and primitive superstition. Live sacrifices to the river. I knew it was here, on some level, but it's still hard to believe. What a nightmare."

"What about those shackles inside?"

"Hmmm? Yes, big iron shackles pinned into the walls. You don't have those black iron shackles I gave you, do you?"

"No, they're at home."

"Pity. I think they might have been part of a set. We can compare them someday."

Takuda moved toward the second cave opening as if in a dream.

"Detective, don't go back in there until you have to."

The sandy bank stopped at the mouth of the cave, where the remaining stones denied the river entrance. Takuda stepped over them into the darkness. Suzuki stepped in behind him, pulling his sash on straight.

"There's a bend here—that's why we didn't see the light from the inside." When they got around the bend, Takuda stood in near darkness before a wall of dried silt, sticks, and stones. "Light that last flare," he said. "We'll use my flashlight after that, but I don't want to run down the bat—Oh, no. Priest, light this up. There's even more."

In the light of Suzuki's flare, the wall rose before them. It was not made of sticks and stones. It was a solid wall of human bone mortared together with black silt. Under Takuda's fingertips, the bones collapsed inward in a rattling mass, leaving behind them a faint, moldy stink and a sound like bowling pins in sawdust, a sound that echoed through the cave like stifled, chuckling laughter.

CHAPTER 17

It was twilight in the rest of the Naga River valley, but the river gorge had been in darkness for hours. Chief Nakamura slipped and slid on the riverside trail.

"This is all very bad business. A cave full of bones? What stupidity!"

Nakamura had complained the whole way. Detective Takuda had ignored most of it. When the chief had become too shrill, Takuda had moved farther ahead.

Behind him, the chief stumbled into the underbrush. "This trail is too muddy. I can't get traction here."

Sergeant Kuma caught up to the chief. He was breathing hard. "That's probably why the detective suggested you change your shoes."

Takuda didn't bother looking back. He was glad of the time to think.

The disappearances were a mystery for generations, but they were wrapped in a sort of shadow. Even when schoolmates and relatives had vanished, even when everyone had been suspicious of the postcards, no one in the valley had questioned it aloud.

Now, even though Takuda and Reverend Suzuki had found the site of the worst mass murder in Japanese history, no one would believe it. If Takuda dragged the local police by the collars and threw them into the cave, they might not notice the human remains.

What was worse, Takuda couldn't really blame them. He knew the murders had occurred, but the more evidence of a murderous conspiracy Takuda found, the less sense it made. *The cult offered sacrifices to the Kappa in return for—what? The hope of good irrigation? The hope of good fishing?* It was stupid.

There was no possible reason for all these murders. *Why did the cult bother?*

There was something else at work. Just as the slicked-back punks on the streets of the city represented the real mobsters in the background, the cult of the Kappa represented something bigger. *But what?*

When the short procession finally reached the sandy bank downstream from the stone pillars, Takuda asked the sergeant to go back and fetch the doctor. They had left him retching up the previous night's drinking among the broken stone lanterns downstream. Nakamura gave a curt nod of assent, and Kuma waddled up the bank. Nakamura hissed at him to hurry and turned a cold eye to Takuda.

Things had worked out as well as they could have, Takuda thought. If Takuda had the chief to himself, without the sergeant and the doctor, he might be able to talk some sense into the man.

It was not to be.

"There is no cave of bones," the chief said. He shifted from one foot to the other. Takuda could tell that moisture from the riverbank sand was seeping into Nakamura's street shoes. "There never was such a thing. Maybe they're remains of people who drowned by accident. In a place with so much water, it's inevitable."

"The people in that cave didn't drown. Not without help, anyway."

"Listen to me." Nakamura stepped closer. His face was twisted with anger. "Don't you dare start talking about some sort of serial killings. Don't even think it! If what you say about some human bones is true, there will be reporters all over this valley very soon. Airing your wild theories would be the height of irresponsibility, and I won't have it. Don't force me to invoke higher powers!"

"The higher powers are already here waiting for us. I left Officer Mori to take pictures while I came to pick you up. He's in there now, taking photographs and laying evidence marking flags, but he called to say the uniforms were gathering outside the cave. At this point, I'm not talking to anyone but you, Chief."

The chief stepped back and bowed. "Ah, I see. Well, that's sensible of you. Yes, quite. It's good that you understand the gravity of our situation here. I suppose our conversation last night helped you see that it's best to let things take the proper channels."

Takuda returned the bow. "I don't care who's in charge, Chief. I just want the freedom to investigate what's really happening in this valley."

Nakamura shook his head in disbelief. Takuda stepped forward to keep the chief from stumbling backward into the river, but he shrugged Takuda off and went around him toward the cave. Takuda followed the old man's uneven progress.

When they came around the last bend, light blazed from the darkened cave like an ironic reenactment of a tale from Japan's mythical past. Uniformed officers scurried on the sandy soil at the base of the mountain. Three men stood talking on the bank opposite the cave mouth. Talking. *Laughing.*

The chief started to cross the river on the rocks below the twin obelisks. Takuda held no hope that the old man would get to the cave without soaking his trousers, at least. He chose not to aggravate Nakamura by attempting to help him.

He studied the three men talking on the bank.

The regional director general was out of uniform. Takuda had received two commendations directly from him, but he knew nothing about the man. The regional director general answered directly to the National Police Agency's commissioner general, so he was in the level of Japanese bureaucracy where management by force of personality no longer existed. At that level, power lay in the inexorable bureaucracy itself, and only the greatest of fools would allow his personal preferences to run afoul of that torturous machinery.

The uniformed officer beside him, on the other hand, could still style himself a leader of men. He was a superintendent supervisor, four ranks above Takuda, and he stood with his feet wide and his fists on his hips. He probably considered himself in charge of the site.

The third man, a broad-shouldered, square-jawed civilian, was a total mystery to Takuda. He pointed at the interior of the cave as if lecturing tourists about an interesting landmark. He wore spike-soled, split-toed fishing boots appropriate to the terrain, and his sportsman's khaki pants and houndstooth jacket gave him an air of local gentry from a bygone age. He ignored Takuda completely, as did the regional director general.

"Takuda, good job bringing the locals into this immediately," said the superintendent supervisor. "You'll give your report to Superintendent Yamada. Take your man Mori home. We're handing it over to the village chief."

Takuda bowed deeply, buying time. While he slowly straightened, the well-dressed stranger murmured to the regional director general and gently led him away by the sleeve.

"Superintendent Supervisor, thank you for relieving me, but I believe Mori has this scene under control, and it's doubtful that the village station has the resources . . ."

"Detective, you are relieved. Go home. Prepare a detailed report for Superintendent Yamada."

"Yes, Superintendent Supervisor, but I thought you

might want to know something of the circumstances here before . . ."

"There's no need for a superintendent supervisor to know more about an archaeological site," the civilian said. He had simply reappeared at the superintendent supervisor's elbow. "Let's go have a drink."

The superintendent supervisor turned toward the stranger, smiling. "Let's go have a drink," he said. "There are a few pubs in Oku Village, but I think we'd do better down in the city."

"Excellent idea, Superintendent Supervisor." They drifted across the rocks and down the muddy trail, the superintendent supervisor and the regional director general chatting amiably as the third man gently guided them along the darkling path. Takuda watched them until they disappeared in the gloom at the bend.

Chief Nakamura was wet to the knees. He stood at the opening of the cave in the glare of portable flood-lights. Beyond him, jumbled skeletons and broken skulls stretched to the depths of the cave. In the middle of the cave, Mori squatted among the skulls. The only sounds were the rapids outside and Suzuki's droning chants from the ruined shrine above.

Takuda stepped up beside Nakamura. The chief stood on stray ribs.

Mori stepped carefully between the skulls. He wore plastic shoe covers and surgical gloves. He placed an evidence flag by the next skull and photographed it with the prefecture's standard camera. He had come prepared.

Nakamura looked from one side of the narrow cave to the other as if unable to comprehend the scene before him. He seemed to watch Officer Mori for several seconds, then he turned his blank, uncomprehending stare on Takuda. His face slowly twisted with rage.

"The foreigner drowned far downstream. What were you doing up here?" Nakamura's hands were shaking. His reedy voice echoed in the cave. "This was already out of hand. This will destroy the village police office. It will bring nothing but bad press, and Zenkoku—Oh, Zenkoku. If they pull out, this valley will die."

"Nothing like that will happen if we handle it correctly. All they'll have is helicopter shots of the ravine. We can keep them out of the valley until things cool down."

Nakamura looked up sharply. He was interested for an instant, but then he growled, deep in his throat, like a dog.

"A fine detective you are. Liar! You tell people anything you need to follow your own insane agenda. First you say you can get the prefecture to take the stinking pervert out of my jail, then you say you can keep people out of the press . . ."

"What?" *Is he talking about Ogawa's wife or about the cave?*

Nakamura shook his head. "I'll have your job if this leaks out. I'll talk to your supervisor."

"I'll tell him you said so."

Nakamura took a breath as if he'd suddenly remembered how. "Detective, you're a fool. You're a fool, just as your father was. Do you really think these old bones mean anything?"

"Some of them are not very old at all," Takuda said.

"They're ancient. They've been well preserved by the conditions of the cave."

"That cave was under water fifty years ago. The only thing that kept the bones in was the stone wall in the mouth. How did anyone build a stone wall right there, right at the rapids?"

"Perhaps it was the Kappa. The Kappa built himself a house. If you meet a Kappa, just bow to it. It will bow in return and spill the water out of the depression on top of its head, and then you can wrestle it! That's the sort of nonsense people told us as children. Are you saying that there are people who believe that? Is Ogawa so crazy that he believes it?"

Mori pretended to work, but he was really watching Takuda.

Nakamura shook his head. "You're insane with grief, just as your wife was insane with grief. It was disgusting to watch. Disgusting. A grown man, a policeman, giving way to grief just as his woman did. You left the valley because she wanted to, because she cut herself. Honestly, acting as if that was a serious suicide attempt! If people want to die, they die. You coddled her, and you became a woman yourself. You act so big and strong, but you're weak, weak and womanly, just as your father was."

Nakamura wheeled and left the cave. Suzuki came to the end of a verse.

Takuda first turned his attention to Suzuki. "Thank you for the chanting, both for the dead and the living. It helped keep me calm during that conversation with the chief. But for your prayers, we might have ended up with another heap of old bones on this floor."

Suzuki ignored him. He was counting beats between verses, just as the whole congregation had counted silently in Takuda's youth. One hundred eight beats, one for each form of human sin. It was the most soothing silence he had ever known.

Takuda approached Mori. "Officer, you're good with computers, with plotting data and statistics and so forth?"

Mori opened his mouth to speak but thought better of it. He bowed in reply.

"Right," Takuda said. "I know I said that incorrectly, but you understood. If I want a result from a certain set of data, could you pull that data into a map? A map of the prefecture and this valley?"

Mori bowed.

"Plot drowning incidents as far back as possible," Takuda said. "If I'm right, these people are from areas where no one ever drowns."

"It's stranger than that," Mori said. "The next time we're both at headquarters, I have something to show you." He smiled without humor. "I have a lot to show you."

CHAPTER 18

"Heh-heh. A policeman of a decadent state and a priest of a defunct sect, both of you in a country jail with an unemployed engineer. It's a very sad scene." Ogawa's eyes glittered in the dim cell. "How sad for the three of us."

"You're like a different man," Takuda said. He stood in the center of the village police station's holding cell, and Suzuki squatted behind him, near the door.

Ogawa beamed. "I'm like a different man? How so?"

"The last time I saw you, you were acting drugged or brain-damaged."

"Acting? I was stunned. High school boys beat me with fencing sticks while the fat sergeant watched. These bumpkins beat me constantly. I believe I have survived a massive brain contusion. Heh-heh."

Takuda recounted what he had heard from patrolmen Kikuchi and Inoue. "Your new story is that the little girl dropped her bag and you were just trying to give it back."

"That is correct," Ogawa said with gravity.

"And she suddenly bit you."

"I am not liked by children or dogs. I'm used to it."

"Yet you confessed," Takuda said.

"I would have told them anything to stop those horrible beatings."

"Stop it. Your confession could take you straight to prison."

"I'm sure we've all seen better days."

"Your wife will probably go to prison as an accessory," Takuda said.

Ogawa laughed. "Never. You'll see. That fat little slut will wriggle out of this just fine."

"You won't."

"Hard times all around. Shouldn't you take a moment to pray for better fortune?"

"Interesting that you bring up prayer," Suzuki said from the doorway. "Where do you pray?"

Ogawa grinned with pleasure as he turned to Suzuki. His gums were an unhealthy gray. "Me pray? I don't pray, Priest, and I don't chant the sutras. Heh-heh-heh! What a waste of time!"

"I wouldn't imagine you chant sutras, no. But you've visited the shrine upriver," Takuda said. "You left your handiwork."

Ogawa hesitated. "Shrine? Handiwork? Did I piss on something again? Maybe I parked my bicycle in the wrong spot. Did I try to help another little girl?" He pulled on his ear and feigned a twitch in his eye, hiding unease behind a parody of unease.

Takuda pulled the photograph from his folder. "You had this photo in your apartment," he said. "We know you've been to the shrine."

"Me? I've never been there. Heh-Heh! I stole that photo from the village historical center. I stole it. Look at the developer's stamp on the print."

Takuda turned the print over. In faded blue characters: *June 1987.*

"That print was made before I came to the valley. I hope stealing it won't add too many years to this prison sentence you're talking about. I've never been to this shrine."

Suzuki's knees popped as he stood. "You've never been to this shrine, but you were so interested that you stole a photo of it. That doesn't make sense."

"You're a priest. You believe in a whole system that doesn't make sense."

Suzuki bowed enough to signal understanding, not agreement. "My system is about life, not death. Your system seems to be all about death."

Ogawa laughed, but he had no reply.

"We know how much you believe in death," Takuda said.

Ogawa cocked his head at him.

"The stink of death is on you, Ogawa. You brought it from beneath the shrine."

"Never been there."

Takuda leaned forward. "We know what's beneath the shrine, and we know what's in the spillway."

Ogawa's eyes widened.

Takuda decided to gamble. "We know that you're trying to revive the cult, and we know you're not working alone."

Ogawa looked relieved. "Cult. The people of this valley once had a healthy respect for native Japanese religion. They had a living religion. A living god. They didn't need fanciful ramblings of dirty Hindus and hairy Chinese." Ogawa leaned forward, glaring at Suzuki. "Your ancestors ruined it for everyone, threw everything out of balance."

"Who works with you?" Takuda asked.

"I'm never alone, Detective. But I'll tell you, I'm not the one you're looking for. I was here in this cell when the foreigner died. I don't know what you've found beneath this shrine you're talking about, but it has nothing to do with me." He swung his feet up onto the cot and leaned back with his hands behind his head. "I'll just wait here for whatever case the yokels can bring against me. Then I'll call my lawyer, and he'll be down here like a fox among the rats. You will fear him."

Takuda folded his arms. "So, all the *heh-heh-heh* is gone, eh?"

"Make me laugh. We'll see."

"What if I could make sure you're never charged?"

"You're lying. You can't do it."

Ogawa had slipped between Takuda's fingers. "All I want is the truth about the cult."

"You wouldn't believe the truth if I told you."

From the corner, Suzuki spoke: "Why do you study Ainu?"

"I'm a student of many different things, Priest."

"Why the changes to the Ainu texts?"

Ogawa ignored Suzuki's question. "For example, I know about your radical sect. It's barely Buddhism at all."

Suzuki ignored him. "It just looks like you're taking modern Ainu, changing the verb forms and removing sounds."

"Most scholars agree that your heretical sect is a thinly veiled crusade against native Japanese religion. Not even the people in the valley believe in it anymore. How do you keep the temple open?"

Suzuki said, "Whose language are you trying to learn?"

"Speaking of cults, now that the detective here has joined you, you're technically a cult." Ogawa turned to the detective. "You've placed yourself in the hands of a radical heretic. Just keep me out of it. Remember that I am a poor swimmer, and I have no claws to speak of."

"I didn't say anything about claws," Takuda said.

"Your face speaks for you."

Takuda tucked the folder under his arm. "There's nothing I can do for you now. You haven't given me a single piece of information I can use here. So let me give you something."

Ogawa sat up with his hands folded in his lap. *An attentive student.*

"Today, we found human remains in a cave under the Shrine of the Returning Apprentice. Hundreds. Maybe thousands. Some of them are so old they've almost turned to clay, but some of them aren't so very old at all. Less than ten years."

"Well, it explains all the empty storefronts."

"You don't seem too concerned," Takuda said, "considering that you're the only suspect in sight."

"I'm quite comfortable here. I'm just joking about the beatings, you know. I haven't had one in days."

"You're rejecting my help, Ogawa. I'm the most useful person you've talked to yet, and you've rejected everything I can do for you."

Ogawa looked at Takuda in disbelief. "You honestly think that I believe you could do anything for me? You must think I'm insane."

"I don't think you're insane. I think you have a definite reason for staying in custody as long as you can, just as you had a definite reason for staying in this valley. Just as you had a definite reason for giving up Okamoto Hydrological Systems, your wife, and your future. Why do you love this valley so much?"

"Love this valley? Who could love this dark, wet, filthy little cleft in the earth? It's disgusting in every way. The people are ignorant and narrow-minded and dull. The scenery is grim at the best of times. Everything is covered with a thin layer of greenish scum, if you look closely enough. The food is . . ."

"Ogawa, why did you stay here? What kept you?"

Ogawa looked up at him mournfully. "I met some-one," he said. "I thought it was love. I really did. But it's not love. It's nothing like love. It's something like the exact opposite of love, but there's not even a word for it. It's ruined me." He smiled. "It'll ruin you, too! I can tell, Detective!"

A heavy body slammed against the door. All three in the cell jumped in surprise.

Takuda was the first to the hallway. Just outside the holding cell, Sergeant Kuma loomed over Officer Mori. Mori guided the massive sergeant backward by the chin, by the elbow, by the rib cage, by the shoulder.

Mori had pushed Kuma's chin and rib cage upward, overbalancing the larger man. Kuma seemed per-plexed. He stepped back from Mori and regained his balance, and then he charged in low, like a bull. Mori couldn't sidestep Kuma in the narrow hallway, so he retreated as he pushed the sergeant's head down, just a little. By the third step, Kuma was stumbling for-ward. With a little more pressure from Mori, he would have landed flat on his face. Mori released Kuma and stepped back, allowing Kuma to regain his balance.

The sergeant's panting, sweaty bulk filled the narrow passage. He looked at Takuda, and Takuda saw the same fat, shame-filled boy he had met in the judo club so many years before. He stepped forward, but the sergeant turned away.

As Kuma disappeared into the office, Chief Naka-mura stepped from the shadows.

He stared at Takuda, Mori, and Suzuki in turn.

"Resisting the sergeant was the last straw," he hissed. "You are all being detained. Sergeant, patrolmen, put them in my office."

Suzuki was the first to go. As he maneuvered through the crowded hallway, he raised his hands over his head, held them out to be handcuffed, and then finally let them drop to his side. Inoue, the shorter of the two patrolmen, ushered him out into the squad room. Mori followed with a bemused expression.

Takuda looked back at the suspect lying on his cot. "I'll see you later, Ogawa."

"In the prefectural hospital mental ward, perhaps."

"I won't be visiting. I'm not a caseworker."

"Visiting? Caseworker? Heh-heh! You'll be in the padded cell next to mine! Stick with it, and this case will break you, Detective." The grin faded, and the light went out of his eyes. "I doubt you'll hold up as well as I have. You still believe the world makes sense."

In the hallway, the chief hissed like an angry goose. The patrolmen came running to fetch the detective, as if they could budge him.

"Listen to me." Ogawa stood on his cot. "This so-called case you're pursuing. It's going to drive you insane if it doesn't kill you. I give you even odds between insanity and death. Do me a favor: Just don't kill anyone. It would spoil all the fun. Stay out of the violent ward, and you know what I'll do for you?"

Takuda looked away. Patrolmen Kikuchi and Inoue

stood at attention in the hallway, ignoring the chief's motions for them to take the detective away.

Ogawa whispered behind him: "Detective what's-your-name, I'll save you a chair in the dayroom. When you finally can't take it anymore, I'll help you braid your own noose! Isn't that what friends are for?"

CHAPTER 19

Detective Takuda said, "Have you secured the cave site?"

Chief Nakamura bared his stained and crooked teeth. "I am asking the questions here."

Takuda, the chief, Reverend Suzuki, and Officer Mori had squeezed into the village police station's dingy conference room. The chief sat almost sideways in his chair to avoid rubbing knees with Suzuki.

"Now, tell me again," Nakamura hissed. "What were you doing so far upriver?"

"We were following up on information from Ogawa's apartment," Takuda said. He handed the chief the photo of the stone columns on the river. "He says he's never been there, and there's no reason to think he's lying. Some of those bones are old . . ."

"Ancient," said the chief. "Probably of Neolithic origin." He shoved the print down in his armchair as if he suspected Takuda would try to take it back. "So there was no reason to assume that there was any crime to investigate, was there? Ha! You were trespassing on private property with no warrant, no probable cause, and in the company of a civilian of questionable intent."

Suzuki looked up, blinking, then returned to his notebook. He wrote furiously. Officer Mori sat beside him, playing with the frayed seam of a yellowed doily. Once he had been taken away from his work in the cave, he seemed distracted and out of sorts. He knew something the rest of them didn't, and it absorbed him much more than the chief's monkey-troop politics. Mori had hinted that important data awaited at headquarters, and Takuda was curious to know what it was.

Beyond his interest in the officer's findings, there was something else nagging him, something the chief had said. Takuda had the strength of a bear, but his wits seemed slower. He was preoccupied, distracted. The chief was still talking about rights, responsibility, and ownership—

"Ownership," Takuda said. "You said we were on private property. I thought the mountain west of the Naga River was owned by the prefecture, all the way up to Eagle Peak Temple."

The chief made a sound like ripping cardboard. "You call yourself a detective, but you know nothing. It's private property. It has been for centuries. The dam is a federal structure, and the prefecture maintains the road, but the rights-of-way are granted in perpetuity.

So there, you see? You didn't even do your basic detective work! You didn't know where you were!"

"Zenkoku Development owns the land," Suzuki said. "The land was deeded to the priests of the Eagle Peak Order by a samurai family from the Chikuzen region. The priests assumed for centuries that they had clear title, but in 1937, my grandfather received word that descendants of the original owners had sold it to a trading company in the 1870s. That company had been absorbed by the Zenkoku group, and Zenkoku had clear title. Even the doubtful records of ownership burned with the village office during World War II, so all the priests had, really, was a spotty scroll with the names of three feudal lords."

"There, you see?" Chief Nakamura beamed with triumph. "Your temple exists because of the magnanimous gesture of the Zenkoku family of companies."

Suzuki bowed. "The temple grounds are leased to our sect in perpetuity, yes."

Chief Nakamura knocked knees with Suzuki. "And here you are, causing trouble, and you don't even know who pays the bills. Ha!"

Takuda sighed. "Speaking of paying the bills, Chief, I'd like to know a little more about your Zenkoku General common stock ownership."

The room stilled. Even Officer Mori paid attention.

The chief leaned forward. "Listen carefully. You are getting into serious business, making allegations about that. Serious business."

"I've made no allegations," Takuda said. "I felt it would be a courtesy to ask you rather than request sealed records."

The chief raised his eyebrows as if amused. "You call yourself a detective? Do the work! I was cleared of all wrongdoing years ago."

"Last summer, the national board denied a request that you receive official censure. That didn't clear you of wrongdoing." Takuda took out his cigarettes, but then he decided not to make himself too much at home. "We just need to know who we're dealing with here in the valley. Sergeant Kuma is reasonably clean. No one knows how he can afford that new car or how he got those great seats at the sumo tournament down in Fukuoka, but it's within reason, if a man is frugal enough. The shares you bought, on the other hand, represent a substantial sum. Your pay rate is public information, and it doesn't add up."

Nakamura pulled himself erect in his chair. "I got an employee discount. I was honored to serve as a security consultant for Zenkoku General's stockholder meeting."

The room was silent. Mori's face contorted with the effort of choking back his laughter, but the chief didn't seem to notice.

Takuda said, "You were working on security for Zenkoku General's annual meetings?"

"Well, yes, just giving my opinions on how to handle things should gangsters try to extort money from the company by disrupting the meeting. The big gangs, like the Yamaguchi-gumi. They do that, you know."

Mori snickered. Suzuki smiled in confusion at first, but a glance at the chief sobered him up quickly.

The chief stared at Mori and Suzuki in amazement. "Well, they do. I'm not making it up. Sometimes they bring bullhorns."

It was too much for Mori. Both Takuda and Suzuki called his name, but he seemed unable to stop laughing. Takuda rose and shouted for him to get control of himself, and he finally stood, shuddering with suppressed giggles. He bowed and apologized as he wiped away tears of mirth.

It was all due to the stress of finding so many human remains, Suzuki said. "I see this at funerals all the time. It's natural, especially among educated young men."

The chief was thunderstruck. "That explains his inappropriate laughter and his scuffle with the sergeant, but it doesn't explain all of you. You're all a bit mad, aren't you?"

"Madmen in a mad world," said a voice behind them.

The well-dressed man from the cavern site let the conference room door click shut behind him. No more houndstooth. He now wore a suit so black it sucked the darkness from the corners of the room. "Chief Nakamura, I advise you not to answer any more questions without a superior officer present."

"But counselor," Nakamura said, "I was just ready to start interrogating them."

"Ah, Chief! Spending your off-hours comparing notes in an informal discussion with brother officers and local spiritual leaders." The counselor nodded to Suzuki. "Going the extra mile to stay abreast on the finding of this purported archaeological site is entirely in keeping with your personal commitment to excellence. What industry and dedication!"

"I was just straightening them out on the old stock purchase question," Nakamura said. "This so-called detective didn't even know that the whole issue was resolved with the affidavit from your office . . ."

"If this discussion has strayed into personal finances, then the business day is done, and it's time to go bend the elbow and sing a few songs."

"I thought you already went out with the superintendent supervisor and the regional director general," Takuda said.

"I could never keep up with high rollers like those two. No, I just pointed them in the right direction, and then I came to see my friend Chief Nakamura. We like sweet potato liquor and singing the old songs, eh? No songs like the old songs."

Nakamura looked at him with something like love.

The well-dressed man opened his arms to the entire company. "You will all come along, of course."

Nakamura's smile crumbled. He shot jealous glances at Takuda, Mori, and Suzuki.

The man introduced himself as Endo. His title was simply "counselor," and his business card was a very plain Zenkoku General design on average stock. The card reassured Takuda. It was meant to show that Endo was beyond caring what his card looked like, but it was much too plain, too deliberately average. It was a sign of inverted vanity. Whatever else this man was, he was proud. That was a weakness.

"Now, come along, gents," the counselor said. "I know a place where there's a little something for everyone."

"But I haven't finished questioning them yet," Nakamura said.

Endo smiled. "What better time to chat than after a few drinks in the company of true loveliness, hmm? As I said, we have something for everyone, especially tonight. For Detective Takuda, we have old-fashioned girls, all beauty and grace. A man could drown in those big, brown eyes and be bound up forever in that long, black hair, and he would still want more. It is an appetite that breeds appetite, yes? A pleasant surrender indeed. For young Officer Mori, we have the modern girls, tough-minded, sassy young things who manage the evening with verve and bravado, but the evening doesn't really begin until you get them alone and they melt with passion for you and you alone. Hmm. Wait just a second." Endo paused with a forefinger in the air, challenging the ceiling in a theatrical mockery of deep thought. "Is the modern girl your type, Officer Mori, or was I thinking of the detective?" He shrugged expansively. "Who really knows what he wants in his heart of hearts? It can be so confusing!"

Takuda, Mori, and Suzuki stood in unison. They faced the stranger in the tiny conference room. Takuda's heart hammered high in his chest. Suzuki was agitated, almost twitchy. Mori wasn't laughing anymore.

"Gentlemen, gentlemen, you *are* raring to go, aren't you? We'll show them a good time, eh, Chief?" Endo slapped the chief on his skinny shoulder, but the chief managed only the palest smile as he stared back at the three unlikely warriors before him.

"Pardon us," Takuda said. "We must get back to the city tonight, and we must detour to drop the priest back at the temple. Our apologies for such an abrupt departure."

Endo bowed in return, apparently delighted with Takuda's strained and perfunctory manners. "Ah, yes, the long, slow drive up to Eagle Peak, up the straightaway and across the narrow, dimly lit dam to the temple. Drive safely," he said. "Oh, and Reverend Suzuki, I'm sorry I seemed to leave you out, but I didn't know what sort of companions to choose for you this evening. Perhaps you yourself are unsure. We will find out sometime, yes? Play the field a little. *Experiment*, as it were."

Suzuki stood very still, a slow flush coming to his cheeks.

Endo laughed and winked broadly before turning his attention to Takuda. "Detective, I'll see you at the meeting tomorrow."

"Meeting?"

"Perhaps I'm thinking of someone else. No matter. I'll see you again. All of you." Endo bowed before easing out of the conference room with Nakamura in tow.

The men began to breathe again.

"Who the hell is that?" Mori's hand trembled as he took one of Suzuki's cigarettes. Takuda didn't know Mori smoked. "I mean, who the hell is that? Who is he really?"

"That's our enemy," Suzuki said. "I didn't know we had one, but that's him."

CHAPTER 20

On the way back to the city, Takuda felt Mori's eyes on him in the rearview mirror.

"Officer, what's on your mind?"

Mori returned his eyes to the road. "What did the suspect say about the changes to the Ainu dictionaries?"

"The priest asked about that as well," Takuda said. "I didn't know you two had gotten together on interrogation topics. It's an interesting tactic, Mori."

"Detective, the priest is well educated in such things. I take full responsibility . . ."

"Forget it," Takuda said. "It worked as well as it could have. We completely bungled it, to tell the truth. Perhaps I should have had you in there with me. Or perhaps instead of me. Anyway, it was a waste. We didn't have any leverage on him."

"Perhaps you never will have any leverage on him,"

Mori said. "He seems as if he's living in a different world."

"He seemed more lucid today. What do you mean by 'a different world,' Officer?"

"You remember drawings of the Kappa in his apartment? It's not just pictures cut from magazines and juice cartons anymore."

Mori handed him a thin folder. "I found these outside the cell before the chief and the sergeant came."

Inside were sheets of writing paper covered with sketches. Starting with the top sheet, Takuda didn't know what he was looking at. He briefly thought it was some sort of insane architecture, an overgrown jungle temple with tubular bridges and vaulted domes hung with vines or ropes. Then he recognized an eye in the middle, and the whole thing jumped into focus. It was a Kappa, but nothing like the cute little turtle-shelled versions that warned children away from the water. Thin wisps of hair hung from the cratered skull. Its dead, staring eyes revealed nothing but hunger. Takuda leafed through the folder. In each drawing, the beak was half-open as if never fully satisfied. There was no fat, no softness to this Kappa. Each bone in the webbed hands and feet stretched the scaled and wattled skin. This was a thin and evil beast, scale and sinew tightly binding angular bones. Ogawa had made detailed anatomical drawings of a creature that lived solely in his imagination, and he had made it as nasty-looking as possible.

"What madness," Takuda said. "This human form on its knees before it—has he drawn himself worshipping the creature?"

"Yes, it's him, right down to the Zenkoku uniform. In better light, it's unmistakable."

Takuda felt a wave of revulsion. "How disgusting. What a disgusting little man."

Mori said nothing.

"How could he draw himself worshipping such a creature? Even though it's mythical, it's as if he drew himself worshipping a sewer rat or a cockroach."

"Detective, if this upsets you, you should stop now."

On the next sheet, the hurriedly sketched human figure held down a smaller figure, like a child. The Kappa, lovingly detailed and starkly sketched, pulled dark flesh from a gaping wound just under the small figure's ribs. That was how Ogawa's Kappa would eat a child's liver. On another sheet, a child floated with hair and garments waving as if underwater. Surrounding the child's abdomen a dark cloud billowed. Blood in the water. The Kappa emerged from the murk with twisted, ropy intestines in its beak.

On the next sheet, a rounded, pudgy foot descended from the top of the paper as if dangling in water. From the bottom of the sheet rose the Kappa's webbed claw, inches away from the unwitting child—

Takuda slapped the folder shut and tossed it to the front seat. "Nasty enough. He's just sitting in jail drawing pictures to incriminate himself in the attempted abduction. He's mocking us in the wake of Lee Hunt's death. Meanwhile, the real killers are going about their business."

Mori pulled to the side of the road and carefully handed the folder back to him. "Look at them, please. Try to spot inconsistencies".

There were no inconsistencies. In each drawing, the Kappa's face was identical. Everything was identical. Even the lank fringe around the cratered and misshapen skull appeared exactly the same in each drawing.

Mori said, "Such consistency is incompatible with most artistic processes like character development or even drawing for fun. The Kappa figure is not evolving in a creative process. Perhaps Ogawa was working from a live model."

Takuda looked at the officer as if amused at the joke. Mori didn't budge.

"Officer, don't repeat that. If they think you aren't taking this seriously, you're done for."

Mori eased the car back out onto the road without a word.

"Officer, you must try to understand."

"I can keep my mouth shut, Detective. Don't worry about me."

Takuda leaned forward. "What does that mean?"

"They're letting you commit suicide, that's clear enough. There will be questions tomorrow, and you'll need answers that will allow them to leave you in charge. Then you and the priest and I can get on with it."

Takuda leaned back in his seat. He never should have doubted the officer. "Tell me what to do."

Hours later, Takuda and Yumi lay on the futon. Headlights of passing cars sundialed through the blinds, sending bright bars scaling their bedroom wall and then shooting backward across the ceiling.

Sometimes it seemed it had always been that way, just the two of them talking late into the night, stifling laughter so as not to annoy the neighbors. It had been so when they were first married, still living with his parents. They had stifled their laughter. They had stifled their lovemaking. Later, she had stifled her grief. In the little six-mat room at his parents' house, she had bitten the blanket to keep from screaming for days and days after their Kenji had drowned. Perhaps it was good she had stifled it. Modern ideas seemed to favor letting feelings out, but some feelings must be contained. If they had let Kenji's death dominate their lives, it would have destroyed them. As it was, grief had never really left them, but it hadn't torn them apart.

Yumi lay gazing at the window, lost in thought. She had no idea of the storm in her husband's heart. He had to tell her what was coming, but he didn't know where to start. On impulse, he reached out to touch the scar on her throat. It was fainter, but it had been deep, so deep, and it would never go away. He could still hear the echo of the knife in her damaged vocal cords.

"Thank you for staying," he said.

She took his hand away from her throat and pulled it between her breasts. "I did leave you."

"You stayed. You could have died. It would have been easier to die."

She didn't reply immediately. "It would have been easier to die," she said.

They waited for a car to pass. He cupped her breast and they turned on their sides. Still another car passed, but he didn't know how to tell her he was planning to smash the cult and punish those who had killed his brother and his son. It would cost his career, his standing in the city, and his family's reputation. If he found the person responsible, found him face-to-face, it would cost Takuda his freedom.

Only the insane saw no choice other than murder. He was probably insane, but he felt strangely calm about the whole thing. After all, he had trained for this all his life. He had spent years building his strength and perfecting his technique. He had taken the defensive art of aikido to a potentially deadly level. Who commits his life that way without some deeper need? Perhaps he had always been insane.

Yumi started the conversation for him. "So you were in a part of the Naga River valley where you had no business, poking around with old Reverend Suzuki's son on private land, and you just happened to find a cave full of skeletons." She turned toward him. "No one else could find it, of course. No one but Detective Takuda would fall into the valley's biggest secret almost two decades after it made any difference. Why are you stirring this up? Why now?"

"I think I know who killed our boy," he said.

She sat up.

"I think there is a cult that worships the Kappa. They believe that there was a Kappa imprisoned beneath the shrine, and they sacrificed to it for years. After the war, when the new dam was built, the river level dropped, and the cave beneath the shrine was just above the water level. They built a wall to contain the cave, and they kept throwing in victims. That's what Suzuki and I found there this morning. Hundreds of them. People you and I knew, kids we went to school with. The cult began to splinter. I think it was partly due to my father's work with the temple. My family became a target at about the time the big Kappa festivals ended, about the time my brother drowned. For another two decades, the old cultists kept dancing, and they kept sacrificing, but for some reason they couldn't kidnap villagers anymore. They started going down to the city. That's how all the abandoned bicycles and scooters end up in the valley."

She looked at him askance. "You're reaching. You're inventing networks of people who kidnap bicyclists, bicycles and all. Why carry the bicycles all the way to Naga River valley?"

"Because there you can scratch off the registration and let them rust in the canal for five years before there's even a chance of that section of canal being dredged."

She stared at him in the half-light. "And you think a cult explains all this."

"The parallel marks. You remember the parallel cuts on Kenji's leg?"

"Of course I do."

"I saw the same marks and the same abdominal wound on a dead American. And I think I know what did it. It's a clawed glove."

"It's not a glove," she said.

"No, I've seen the results three times now."

"I've seen things, too. You didn't go to war based on what I saw."

He felt his cheeks go red in the darkness. She was still angry that no one believed her story. *Who would believe such a story?*

The answer came quietly, in the dark: *I should have believed it.*

He pushed the thought away. "I might have to go outside the law if I find the killer."

She made a sound of disgust deep in her husky throat. "Like some stupid period drama. You take off for revenge, and I stay home and cry? No, no, no."

"I might not come back."

"You're already gone. You're insane. I'm going to call your boss."

"He won't hear you. Nakamura has been calling daily, and he . . ."

"Leave Nakamura out of this," she said. "You can't unbalance me that easily."

"Nakamura is part of this. I think he's been part of it for decades."

"Stay away from him," she said. "He'll be brittle by now, and I don't want you jailed for breaking a brittle moron."

"He's not the one. He doesn't have the strength to wear diving gear, much less swim against the current to take down a struggling victim."

"Diving gear?"

"Yes. That's the only way they could have taken down their victims. Now they don't bother. They just pick people off the road, bikes and all."

"But the American was swimming."

"Special case. The killers missed Hanako Kawaguchi, and it was time for a sacrifice. They lured the American to the river."

She frowned in the half-light. "You said there was a clawed glove to make the parallel cuts."

"That's right. And stress might have made a diving mask look like that face you saw in the water, like the drawings you made for Nakamura." Ogawa's horrible drawings came to Takuda's mind.

Yumi shook her head. "No, no, no. I'll tell you again. I looked at hundreds of diving masks in every catalog I could find. There was nothing like that available in Japan." She sat up with exaggerated care, as if it took all her strength to remain calm. "You remember the

Kappa costumes for the old festival dances? Just before we left, they broke off the left forefingers. That was when the farmers lost their forefingers, too."

"I remember that."

"Well, those farmers believe in the Kappa even if you don't. Even if you don't believe your wife's eyes and the scars in your own flesh. They believe. They aren't worrying about bicycles and masks and clawed gloves. They cut off their own fingers in an act of devotion. That's how you'll recognize the ones who observe the old ways. Those men will be dangerous even if they're old. Even the oldest dog still has one last bite." The muscle jumped on the side of her jaw. "And if you have a choice between killing them and coming home, don't kill them. Just walk away. Our family has gotten smaller and smaller. Don't destroy it just for revenge."

CHAPTER 21

The prefectural police department faced north, toward the sea. It had been built in the exhilarating years between the Tokyo Olympics and the Osaka Expo, when all of Japan had been looking toward the bright future overseas, toward Japan taking her rightful place in the family of nations. Of course such an imposing new building would face the sea.

The bright future never materialized in that prefecture. The prefecture lay in the *san-in*, the mountain shadow, so while the rest of Japan faced the bright future, the dark valleys held secrets that would always drag the prefecture backward.

From the walkway to the entrance, Takuda could see the window-sitters, five useless detectives who sat far from the action in the heart of the office. They showed up every day, even on this sunny Saturday morning. They would continue the formality of showing up until they could collect their pensions. This morning, one of the window-sitters was trimming his toenails with his foot on the sill.

Takuda sprang up the stairs. That window-sitter would go, and another would take his place. Takuda pressed the elevator button. The "3" was almost worn away. *Why think about the window-sitters, of all people? Why today?* There were bigger things at stake.

Takuda realized why window-sitters came to mind when the elevator doors opened and he walked down the familiar beige-and-gray hallway. In his own way, he had become worse than a window-sitter. *At least window-sitters never make any trouble.*

Takuda exchanged the usual nods and grunts with the other detectives, but the office mood was anything but usual. Even with his deadened senses, Takuda could feel the chill.

Superintendent Yamada was not at his desk. The conference room door was closed.

Takuda didn't even have to look at the conference room schedule. He went in. As expected, his boss, Superintendent Yamada, sat at the head of the table. Chief Nakamura sat in the seat of honor, facing the door. At Nakamura's left sat Endo, the Zenkoku General counselor Takuda had met the night before.

Only Endo rose to return Takuda's bow. Takuda backed out for a moment to get his own chair.

Nakamura started talking as soon as Takuda sat. "Certain questions have arisen about the official . . ."

"This is not an official meeting." The superintendent sat forward without a glance at Nakamura. "Chief Nakamura requested a meeting today, and he took it upon himself to bring an employee of Zenkoku General. Please, honored guests, let me first introduce one of our most decorated and experienced detectives."

As they introduced themselves, Takuda studied Endo. The suit was worth a month of Takuda's salary, at least, but the man who wore it was brown and weathered. Even though his hands were hardened with practice, there were no broken knuckles, no scarring on the striking surfaces, and no swordsman's calluses between the thumbs and forefingers. The stranger sized up Takuda as well. His eyes revealed nothing, but a slight smile played at the edges of his lips as they exchanged business cards for the second time.

Nakamura cleared his throat and began again. "A tragedy of this level seems to speak of foul play, but experts who have viewed the site say it's entirely possible that this underwater cave trapped bodies from upstream, perhaps from the vicinity of Eagle Peak Temple, for hundreds of years. There's no telling where all these bones came from. Some of them are so old that they couldn't have been put there by anyone alive today."

"Experts," Yamada said.

"Yes. These experts say the first skulls they examined are more than five hundred years old. There's no telling how old this site is. The bones would have stayed in that cave forever had the detective and his friends not destroyed the shrine above it."

On the table before Nakamura lay a crime-scene map hastily sketched on graph paper. Asterisks appeared at the sides of the cavern and at the end farthest from the entrance.

Takuda pointed to Nakamura's map. "Officer Mori plotted a detailed crime-scene map. It was very different from this one."

Nakamura nodded. "We do what we can out in the country."

"The officer also put crime-scene flags on distinct remains, starting with the bones that appeared newest. He started at the top of the heap, in the center of the cave, then moved downward and outward."

"He is very systematic," Nakamura said. "However, such a system prevented us from getting to the lower levels of the crime scene."

"Testing remains from the farthest reaches of the cavern ensures that you'll be testing the oldest remains first," Takuda said.

"What's your point, Detective?"

"If you dig the older remains out from under the newer ones, the media attention will disappear. No one will even be thinking about the site when you get to the freshest remains."

"That's nonsense."

Endo cleared his throat. "Gentlemen, may I have a few words?"

All eyes turned to Endo.

"This is a matter of mutual concern. The Zenkoku family of companies has financial interests in the Naga River valley. However, we have deeper relationships to the land and to the people. As Japanese, all of us here today understand these deeper relationships." He began to interweave his fingers: "Our people, our land, our faith, and our culture." He ended with his hands clenched above the table. "These are all interconnected to make us strong, especially when we all work together for the common good."

Yamada scratched his ear. He looked as if he might fall asleep.

Endo smiled and spread his hands on the conference table. "Chief Nakamura was kind enough to bring me here today precisely because we all wish to serve the common good. You wish to keep the peace. You wish to protect the people of this prefecture. We want to help in any way you choose. Because of our various holdings here in your prefecture, including the Zenkoku Fiber plant in the Naga River valley, we are part of the prefecture. Part of your larger family if you will. We also need your help and protection."

Takuda sat forward. "Do you want us to come in and solve the water safety question? We could do that."

"That's enough, Detective." The superintendent regarded Takuda from under heavy eyelids.

"We could start with the canals and work our way down to the spillways and the runoff pond."

Nakamura leapt to his feet. "That's preposterous! That's completely off-limits! You could find yourself in huge trouble there, Detective!"

Endo tugged gently on the chief's sleeve. Nakamura collapsed into his chair without a word.

The superintendent was still looking at Takuda. He looked bored, but Takuda knew better. Finally, the superintendent sighed in resignation and sat forward. "Who am I talking to? Zenkoku General or Zenkoku Fiber?"

Endo bowed. "In this matter of our mutual concern, I am honored to represent the corporation as a whole."

Yamada bowed without a trace of sarcasm. "So, does the corporation as a whole have any information for us?"

"Perhaps we can lend our support. It's not generally known, but we have holdings reaching far back into our country's medieval past, long before we were unified under the Zenkoku banner. We were still doing brisk business with the Vietnamese in Hoi An when the Dutch set up shop at Nagasaki, so you might call us the oldest continuously operating multinational corporation. Over time, we have developed specific methods of balancing progress against the preservation of important cultural assets."

"What does that mean?"

Endo didn't smile. He could read the superintendent, too. "Japanese history is under our feet every day, gentlemen. Every time the Zenkoku family puts up a building or digs a tunnel, we find archaeological sites that must be preserved. We have partners at most major universities, both here and abroad. These men and women drop what they're doing when we find something interesting. They can quickly and easily evaluate most situations. That way, we can effectively help local governments make difficult decisions."

"But it's a crime scene," Takuda said.

"Actually, the head of the archaeological department at your own university here in the city has written a brief position paper on that very topic."

He whisked it from his briefcase.

"He believes the remains are all more than seven hundred years old, not five hundred. That's older than much of the Zenkoku family itself, gentlemen, and we are quite old."

Yamada was frighteningly still. "So you shipped in an academic to trespass on a crime scene."

"The land belongs to Zenkoku Development. We have clear title since 1937, I believe. My presence could hardly be called trespassing, as I was invited to consult on this matter even before I ran into my old friend the regional director general. From what I was told, there was some doubt as to whether this was a crime scene at all."

The superintendent turned to Nakamura. "So you pulled in your corporate friends to reclassify a crime scene as an archaeological site."

Nakamura squirmed under his gaze. "Well, we don't have the resources to deal with this kind of thing, even to guard the site. We weren't sure what to do."

"You could have left it to the prefecture." Yamada's expression was blank.

"Left it to the prefecture? Your maniac detective here was trying to tie it all together. But it's preposterous! The skeletons in the cavern have nothing to do with the pervert Ogawa. The pervert Ogawa has nothing to do with the tragic drowning of the Zenkoku English teacher. Only the drowning is related to the water safety question, which has shown steady improvement since Zenkoku first came to our valley, I might add."

The superintendent glanced at Takuda.

The chief puffed out his chest. He thought he was winning. "Your man Takuda has been driven insane by shame. He wants to tie all our problems together, but it's preposterous, isn't it? That would mean that the pervert Ogawa is a seven-hundred-year-old killer who can slip out of his jail cell at will. At seven hundred, he would be too feeble for that, ha!" Nakamura straightened his tie and sat erect in his chair. "In my professional opinion, Detective Takuda is no longer fit for duty. He wants to make sense of the tragic events in his family's history. Unfortunately, misplaced blame cannot bring back his brother, his son, or his parents. He should put aside blame and face his own shame. He has failed his family, first as an older brother, then as a father, and finally as a son. Perhaps shame has driven him to failure as an officer of the law as well."

Nakamura held his chin up, but his eyes shifted quickly from Yamada to Takuda to Endo.

The silence stretched on. Takuda had nothing to say. As far as his failures were concerned, Nakamura was right. He had failed his family in every possible way, and he fully intended to fail as an officer of the law. However, there was still work to do.

He spoke slowly into the silence. "Chief Nakamura, when Lee Hunt disappeared, and also when his body was found, you referred to him as a tourist. When I asked why he was in the Naga River valley, you said he was on holiday with his wife. Just now, you referred to him as a Zenkoku English teacher. Was he in the employ of Zenkoku? If so, why did you keep this information from us?"

CHAPTER 22

The blood drained from Nakamura's face. He sputtered to the superintendent: "The detective was out of control. I didn't tell him the foreigner was working for Zenkoku because I didn't remember—I didn't have enough personnel to deal with the details." He cut his eyes at Endo. Takuda couldn't tell if he was begging Endo for help or for forgiveness.

Endo's black eyes glittered. He relished Nakamura's squirming with some base pleasure beyond simple amusement.

The superintendent cleared his throat. "Can the Zenkoku General representative help us with this? What was the foreigner doing there?"

Endo tore his eyes away from the tortured police chief. "Ah. Yes, yes, of course. I may be able to assist here in several ways. Let me say at the outset that we at Zenkoku have no opinion on Detective Takuda's fitness for duty. If we did, we would communicate our concerns through the appropriate channels." He smiled at Takuda with large, yellow teeth. "My superiors would see to it personally."

Takuda bowed in acknowledgment. He did not look forward to the day when Endo's masters took an interest in his career.

Endo stood and buttoned his beautiful suit coat. "On behalf of the Zenkoku family of companies, I would like to clarify two misunderstandings. First, the foreigner was not a Zenkoku employee. He was an employee of ActiveUs, a teaching and testing firm that we retain for corporate training. He had just completed teaching the spring intensive English course for new employees. Like so many of us, he found Naga River valley charming, and he brought his pretty young wife along to enjoy it. Unfortunately, his Japanese skills were poor. He obviously misunderstood warnings about the cold, swift flow from the spring thaw."

Takuda sat forward. "And what about his liver? What about his intestines?"

Endo bowed. "I regret my inability to make definitive statements about the individual internal organs of foreign workers." He addressed the entire table. "At any rate, it should come as no surprise that this unfortunate accident victim had indirect ties to our corporate family. The Zenkoku companies and their various holdings employ only a tiny fraction of the population, not even four percent, but we eventually touch the lives of everyone in Japan."

"I'm beginning to believe that," Takuda said.

"The other point that requires clarification is the assumption that our academic friends could reclassify a crime scene as an archaeological site. That would take a court injunction." He drew a large, official envelope from his briefcase. "It's unusual for someone like me, a simple salaried worker, to act as an officer of the court. However, the judge felt that urgent action was needed to preserve the archaeological integrity of the site. Copies have already been sent to your superiors, but they will want the original, of course." He offered the envelope with a bow to the superintendent. "If you would, please accept this injunction to cease all activities in the cavern or the shrine above. The consequences of trespass on the site are listed here, with references to national and prefectural statutes on the protection of antiquities."

"So, you're a corporate lawyer as well," the superintendent said.

"I have the great fortune to serve the Zenkoku family in multiple capacities."

There was nothing more to be said. Endo bowed to Detective Takuda and Superintendent Yamada, and then he strolled out with Chief Nakamura following. Nakamura was grinning, and he turned to say something to Takuda, but a touch on the shoulder from Endo made him fall in line.

As the door swung shut, the superintendent turned to Takuda. "You disappear just when I need you on the ground in that valley. You stumble into a cave full of bones. Then I start getting the phone calls. Everyone except the prime minister has called me about this nasty business. Maybe he did. I haven't checked my messages for fifteen minutes now."

"You told me to stay out of the way."

"You're making a rotten mess of it. You reports are perfect, but they don't say anything. I can't even tell people what you're doing because I don't know."

"I'm not sure I do, either."

"Okay, Detective, what do you know?"

"The suspect Ogawa was attempting to kidnap the Kawaguchi girl. He has been incarcerated too long to be involved in the drowning of Lee Hunt."

A muscle jumped in the superintendent's jaw. "The foreigner whose intestines interest you so deeply."

The clock ticked loudly.

Yamada said, "What else do you have? Tell me you have more."

There was more, but he couldn't tell the superintendent any of it. He wasn't sure he understood it himself.

"Takuda, here's what they tell me. They tell me that you're misrepresenting your position as a detective. They tell me that you're interfering with regular investigations. They tell me that you had Mori illegally retrieve evidence from Ogawa's apartment. Now, here's what I know firsthand. You aren't coming in, you aren't staying in touch, and your paperwork is suddenly textbook perfect. You did a half-baked interview with Ogawa's ex-wife, and your report for that one is missing altogether. Now she's disappeared. We may never know what she could have told us."

Takuda didn't allow himself to smile.

"Takuda, you let a Buddhist priest pray over the body of a foreign national."

"He had the wife's permission."

"It was a bad idea in the present circumstances. People are asking me what our policy is on such matters. Now I have to find a policy. For review. I don't know whose review. Way, way up, maybe not even in the prefecture. I can't see that far."

"Reverend Suzuki happened to be there. It was a humanitarian act."

"The governor's office asks if we consider Japanese religion better than foreign religion."

Takuda shook his head. "That's stupid."

"They ask why you didn't call a Catholic priest."

"Reverend Suzuki just happened to be there."

"As he just happened to be there when you found the shrine?"

"The cavern might not have been found otherwise."

"No one will soon forget that fact, Detective. They tell me that you two have partially destroyed an important cultural artifact, some altar at the shrine above the cavern, and that you allowed the priest to trespass on a crime scene. Or you thought it was a crime scene."

"How did they know we broke the altar?"

"So you admit it."

"There were a lot of human remains. I thought the

prayers of a priest were as appropriate as Officer Mori's crime scene flags."

"Takuda, don't bring up Mori in my presence. Just don't say a word about him. If you've got some sort of mania about that valley, that's your problem, but you're dragging him down with you."

"I don't understand."

"You know that he's been following you around for a year now, and you've got him staked out as your personal driver."

"He's a very bright young man."

"He's smarter than both of us put together, and we're lucky that a man like him wants to be a detective. He could have been a damned fine one, too, but you've probably already ruined his chances."

"How have I done such a thing?"

"Takuda, you had him steal evidence. Right in front of a sergeant, apparently. I have to deliver the papers back to Nakamura. With an apology."

"Shouldn't I return them?"

"You won't be going back there. You're useless in that valley, Takuda."

"I was only asking simple questions. Why are they so upset? Isn't that strange?" Takuda leaned forward. "What about this counselor, Endo? He has friends in high places. Is the pressure coming from him?"

"Don't worry about where the pressure comes from." The superintendent folded his hands neatly on the table. "The pressure comes from me, Detective." He regarded Takuda with dead, expressionless eyes. "The only pressure you ever need to think about comes from me."

It was a bad time to ask questions, but Takuda was beyond caring. If he was going down, he might as well go down swinging.

Just as Takuda opened his mouth, the superintendent's phone rang. Yamada looked at the phone's tiny screen for several seconds before motioning Takuda out of the room.

Takuda stood outside. Detectives passing him in the hallway returned his greetings but did not look him in the eye.

The superintendent called him back in. "You're off the hook, Takuda. There was an accidental release from the southern dam, and the water has sluiced out the cavern. Washed it clean, apparently, and the walls have collapsed. It would have been a mess anyway, so it doesn't matter, whatever you and Mori and that half-homeless priest did up there."

Takuda blinked. "An accidental release."

The superintendent nodded. "Don't start, Detective. You're thinking like an insurance adjuster, not a policeman. The real question would be why Zenkoku ever built a plant there to start with, but that's not our job."

Takuda sat without being asked.

"So that leaves us with the question of what comes next. I remember when you were a rookie, and you patrolled the bar district. Do you remember that?"

Takuda nodded.

"Mori is taking his exam pretty soon, and I expect that he'll be an assistant detective. I'm partnering you two for the bar district. You'll bring a lot of stability to that area."

"The gangsters bring stability to that area. You send us there, and your stability will be gone."

"Steady, Detective, steady. It's not war, not since the new gang laws went into effect. You'll be surprised at how things have changed. This is the best way to keep Officer Mori's record clean and to bring him up through the ranks. Brushing elbows with thugs in the bar district can teach him a thing or two without plunging him straight into anti-gang work. You know there are several ways to temper a sword, and we want to be careful with Mori. We want to bring him in smoothly."

"And where will I fit? Do I end up window-sitting, with a nice view of the water?"

The superintendent rolled his eyes as if hearing an old joke. "We can do it that way if you choose, Detective. It's all up to you." He laid his hands flat on the table. "You know why you never got ahead? Why no one ever tapped you for bigger things?"

Takuda paused. "I noticed that I was passed over for a few things, but no, I never knew why."

Yamada looked at his hands. "You were passed over for everything. Did you wonder why the Organized Crime Division sent you back early?"

Takuda said, "I thought you requested my return."

Yamada didn't smile. "I pulled enough caseload

from other detectives to make it look that way. They requested that I take you back. You were quite the hero. Leading every single big bust, the first one through the door every time, on the front line against the most hardened criminals in the country. It looked like leadership at first, but after a few busts, the guys backing you up got a little nervous. After a few more, they started thinking you were reckless. Finally, they started to think you didn't want to go home. They thought you wanted to die. Were they right?"

Takuda was silent.

Yamada sighed. "It's a hard pill to swallow, but there it is. Take Mori to the bar district. Don't get him killed. Help him get his feet wet and keep his nose clean. Then we'll see if you have a career."

Takuda rose from his seat. He turned to go, but something struck him. "You remember everything about my loan to the Organized Crime Division, but do you remember the name of my hometown?"

The superintendent frowned. "Some little village to the south, as I recall. I remember you were pretty green when you got here, even after a few years in a local force. Why do you ask?"

Takuda said, "Who said you should let me go to the Naga River valley? Who told you I was a good man for the job?"

"You volunteered to go, didn't you? Did you ask for this?"

"You never forget an assignment. You never forget anything. But you've forgotten twice that I grew up in the Naga River valley. Now you forget whether I volunteered or not. You don't think it's odd that your mind is so foggy about this?"

"I'm not foggy about anything, Takuda. I want you in the bar district until you get settled, you and Mori. Now get to it, and don't let me hear a word from you until you're in. Do you hear me?"

CHAPTER 23

Takuda walked the corridors of the prefectural police department, probably for the last time.

Beige-and-gray or gray-and-beige, take your pick. I won't miss this.

He would be fired if he didn't take Mori to the bar district. So would Mori, unfortunately. Then again, if the bizarre forgetfulness that had stolen over his supervisor was any indication, they might keep drawing pay for months after they quit showing up.

As if I wanted anything extra. I just need to be sure Yumi is taken care of.

He found Mori camped out in a darkened conference room. "Hey, Officer, I'm cutting you loose. Thanks for everything you've done."

Mori stared at his computer. "I have something to tell you."

"Forget it. You're back on the regular duty roster."

Mori looked up sharply. "Have you already done it? Am I already back on the roster?"

"No, but it's all over. Not only have they designated the cave an archaeological site, they've washed it clean. Sluiced it out and collapsed it. There was a release at the upper dam."

Mori's face clouded.

Takuda continued. "They're calling it an accident. It might be worth trying to retrieve remains from the river and the canals. Perhaps there's something to salvage . . ."

The officer barked laughter. "There's nothing to salvage. Those remains are already ashes in the bottom of a kiln, but that's not the end of our work in the Naga River valley. I know whose bones they are."

Takuda sat across the conference table from Mori.

"I also know how the good people of that valley covered up the murders of their neighbors," Mori said.

Takuda felt suddenly sick to his stomach. *Why nauseated now? This is what I've wanted to know all along, isn't it?* "Tell me, Officer."

"I can show you." Mori presented a sheet of paper.

It was a copy of a family registry faxed from Hyogo prefecture. It was an old registry, and there hadn't been births, deaths, or marriages recorded in almost thirty years. Otherwise, there was nothing unusual about it, just the record of the marriage and births of two sons to Kamekichi and Junko Kuma . . .

Kuma. Takuda looked at the sons' birth dates. There

was Tadanori Kuma, with a birth date less than a month after Takuda's own.

Little Bear, with your overbearing mother and your tears and you chopstick-thin arms. So that's where you ended up.

Mori said, "Tadanori Kuma and his whole family were murdered when you were a boy. Probably dragged out of their farmhouse in the middle of the night. They died in the canals if I'm right, but their bodies went down that hole under the shrine among the bones and the rotting bodies of their neighbors."

Takuda stared at the fax without really seeing it. *Little Bear didn't deserve such a death. No one deserves such a death.* "How did you find this?"

"Sergeant Kuma gave me the time frame for Little Bear's disappearance. I searched newspapers on microfilm for disasters around that time. In the same month, I found a massive landslide in Hyogo prefecture, in the middle of nowhere. I called the county office and asked for the Kuma family register, probably in the 'dead' register file, meaning there was no address registry associated with it. They faxed me this twenty minutes later." He pushed up his glasses. "I used your name, by the way."

The fax was shaking in Takuda's hand. When he focused on it, he noticed that the registry was a transferred document, not from Oku Village but from Osaka. "They didn't live in Osaka."

Mori smiled without mirth. "That's the clever thing here. The copy on file with our prefecture says the Kuma family moved to Osaka. Hyogo prefecture thinks they moved from Osaka, but who knows? If anyone asks Osaka, Osaka has never heard of them."

Takuda said, "And you asked Osaka."

"All twenty-four wards, just to be sure."

Takuda sat back. "Why fake a broken paper trail from Oku Village? That's stupid. That's a waste of time."

Mori nodded. "Unless you're trying to protect your fellow villagers."

Takuda said, "Officer, do you have a name? Can you give me a name?"

Mori was very still as he spoke. "To make this seamless, the village office had to retype the appropriate pages and reapply personal seals. But if they murdered these families, using their personal seals one more time was no big deal—then they probably tossed them into the fire with their clothing. Ivory seals would go up like wood, and even the hardest stone seals would chip and break up in a kiln . . ."

"Officer, you've been working on this alone for too long."

Mori looked at Takuda with quiet rage. "You have no idea. Look at the names, all the vital information here. All retyped on an old Zenkoku Q–35 typewriter. It's unmistakable."

Takuda examined the sheet. "The Q–35 was a three-thousand-key nightmare. That's not casual labor. The head clerk at the village was probably the only one who could work that old clutch-control beast."

Mori exhaled in a stuttering way. It was something

like laughter. "There was a steep learning curve with the old clutch-control typewriters, yes."

"Well, we might be able to find that head clerk."

"It should be easy. You were standing out in front of his house the other day."

"Gotoh!"

"Gotoh."

She has to pray twice as hard to make up for her husband. Finally, Takuda understood his mother's words about Miyoko Gotoh, far too late to help his family or himself. His mother had known. Suzuki had known. Even Mori—

"Officer, you didn't pull this together overnight."

"No, I didn't," he said. "I've been working on this since the disappearance of my sister, Yoshiko."

Takuda gathered himself and stood. "Well, now I understand your interest in the Naga River valley. I also understand your interest in me and my history."

Mori frowned. "Detective, there's a lot more to it than you seem to understand."

"Well, no matter. We can make sure no one ever loses another little sister to that valley. Let's go see the Gotohs."

Mori looked at him in surprise. "It's not that simple."

"What do you mean?"

Mori closed his laptop. "There's more. There's much more. The priest has a great deal to tell us. He's meeting us downtown in twenty minutes."

Sunshine poured into the community center practice hall through mezzanine windows. Suzuki stood in the center of the room waiting for Takuda and Mori. He looked like a traveler from a fairy tale with his priestly robes and embroidered rucksack, but he grinned like a teenager as they approached.

"We're sorry to make you wait, Reverend," Takuda said as he bowed. "We hope this is a good place to meet."

"It's perfect, Detective." Suzuki unslung his rucksack. "There are a few things I need to show you in the light of day, and we might need a little elbow room."

"Show us later," Mori said. "You're the only one who'll tell us anything about the cult and the Farmers' Co-op."

"Officer, the cult is dead, even though the Co-op survives. If there were any former cult members among the worshippers at my temple, I couldn't tell you anyway. I'm sorry."

Mori frowned. "Then give us names of cult members who weren't members of your temple."

Suzuki smiled. "I wish it were so simple."

Takuda nodded. "It's a sacred trust, isn't it? I understand your position."

"I'm sure you do."

"Now, Priest, you must understand this," Takuda said. "The cult murdered for decades, and someone is still killing. You saw the bones, and you saw the dead

American. If we don't get to the bottom of it, the killings may continue." He put away his pen and notebook. He had pulled them out of his jacket pocket specifically to put them away when the time came, just to show Suzuki that everything was off the record.

Suzuki grinned about the pen-and-notebook trick. He sat on the straw matting and gestured for them to join him.

Takuda sighed and sank to the matting. "Give us names from the Farmers' Co-op. The core members. The ones responsible. You must know. I'm sure your father knew."

Officer Mori sat with his hands on his thighs. He seemed resigned to letting Takuda and Suzuki resolve the nonsense so he could get to work.

Suzuki smiled. "Very well. First, I have gifts for you. Then I'll give you the name of one man who quit the Farmers' Co-op when he became bedridden."

Suzuki pulled three swords from his rucksack. Their scabbards were wrapped in lengths of silk.

"These are part of my temple's history, but they are private property, my property. I can do with them whatever I please." He laid them on the mats. "Three minor warriors of the Kuroda clan of Chikuzen were lost on a pilgrimage to Sado Island, and their horses drowned in Naga River valley. They barely escaped with their lives. They donated these swords to the temple to fight the evil in the river. This was long after the days of the warrior-monks, but it was a fine gift anyway.

"There are three of them, a matched set. It was unusual for blades so different to be made as a matched set for three men, but men of the Kuroda clan practiced various styles. This kind of sword, for example, is sometimes called a 'laundry-pole sword.' It's uniquely suited for a modern swordsman of unusual height. Someone my height, for example."

The sword was lean and streamlined as if for flight. It was almost ridiculously long. The scalloped pattern along the cutting edge was very narrow, showing that the blade was tempered for maximum flexibility, not hardness. He set it aside, unsheathed, before he took up the next scabbard.

Mori glanced at Takuda. The officer was clearly not pleased about the naked blade lying on the straw matting.

Suzuki seemed oblivious. "This one, the smallest one, is better suited to a more modern duelist." Suzuki drew the sword and rested the spine of the blade on his thumbnail. That allowed him to show the blade without smudging it. He then carefully removed his hand from the hilt. The blade balanced on his thumbnail.

Takuda and Mori leapt to their feet and stepped back. This was a foolish way to handle a true sword, but Suzuki seemed pleased with himself.

"It's the closest thing to a perfect blade that I've ever seen. It was designed for precision, finesse. A younger man, someone of slighter build, might put it to good use. It would be almost dainty in the hands of a man like you, Detective."

He grasped the sword properly, sheathed it, and passed it to Mori. Mori accepted it with obvious surprise, but Takuda noticed that he handled it with familiarity. This was not his first sword.

Suzuki stood. "This one suits you nicely, Detective." He bowed and passed the third sword to Takuda.

The scabbard was heavier and plainer than the other two. The sword itself was a brutal caricature of a classical Japanese weapon. The blade was two-thirds the width of Takuda's palm. The scalloped tempering pattern went from the cutting edge almost halfway to the blood groove. It was a hard tempering, almost mirror bright. The maker had carefully sacrificed flexibility for sheer cutting strength. The sword was not a work of beauty. It was a grim and merciless instrument designed for a single purpose: hacking through armor, flesh, and bone.

"It does suit you," Mori said.

"As if it were made for him," Suzuki answered.

Takuda grasped the hilt properly, and even though it felt *right*, even though it seemed to close a circuit so that even more power flowed through his hands, a wave of sadness washed over him.

The sword didn't suit what he wanted to be, but it suited what he was becoming.

Has it come to this? Is there no other way?

"These are gifts to you," Suzuki said. He casually rested the unsheathed laundry-pole blade on his shoulder. Takuda and Mori stepped back again. Takuda thought Suzuki might cut off his own ear.

"I'll give you the paperwork as well. The hilts, guards, and scabbards are more modern. They're almost worthless. The blades, though, are perfect, as you can see."

Takuda said, "Reverend, these are gifts worthy of heads of state. These swords are unique masterpieces. We can't accept these."

Suzuki shrugged, a frightening action from a man with a razor-sharp blade centimeters from his unprotected throat. "The temple is bankrupt, and I'm the last priest of my sect. These are just a few of the treasures I'll have to liquidate. Besides," he said, "these swords seem to belong with you. I have the feeling something good will come of this. Don't you?"

CHAPTER 24

Takuda, Mori, and Suzuki had the coffeehouse to themselves. Suzuki's robes and Mori's uniform couldn't dispel the charged air around the three; the room had fallen silent as they entered. The customers had drifted out one by one, and the manager had quietly disappeared after serving their coffee. Gangsters flashing their tattoos seldom emptied rooms so efficiently.

Suzuki toyed with an udder-shaped creamer. "I'm sure you've seen and heard disturbing things. The gangsters, the prostitutes, the drug users, the murderers—I can only imagine. I don't know how you do it, you and men like you who face such suffering in your daily routines. Even I have seen and heard things in the course of my work that raise the gooseflesh as I think about them, right here in the sunlight."

Takuda thought of Ogawa. "I've had gooseflesh once or twice, Priest. Where are you going with this?"

Suzuki's smile didn't fade, but his gaze drifted to the creamer. "As policemen, you deal with suffering caused when people break the laws of Japan. In my work, I deal with suffering caused by transgressions against Universal Law. You meet sufferers while their pain and delusion still drives them to destroy the lives of others, and that is very sad. On the other hand, I meet these people when their suffering finally drives them to Buddhism. It's a joyous day."

Mori slurped his coffee.

"Let me read you something." Suzuki pulled out a sheet of yellowed onionskin paper. "This is my father's adaptation of the second scroll in our sect's legacy. He was taking his own fully annotated version to the publisher when he left the temple that day." As an aside to Mori: "He was drowned, of course. They found his robes caught on a canal gate, but he was gone, as was his manuscript. He is still officially listed as a missing person."

"I'm sure you eased his pain with prayer at the cave," Mori said.

Suzuki bowed briefly before reading from his father's adaptation:

"As swift spring waters sweep away debris choking the rivers and streams, so let truth thunder downward from Eagle Peak Temple to sweep away lies spread by practitioners of unclean ritual.

"It has been said that Kappa are charmed monkeys. This is superstition. It has been said that they are stillborn babies cast into flowing water. This is superstition. It has been said that they are servants of the heavenly Dragon King, the harbinger of all rains and of all waters, whose daughter achieved enlightenment in her earthly form as related in the 'Meeting in the Air' chapter of the *Lotus Sutra*, but this is a lie designed to confuse the faithful. There is no connection between the Kappa and any part of our venerated Buddhist liturgy.

"Kappa are the damned apprentice priests who traveled to Xi'an to study Buddhism, who fell under the influence of Chinese pagans, who forsook the light of Buddhism and attempted to learn secrets of eternal life, and who, for their blasphemies, must live eternally as Kappa, trapped between the worlds of men, the worlds of beasts, and the worlds of Hell . . ."

Mori cleared his throat. Suzuki looked up from the paper. "Ah . . . I can skip a few pages . . . ah. Here we go:

"There is much disagreement as to the shape-shifting abilities of Kappa. It was long believed that they could only appear as beautiful women, young boys, or apprentice priests. In human form, they speak a corrupted form of an ancient tongue made comprehensible to men through magic, but they seem unable to read or write. Much has been said of what Kappa do with their victims. The *yamawaro*, or mountain Kappa, is so adept at hiding its victims that they are often never found. The claw marks—" Suzuki's voice trailed off. He folded the paper. "There's really nothing else here we didn't know."

They sat silently. Finally, Takuda said, "Is that it?"

Mori said, "You have one more treasure in your rucksack, don't you?"

Suzuki frowned at Mori and drew a small cedar box from his rucksack. He lifted the top to reveal a stained silken bag. A familiar fishy stench cut through the aroma of the cedar box itself.

"This is the newest treasure at my temple, and probably the last." He reached into the bag with disposable chopsticks and drew out a desiccated talon.

"A boy visiting the Naga River valley once managed to cut a finger from the Kappa, and he donated it to the temple." He turned the grisly relic under the light. "He actually slipped it to my father when no one was looking. A biologist from the city said that it was a human finger, despite the length and slenderness of the bones. She said the discoloration of the skin and the extreme thickening and vertical ridges of the nail indicated that it was from an elderly subject with thickening of the cuticle due to bacterial or fungal infection."

"That's not a human finger," Mori said. Suzuki nodded in agreement. They looked at Takuda.

"What do you want me to say? You're telling me a mythological creature is doing the killing?"

Mori said, "Yes, that's it."

"So next we're going to chase shape-shifting foxes and enchanted raccoon-dogs?"

Suzuki looked exasperated. "Detective, it explains why it went on for so long and why they kept it all secret. It also explains how the Kappa's caretakers messed it up. They got too old, and a newcomer tried to grab a local girl."

Takuda looked between them. They were dead serious. "Right then, Priest, gather your things. We're going to point that dried-up old finger at a man named Gotoh."

"Gotoh?" Suzuki looked confused. "You already knew, then."

"That Gotoh was in the cult? Yes, Officer Mori's work made clear Gotoh was helping to cover up the disappearances."

Suzuki slipped the finger back into the bag. "Detective, I don't know how showing this finger to a retired village clerk would help. I just showed it to you to point out that the creature can be hurt."

"Let's not get too in love with this idea of a creature," Takuda said. "If the cultists believe in it, it might be useful. Maybe the Gotohs can tell us what to do about it."

"We know what to do about it," Suzuki said.

"No, we don't," Mori said. "That finger lived for a week after it was cut off. If you put it in water right now, it would be full and fleshy again in an instant, and it would claw your eyes out, if it could find them. We don't know how to kill something like that."

Suzuki stood. "Now I understand! The boy who cut off the Kappa's finger was not from the valley. He was from the city. His name was . . ."

"Mori," the officer said. He stood and bowed as if introducing himself for the first time. "I was looking

for my sister Yoshiko. I finally found her bicycle abandoned at the spur line station, the old line that led into
the valley through a tunnel under Eagle Peak. I think
her bones ended up in that cave, probably a couple of
layers down."

Takuda and Mori regarded each other silently. Mori
was expressionless.

"Officer," Takuda said. "You knew about me all
along. You knew before you met me."

"Yes, I knew. Now it's time to finish my work in the
Naga River valley. Our work."

"So," Suzuki said, "we three are chosen, brought
together by forces beyond . . ."

"You're not done in the valley, either, but we can't
just drive you there," Mori said to Takuda. "They'll be
waiting for you. That's what the superintendent was
trying to tell you."

"So how will I get in?"

Mori looked pained. "It's not simple. I can get in just
by giving the priest a ride home. I can explain that,
even if they've set up a checkpoint at the top of the
straightaway, and then I'll just go down into the valley
instead of crossing the dam. You, on the other hand,
wouldn't get that far."

"So how will I get in?"

"We can put you in the trunk," Suzuki said. "It
would be a little crowded—" His words trailed off into
silence under Takuda's stare.

Takuda looked down. He hadn't meant to glare at
Suzuki. "Excuse me, Priest. I'm not going anywhere in

the trunk of a car. I'd fight my way in before I would let myself be smuggled into the valley of my birth." He smiled. "I hope you understand."

"There's another way in," Mori said.

They turned to him.

"It's an abandoned railroad tunnel."

Takuda nodded. "The old spur line. I've seen the mouth on the mountain side of the west branch canal. You'll already be in the valley, so I'll just call when I get out of the tunnel. It's perfect."

"Yes, perfect," Mori said. He looked thoughtful.

Suzuki leaned forward. "What's wrong with perfect?"

Mori grimaced at him. "Just take the sword with you, anyway," he told Takuda. "It was dark and cold when I was a boy, and somehow I think it will be even darker and colder now."

CHAPTER 25

An old woman got on the train so slowly that she appeared bit by bit: first, the spotted hand gripping the railing, then gray hair in a neat bun, then her pale, wrinkled face, then the smock that protected her kimono, and then clear plastic spats over white silk socks and high wooden sandals. She had shaken the worst of the rain off her umbrella by the time Detective Takuda realized he should have helped her up the steps. She shuffled toward him and bowed slightly before she put her package on the seat between them. He thought of saying something about the weather, but she had seen rain before.

She was no bigger than she had to be, very neat and self-possessed. He was huge and clumsy beside her. He watched her in profile as she wiped her hands and her glasses with a small, embroidered handkerchief. She caught him looking, and he bowed briefly. She glanced at his golf bag on the overhead rack and eyed him critically. She returned her attention to her handkerchief.

It was going to be a long ride.

It took at least two hours to get to the Naga River valley from anywhere else. The national expressway ran along the coast, far north of the valley, and prefectural highways narrowed and their number decreased as they wound south toward Eagle Peak. Finally, only one two-lane road hugging the face of the mountain crossed over into the valley itself, and even that way was closed to Takuda. He had taken the train, the slowest way possible to reach the village, and now he had to go in through the back door. He sincerely hated the idea.

The back door was a railway tunnel that had been dug into the mountain during the tenure of an ambitious and optimistic governor. The governor had convinced the national railway service to operate a spur line from the nearest east–west line through the tunnel and to the valley. There was no financial incentive to build the tunnel. It was purely an effort to bring the Naga River valley into the twentieth century. Now the east–west local line still wound through the mountains on its eccentric schedule, but the narrow-gauge line into the valley itself had been abandoned before Takuda entered grade school. The tunnel was still there, along with its decrepit transfer station, but the nearest serviced stop on the local line was twenty-five minutes farther along the base of Mount Tensai, just northwest of Eagle Peak.

Takuda disembarked from the local train and exited the station, but he had only the roughest idea of how to find the tunnel. Walking along the tracks of the east–west line was out of the question. The old woman, who had gotten off the train just behind him, sat on a bench. Takuda glanced at the schedule board. The station was almost as remote as the old spur line itself; the next train wasn't for another two hours. If someone were picking her up, she would wait outside the station, not on the platform. *What was she waiting for?*

Takuda went to relieve himself. Unattended little stations like this had filthy men's rooms. He lit a cigarette to cover the stench.

He had just finished washing his hands when he heard the woman pass the men's room door, and he walked out quietly behind her. She wore sturdy walking shoes that didn't match her kimono. Of course she hadn't been waiting for anyone. A modest country woman, she had let the rest of the passengers leave before she changed her shoes.

She walked up a narrow lane by the station, the same way Takuda was going. After passing the noodle shops and pubs that clung to the side of the station, the lane wound up and over the foothills of Mount Tensai. Takuda slowed down and let the woman get well ahead of him. He wasn't following her, and he didn't want to alarm her. He knew the trail to the spur line station had to be somewhere up that way.

Squat houses with stucco walls lined the street. As

they approached the base of Mount Tensai, the houses dropped away on the left, and the mountain rose in their place. It was quiet here. The last of the plum blossoms were almost gone. The songbirds weren't back yet, but hardy sparrows flitted through the bamboo. As the grade steepened, Takuda felt better and better. He let out his stride, reveling in the crisp morning air. When he spotted the trailhead Mori had told him about, he would turn around and get some noodles back down at the station. The fresh air and the midmorning walk had already made him a little hungry, and he wouldn't mind walking up this pleasant little stretch again. Perhaps he was killing time, but who would want to go back into that valley before he had to?

He didn't notice that the woman had turned to face him until he was just a few paces down the hill from her. Her face was grim and lined. Her kimono sleeve hung like a curtain as she pointed out a gap between two squat, decrepit houses. A garbage-strewn trail curved out of sight.

The woman stared back at him, her expression so forbidding that he stopped mute before her. Her eyes were black even at this short distance, and she pointed to his path with a stiff, bony finger. She was younger than she looked, but a hard life had made her formidable.

Still, he called out, "How did you know?"

"You were conspicuous even on the train, but here, you're downright suspicious. Everything is wrong. You're some kind of soldier dressed as a clerk carrying a very light golf bag in a mountain village where there's no golf."

He felt himself flush. His sword was in the golf bag.

"You blush like a schoolgirl. If you have business in that valley, you had best prepare yourself."

He growled. As he turned toward the path, she told him to wait.

"Listen," she said. She stepped closer. "You should dress as a fisherman so that it's not a surprise if you're dirty from the tunnel. Also, a heavy fishing tackle tube would be less conspicuous than a light, bouncing golf bag. There's a store on the other side of the station. You can buy your fishing outfit there and store your city clothes in a locker at the station. Lose the golf bag."

He frowned. "You know Naga River valley is rotten. Everybody knows it. So you just never cross the mountains, and everything is all right for you?"

She frowned back at him. "Don't get so high-and-mighty. We stay alive. We don't disappear in the middle of the night like they do in the Naga River valley. That's what I know about the Naga River valley." She started back up the hill. "Remember this, fisherman: don't chase the fish into the water. Let the fish come to you."

"Believe me, auntie, I'm not going into the water."

She called over her shoulder, "Buy waders, too. If you're going into the tunnel, you're going into the water."

An hour later, he once again approached the trailhead the old woman had shown him. His sword was slung over his shoulder, snug in the biggest tackle tube he could find at the sporting goods store near the station. He carried waders ending in spiked, split-toed fishing boots. He doubted he looked like a fisherman.

As he stepped off the road, he was struck by the decrepitude of the houses on either side of the trailhead. They weren't simply abandoned. They were dead and rotten. Stucco had popped off the lath to reveal dark, fungal masses in the wood underneath. The window frames were bent outward, corroded aluminum still bristling with bits of filthy glass. The eaves sagged as if ready to fall into the dark, fetid undergrowth slowly overtaking the gardens.

Takuda hunched his shoulders in the drizzling rain and turned to the trail. The first fifty paces was littered with cigarette butts, alcohol containers, pornographic comic books—the leavings of garden-variety juvenile delinquents. The trash ended in a small clearing where the trunk of a fallen cedar blocked the path. Here was a small fire pit and a small mountain of beer cans and saké jars. In the clearing, the hard-packed earth was free of trash. The kids apparently threw it all into the fire.

As Takuda climbed over the fallen tree, he saw that the tree had been felled with axes. Someone had worked very hard to block the trail.

On the other side of the felled tree, the forest had nearly retaken the trail, but there were old footprints in the soft bed of cedar needles. Takuda wasn't the only one to use the path this spring.

The path led to the transfer station, a cement platform between the local line and the rusting tracks of the spur. The spur line had been disused for decades. A tiled roof supported by rotting wooden pillars ran the length of the platform. At the end of the platform squatted a ticket office big enough for one employee and a kerosene heater. The ticket window had been filled in with plywood. A faded, hand-lettered sign requested that disembarking passengers drop their tickets into a slot long since boarded over.

The station and everything around it cut sharp angles in that gray midmorning light. On the local-line side, a sheer retaining wall of wet concrete blocks rose at a forty-five degree angle. On the spur-line side, a stand of bamboo shone green through the drizzle. The face of Eagle Peak humped with remains of terraced fields, some overtaken by kudzu vines. Houses of time-blackened cedar with heavy tile roofs crumbled above those abandoned terraces.

At the base of the mountain, tracks choked with underbrush and debris led to the tunnel's black, gaping mouth. He squared his shoulders and walked toward it, ready to enter the darkness once again.

CHAPTER 26

The tunnel mouth yawned like the maw of some primitive cave, a lair for savage beasts. The rusted gates hung from their hinges with no evidence of chain or lock. Water covered the gravel railway bed almost up to the black-slimed concrete ties.

Mori didn't say anything about water. The old woman did me a favor.

Detective Takuda put on his waders and packed his slacks tightly into the tackle tube. After a moment's thought, he put in his keys, handcuffs, badge, notebook, and cell phone as well. The sword barely fit. He watched the tunnel mouth the whole time.

The rusted rails curved away into dead black.

Spring wind died as Takuda stepped under the mossy concrete arch into still twilight. He looked over his shoulder at the platform behind. He felt somehow as if he had crossed more than a few slimed railway ties to enter this tunnel, and going back to the platform wouldn't bring him back, not all the way.

What nonsense! It's just a shortcut. It's foolish for a grown man to be afraid of the dark. He stretched his shoulders and tilted his head one way, then the other, just to feel the vertebrae pop. In a smooth motion, as if he had done it all his life, he reached between his shoulder blades and drew the sword from its scabbard in the tackle tube. *Just to be on the safe side.*

It had seemed like a reasonable way to get into the valley. He couldn't take the high road for fear of being spotted, and he couldn't hike over the mountains in less than a day. This would be shorter. Takuda figured that the tunnel through the mountain's shoulder had to be less than two kilometers long. If the tunnel was less than two kilometers long, it would be a twenty-minute walk. Feeling his way along the slimed ties would make it half an hour. Anyone could do that. Miyoko Gotoh could do that, leaning on her broom.

Five steps into the tunnel, Takuda was in shadows. Ten steps into the tunnel, he couldn't see anything beyond the tiny pool of light from his penlight. The water on either side of the tracks was impenetrable black. The silted gravel between the ties seemed to absorb the light itself. The only sounds were his breathing and the grating of his spiked fishing boots.

He was surprised that he was afraid. He was used to the dark, and he trained for it. When a suspect could not be flushed out into the light of day, Takuda's work took him into the shadowed lairs of gangsters, pimps, and drug addicts. These people, by the time they became hazards to public safety, seemed to prefer living in the twilight underworld.

His colleagues had sometimes compared dark-seeking criminals to cockroaches, but more than once, Takuda had knocked on a darkened door with a crash squad crouched at his back, and he had survived by taking every threat seriously. No matter what else these suspects had done, they had managed to bring the battle to their home turf, where they knew the terrain and controlled the conditions. Such clever fighters were hardly cockroaches.

No, he had walked into the dark too often to be afraid of the simple darkness. He would live or he would die. It was the unknown he feared, not the dark.

Not the unknown, not anymore. Now it's just the suspense.

None of it really made sense. Why was he the one to walk the dark tunnel? Why did everyone just accept that he would? Yamada, Mori, Suzuki, even Yumi. They all just assumed he would follow the trail to the end of his career. Everyone just assumed that it would come to this, and everyone was letting it happen. The only ones actively opposing it were the ones who stood to lose out financially. The others just let him destroy himself.

The whole thing was insane. Everything his family had wished for him, everything he and Yumi had worked and sacrificed for was coming to an end. His parents had died of grief—cancer had been a symptom, not a cause. Takuda had mourned them daily, in his heart. Now, for the first time, he was glad they were dead. At least they hadn't lived to see what was happening to him.

He would lose his position, his livelihood, his status, his retirement. He would lose everything, including the respect of his colleagues. In a different age, he would have had to commit suicide as soon as the job was done.

Times had changed, and he had already decided to live. *That will stink things up, won't it?*

Water glinted in the corner of his eye.

He stopped and played his flashlight beam over the inky surface. *This water shouldn't be moving.* A fish? A turtle? There had been a ripple, but it had gone as quickly as it had appeared.

How deep could this water be? His hand tightened on the sword. It was about two meters from the rails to the tunnel wall. If the gravel fell off from the ties just as it had outside the tunnel, then the water couldn't be more than half a meter deep.

Fifteen minutes more? Twenty minutes more? There was no way to tell. No matter what, he would get out of the tunnel sooner by staying on the tracks. He returned his flashlight beam to the rails in front of him. He resisted the urge to run. He trusted his physical abilities, but running in complete darkness with a drawn sword should be avoided if possible.

He walked onward, scanning the water on either side of the rails. Maybe it had just been a drip from the ceiling. He resisted the urge to play the flashlight beam on the tunnel ceiling. He conjured again in his mind's eye the rippling water: concentric rings as from a falling droplet? No, it had been a wavelet, almost triangular, caused by movement from beneath the surface.

He let out a deep breath, and it rattled out of his chest. His heart was thudding.

Three steps later, the water seemed to creep up the rails as the grade of the rail bed changed. Ten steps later, the rails disappeared under the surface. Beyond, there was darkness, the black face of the water.

Takuda, up to his ankles in water, heard a faint sound behind him, like a ripple, a single droplet. The stench of rotting fish wrapped around him. He turned, pointing the flashlight back the way he had come. Beside the track, a shape rose from the water.

Takuda knew what it was.

In a way, he had always known what it was.

It was like a boy, but it was not a boy. Its head was much too big for the spindly neck. Its arms were much too long, and its huge hands hung limp by its bony, wide-splayed knees. It was altogether sexless.

Takuda moved the flashlight beam up to the head. The skull seemed spongy and misshapen, with lank, dark locks hanging like strips of seaweed. The eyes were too large and too far apart. The mouth was a gaping wound hardened and cracked at the edges.

"*Azhi,*" it hissed. It shuffled toward him slowly beside the track. The sound was meaningless, but Takuda understood anyway: *big brother.*

And deep in Takuda's chest, there was a satisfaction, a glow. *It has stolen my brother's voice, and it tries to look human. It really is a devil.* In that instant, with his heart in his mouth and blood ringing in his ears, Takuda's life became whole again. Everything made sense.

He held his sword low, almost behind him as he backed along the tracks into deeper water.

"Demon," he said. "Murderer. Monster. Come to me. It's been a long time."

The creature hissed with pleasure. Its mouth contorted into something like a smile. Takuda was going to deeper water, just as it had hoped.

Takuda tightened the lanyard of his little flashlight around his wrist. The water was past his knees. He was going exactly where the creature thought it wanted him.

Legend had it that the creature was strong enough to pull a horse underwater. Takuda knew from painful experience that it had poisoned talons.

The water was up to his hips, and the creature was slowly closing the gap. He smiled to himself despite his hammering heart. *It's going to have its hands full. If I get a good grip on it, I'll tear it to pieces right here.*

He let the flashlight dangle as he gripped his sword with both hands. With a strangled shriek, the creature dove for him.

Takuda whipped the sword through the water, and the impact jolted him backward. The creature had impaled itself under the left shoulder, and it writhed on his blade. The flashlight beam shuddered on the roiling black water as Takuda struggled to keep his balance. As he regained his footing, he dug in with the fisherman's boots and heaved the squirming thing into the air.

It wasn't a little boy. It wasn't a boy at all.

He didn't dare release the blade to take up the flashlight, but in the quivering half-light, he saw enough: The cracked and blackened beak snapped at him, and the long, paddle-like hands swished past his face. Bandy, knotted legs pumped in midair, searching for water with the long, webbed, feet.

Webbed human feet. Taloned human hands. Frog-lidded human eyes. And a human mouth, ruined and tortured, now a snapping beak.

Lord Buddha help us. This thing was once a man.

The talons swung closer as the Kappa slid down the blade toward him. He dug his feet in deeper and coiled in upon himself, concentrating all his power at his center of gravity. At this time, at this place, drawing strength from the mountain, from the water, from all corners of the universe, he was stronger than twenty men, stronger than fifty. With every bit of that strength, he coiled himself even tighter. Then he picked a spot on the tunnel wall and exploded toward it, releasing his entire energy as he slung the creature from his sword.

The creature hit the wall. The impact made Takuda's ears ring and drenched him in fish-stinking muck.

He wiped the foul liquid from his eyes and regained his little flashlight. The Kappa had exploded against the wall, but he needed to make sure there was no life left in the pieces. There was more than biology keeping the thing alive, and he needed to be sure it was gone for good. Perhaps he should collect the pieces and take them to Suzuki.

He rinsed the creature's foul blood from the sword and wiped it dry before he sheathed it and capped the tackle tube tightly.

Black ooze ran down the wall, but the creature had disappeared. Takuda stood dripping in the tunnel, not moving a muscle. It didn't make sense. It couldn't have simply dissolved into muck and filth. It had hit the wall very, very hard, but skin and talons and bones should still be near the surface of the water even if they had slid off the wall.

As he stepped forward into waist-deep water to find the broken corpse, he felt the motion behind him.

The claws bit into Takuda's boots at the ankles, and the Kappa pulled his feet out from under him.

He flailed and went down in the hip-deep water as the Kappa clawed its way up his body. The flashlight flickered and died, and the last thing Takuda saw was the Kappa reaching for his face through the murky water.

CHAPTER 27

Takuda spun and spun in airless cold, tumbling blind as water filled his nose and his ears. The creature turned them both as it clawed its way through canvas and rubber. Takuda's hands reached for the monster even as he fought for balance in the darkness. He caught a slick, bony elbow, but it jerked away from him. His hands slid off its scale-slimed ribs as the creature dug at his midsection, and the claws raked at his chest through his fishing outfit.

Takuda curled into a ball to keep the creature away from his throat and his liver. And in a ball he sank, with the creature swirling around him, trying to wriggle under his guard.

Even as he realized he might drown in that unlit tunnel, memories of chasing his brother and his son through murky water came rushing back sharp and clear: *We've been here before, the Kappa and I. But I was just a boy then. The beast has a surprise coming.*

Takuda's rounded back touched down on gravel. He rested there lightly, buoyed by the air in his lungs and in his rubberized waders and by the squirming of the monster. Every time the beast reached in, he parried, deflecting the claws with his shins and forearms. He let go with his mind and allowed his arms and legs to take care of themselves. He was fighting blind, but the creature had two arms, two legs, and a biting mouth, just like any other fighter.

The creature paused, just for an instant.

It renewed its attack from the left, then tried to dodge in on Takuda's right. Frustrated at every turn, it tore at him in a full-on frontal assault. Takuda could hear its rattling hiss through the water itself.

Not used to fighting grown men, are you? It makes you angry when it's not an easy kill. Make a mistake, and I'll tie your rubbery bones in a knot.

His lungs screamed for air, but he could wait. Water was trickling through his nose to the back of his throat. The urge to cough was almost overwhelming. He let it overwhelm him, then wash over him, then recede. He could wait.

The creature's fury seemed to spend itself. Again, it paused, just for an instant, and again, it attacked from the left.

Now.

Takuda's left hand closed on the creature's throat,

and his right hand caught its flailing left arm. He rolled it onto its back, with its head against the steel track. The creature screamed in the water.

Now all I have to do is live long enough to kill you.

Its feet raked at Takuda's belly, and its free arm flailed. Takuda pulled its captive arm across its body, twisting the creature facedown, away from him.

Takuda needed air. His head throbbed. Blue-and-orange spots swam inward from the edges of his vision, disappearing in the center, into a hole, a tunnel, a dark tunnel within a dark tunnel within a dark tunnel—

Beast first, then air.

Takuda worked his left foot into the gravel until his fishing boot wedged beneath the rail. Then he planted his right foot on the back of the creature's head, digging the steel spikes into its slimy flesh. It shrieked in the water.

Takuda exploded to the surface. He coughed and gagged, blowing outward with empty lungs. That was the hardest part—not taking that first gasp of air until his throat was clear.

When he finally inhaled, it was a sweet breath, even tainted with mold and decay and the stench of rotten fish. He gasped and retched, wiping water from his eyes. It was good to be alive.

He stood gasping until his head cleared and his breathing slowed. That gave him precious seconds to think, standing in the dark, his weapon in a tackle tube somewhere in the waist-deep water, a mythical water beast pinned beneath his boot—

Now what?

The creature squirmed, gaining a foothold in the gravel. Takuda shoved his boot into its neck, grinding its face against the rail. Even standing out of the water, Takuda heard it screaming. It sounded almost like a human sob. *Almost.*

It screams because steel—burns it? Weakens it? What a strange thing. The shackles Suzuki had given him—*of course. Iron shackles.*

He needed iron or steel to bind this creature, but his handcuffs were in the tackle tube. They might as well be on the moon. Handcuffs would have made it simpler, but he could wrestle it . . .

. . . out of the water. He would hold it out of the water. It would grow weaker with every step.

It was a sorry plan, but it was the only plan he had. The beast had been run through with good steel, slammed against the wall with enough force to pulp a human, and had its head pinned between a steel rail and steel spikes until its screams had died down to a plaintive mewling. It was waiting to slash him to ribbons if he let down his guard.

There was nothing else to be done. He couldn't pin it to the rail forever, and it certainly wasn't going to drown.

"Let's see how you do out of the water, little fish."

He plunged his torso under the surface and grabbed the creature above its slimed, bulbous elbow joints. It was a grip that would have splintered a man's bones and split the skin, but the fish-flesh squirmed under

Takuda's fingers. *Too strong. It's too strong.* Then he pulled its elbows together and tightened his grip as if to squeeze the Kappa out of its own skin, and the beast shrieked in the murk.

He took his boot from the back of its neck and hoisted it up out of the water and above his head in one motion. It howled and squirmed, flailing its long, web-toed feet.

Takuda struggled forward in the darkness. His fingers were numb and tingling. His grip strength seemed to be failing, and he didn't know why. *No matter.* It would be enough. He was strong enough.

He was completely turned around. After a few labored steps, he felt as if he was going back the way he came. On impulse, he turned and headed in the opposite direction.

He bumped into his tackle tube, and he carefully stepped through the strap hanging beneath the water's surface. It bumped against his thigh at every step. It was the most reassuring thing he had ever felt.

The creature seemed weaker and slower, just a little. It hissed and growled like an angry cat: *"Heh ho khu! Heh khiru khu hariri!"*

Takuda couldn't understand the words, but he somehow knew what it was saying. He saw flashes of his past as if the creature was putting ideas in his head.

It knew who he was, and it had killed his family.

It bubbled as if in pleasure. It knew that he understood.

"Heh khudo tan khuhuhu—"

It had eaten his brother's liver.

Takuda twisted its elbows one underneath the other until he heard the rubbery bones grinding in their sockets. At that moment, the beast pitched sideways in an effort to escape. It was as weak as a baby, but it had taken him by surprise, and he had almost dropped it.

He felt his way onward. If the Kappa got into the water, it would regain its strength and kill him. He dug the iron spikes of his boots into the gravel as best he could on each step.

The curved wall ahead grew brighter. The light made an irregular halo around the lumpy, misshapen head of the creature he held in front of him.

"Wait till I get you up on the dirt," he told the beast. "I'll take you in one hand and my sword in the other, and I'll cut a piece off you every twenty paces, all the way up to the temple, and then I'll drop your ugly head in the parking lot. After the priest is done reading sutras over it, he'll open it up and use it as an ashtray."

It breathed heavily. Its voice was a dry rattle in its throat. *"Heh khu khozann kho tan—"*

It planned to eat Suzuki's liver, too.

"The priest is a drinking man. You'll need more than your little turtle beak to eat a liver like his."

The Kappa laughed, a sound like cracking bamboo. It chilled Takuda, so he held his tongue until the tunnel mouth was a huge arc of green before them, a sunlit world, a world of freedom from the hideous monster in his grasp. It was unfamiliar territory, not the spur line station. He had chosen the right direction, and he was heading for the Naga River valley.

In the sunlight slanting inward through the rusted gate, Takuda took another look at his captive.

It was gray and shriveled. Out of the water for so long, it had drained like a squeezed sponge, and the skin hung on its thin frame. Its misshapen head flopped on its shoulders. He turned it to face him. It snapped weakly. It opened one eye, a clouded, yellowed little orb that had once been a human eye. Takuda could read nothing from it but hatred. *What else could be left in a creature like this?*

He would kill it quickly, of course. He felt no mercy for the Kappa itself, but enjoying its death would make him just as evil.

At the mouth, the water was only up to his knees. Takuda used the Kappa to push open the unlocked gate. As he shoved the creature against the rusted steel, its groans were lost in the squealing of the hinges. Water spilled from the corroded frame above, and most of it went down Takuda's collar. He swore and stepped into the sunshine.

The flooded rail bed turned south, running parallel to a canal. Here, in sight of the trees and bamboo and flooded rice fields, Takuda could hardly believe the nightmare of the Kappa.

Except that he held it in his own two hands.

Takuda walked forward until the water was only up to his ankles. He held the Kappa aloft with one hand as he retrieved and uncapped the tackle tube. His eyes seemed dim, almost unable to focus. His forearms were covered in blood, human blood. His own blood. He was very weak, but he could still wield a sword.

The blade shone bright in the morning sun, and the Kappa's eyes followed it as Takuda raised it for the strike . . .

. . . and then the Kappa's yellow eyes met his. It gurgled like a happy child.

He felt the blow before it came. Just barely. He moved his head back, and the sharpened claws whizzed past his chin and slammed into his shoulder.

The water, Takuda thought. *Just a trickle as we passed through the gate, but it was enough.*

The Kappa laughed aloud. That sound was almost worse than the pain.

Takuda dropped to his knees as the second claw zipped over his head.

The Kappa wriggled free of his weakened grasp as its feet dipped into the shallow water. It twisted its claws into Takuda's shoulder, and the sudden, shocking pain made Takuda release his sword.

Now they were together on the flooded rail bed, and the Kappa had regained its strength. Its skin tightened up before Takuda's eyes as if it were soaking up water through its webbed feet.

The Kappa made something like a smile. *"Ho kho dokho ya. Heh ho khu kho zhita."*

It would start by eating Takuda's tongue. It reached for his throat.

CHAPTER 28

The Kappa's voice rattled with joy as it wrapped its slimy fingers around Takuda's neck. A thin, black trickle of sticky spittle dangled from the corner of its beak.

Takuda collapsed backward onto his back in the shallow water between the railroad tracks. Even as his vision began to blur, Takuda realized how stupid, how blinded by hatred and bloodlust the creature had become. It had poisoned him, and he would soon be immobilized, but the creature wanted to prove its strength. It wanted to watch him die up close. Takuda had no fear, not any longer, and only a little pain. He looked quickly for the weapon he was sure would appear.

And poking through the zippered opening of the pocket on his right arm, just below his shoulder, a bright steel cylinder shone in the morning sunlight:

the pen he had accidentally stolen from the distracted salesman at the sporting goods store.

Now it was just a matter of delivering that pen to the Kappa's brain stem.

He rolled on the gravel and worked his left hand between himself and the Kappa, up to the protruding pen. His hands were curiously numb. As the Kappa turned its head to see what he was doing, Takuda pulled the pen free and backhanded it into the Kappa's face.

The Kappa howled and stumbled through the shallow water, pulling feebly at the bit of steel.

Takuda scrambled over the rail for the sword, but he moved in slow motion. He took it up in his left hand, but his fingers were so numb that he almost dropped it. He crawled painfully to the embankment.

When he looked back, the Kappa crouched in the shallows, yanking at the pen. It finally got a grip, and it shrieked as it pulled. The pen came free in a gout of black fluid.

The Kappa looked at Takuda and hissed in rage.

Takuda held the blade aloft. "Come on, this is for you." They stared at each other as Takuda struggled to his feet.

The creature dropped to all fours and scrambled away from him, toward the canal.

"Wait for me. I'll take you to a magical land."

The Kappa slipped over the embankment and out of sight.

Takuda's legs gave way. He was suddenly—

saddened? What a horrible thing, that a creature like that could exist. What a horrible world that could produce that kind of torture. An endless cycle of pain and fear and doubt, all culminating in death.

It would be better to simply die and get it all over with. He should have let Yumi bleed to death when she had stabbed herself in the throat. Perhaps he would just sit in the water and bleed to death himself.

What did he have to live for? Day after day, waking up, working, all of it was just a torturous, monotonous ordeal. There was nothing more. Life was work, and he was exhausted by it. Perhaps if he opened a vein, he would finally find peace.

He rolled up his sleeve, clearing the shredded fabric away for a cut.

Vertical, vertical, not horizontal. Up the road, not 'cross the street. You want the vein, not the meat.

Somewhere, in the back of his mind, he was insistently surprised by all this. He hadn't thought this way since the days following the death of his son, Kenji, but now he couldn't imagine why he should think anything else. He had never believed in anything, not really. Death was just the end. Darkness. In the end, there was nothing but death.

He had to rest the blade on his shoulder to get the point on a good vein in his wrist. As the heavy steel dug into the base of his palm, ready to slice along the vein up to the elbow, the flat, cold blade rested against his cheek for just a moment. Just an instant. It felt good. For no reason in particular, he thought of Yumi's hand on his forehead when he was feverish. Yet he was not feverish.

But I am certainly ill. I am poisoned. I am poisoned by evil.

He stopped to examine that thought. His hand remained on the spine of the blade, ready to slice himself open.

Even if the Kappa's poison had somehow affected his thinking, it did not mean he was incorrect. Buddhism was the only religion that explained human suffering, but Buddhism was complete nonsense. *In the long run, no matter what humans want to believe about love, mercy, and justice, the savage universe is always out there, just outside the door, a swirling vacuum of chaos waiting to take our children, take our lives, break our hearts.*

My little Kenji. My sweet little boy. He was a good boy. He did not deserve to die that way.

I am so tired of grieving for him.

He grasped the blade tighter, and the cold steel brushed his cheek again, like Yumi's cool, slim fingers.

What about Yumi? What will she do?

—*Detective, if you get up and do your job, she can stop grieving.*

It was another voice in his head, and it was startling. It was—Suzuki? *Now I know I'm insane. Suzuki is in my head.*

The Suzuki in his head laughed.

—*Relieve the suffering of others by ending this water-imp's killing spree. If you don't feel better after that, then go kill yourself.*

Takuda shook his head. *That doesn't give meaning to life. It's all nonsense. Buddhism is nonsense.*

—*Of course it is. That means all we have is this life. Thanks to that foul little creature over in that canal, you've wasted more than a third of yours in mourning. What a pitiful existence. If you end it here, how many more lives will be wasted in the same way?*

Purplish blood had welled around the tip of the blade. Takuda was still unready to lift the steel out of his own flesh.

I decided to live, despite my situation. I decided against suicide, but wouldn't my suicide make it easier for everyone?

The Suzuki in his head was silent. Takuda opened his eyes. The Kappa stood stiff on the embankment. Its face didn't change, not exactly, but its form seemed to shift, as if some obscuring shadow fell over its hideous deformities. It suddenly looked like a young woman.

Takuda stood. The Kappa's hands were too long, the legs were too short, the head was misshapen, and its mouth was a horror, but it looked like a young woman nonetheless.

"*Dono zhan. He kho dono zhan.*"

It wanted to be his friend.

He was on his feet before he realized he was going to stand. The Kappa squealed as he advanced with the sword. He chased it to the edge of the embankment, and it skittered into the canal like a skipping stone. It disappeared, carried away in the swollen stream.

Takuda turned his back on the canal. Foolish to turn his back, but he was so tired—

His shoulder was oozing blood. He needed to have it irrigated and the surrounding muscle pumped with antibiotics. He probably needed a tetanus shot. He would find if there was another doctor in the valley these days. He wouldn't have the butcher coroner treat him.

As he looked at his hands, there was too much blood. It wasn't just from his shoulder. He tried to peel back his sleeves, and they seemed to fall apart under his weakened fingers.

The Kappa had torn his forearms to pieces. He was slashed to the bone in spots.

He tried to bind the wounds with the dry trousers in the tackle tube, but his fingers felt too thick. He wasn't bleeding to death, but he needed stitching.

Blood and poison. This is bad bad bad.

He wasn't sure he was breathing deeply enough. He tried to fish his phone out of the tackle tube and finally just poured everything out onto the dirt. He could barely focus on the screen. His fingers flexed senseless against the phone, and blood oozed onto the keypad.

He used his thumb knuckle to find Mori's number. Mori's away message answered on the third ring.

"Mori, it was waiting for me, and I'm in bad shape. I'm in the valley, at the mouth of the old railway tunnel. I'll just rest here."

He tried to hang up, but the phone fell from his fingers and into the dirt. He thought of Yumi and Kenji.

He hadn't realized it would be so easy to let go and slip away. Five minutes before, the point of the blade had been poised to slice a vein. Now, he didn't want to die, but he probably would anyway. It was—*ironic*. He thought to close his eyes, but they didn't seem to respond, and it didn't matter. His breathing was shallow and ragged in his own ears. He fell and lay sideways on the dirt. It was warmer there.

Darkness overtook him.

CHAPTER 29

Detective Takuda woke to pain and incense. He lay on a thin mat in Suzuki's sitting room. Fujimoto, the village doctor, knelt at his side.

"Oh, no, I need a real doctor," he said as he tried to sit.

The doctor restrained him with a single hand. Takuda collapsed, gasping on the mat.

"The poison has weakened you. You slept for two full days. This is Wednesday."

Takuda said nothing, so the doctor continued: "Most of the wounds on your forearms are superficial. A few are very deep. They are clean now, and they may heal quickly."

Takuda lifted his leaden arms. Beneath the bandages, his arms were swollen like bolsters. *I look like Astro Boy.* He dropped his arms to his sides, and he felt a sudden twinge of pain.

"Take it easy," the doctor said. "You have a few deep mattress stitches."

The breath rattled in Takuda's throat. "You know a lot about this kind of wound, don't you?"

"Not about treating them. I've never seen them on a living patient," he said. His hands shook as he filled a hypodermic needle. "This is a massive dose of antibiotics. Another one. You're a big man, and I think you can take another."

He slid the needle into the vein at Takuda's left bicep.

Takuda gripped the doctor's windpipe with his right hand. *Well, there's still enough strength for this.* "Pull that needle out slowly, Doctor."

The doctor's eyes widened, but he didn't move. "I've already stuck enough needles in you to sew a winter kimono. If I wanted to hurt you, why would I wait till you woke?"

"Maybe you had someone at your shoulder."

Suzuki spoke from the kitchen: "We haven't been watching him. We've been sitting in here chatting about monsters."

Officer Mori stepped in. "Don't hurt the doctor," he said. "He has something to tell you."

Takuda looked up at the doctor's averted eyes. His fingertips were tingling as if feeling had just returned. "What do you want to say, Doctor?"

"May I finish administering this antibiotic first?"

Takuda released the throat. He felt pressure and a little cold as the antibiotic flowed in. The doctor removed the needle and covered the puncture mark with a circular adhesive bandage printed with the face of a cartoon pig.

"I know very little," the doctor said. "I know that your brother and your son bore these wounds. When your brother died, it was tragic, but I didn't see anything odd about it. Your father was a reformer, but there was no reason to believe that anyone would kill his son."

Takuda looked away from him.

"But after your son—I thought you and he hit the same rocks. The swelling and the paralysis of your face—I sent swabs from his wounds to the city for toxicology. I had to pay for the tests myself because the village wouldn't pay. The police reported a simple drowning, you see. No foul play, no snake, no spider."

"What was the result?"

The doctor snapped his bag shut. "The result was that I should be quiet."

Takuda sat up.

"The samples were tampered with," the doctor said hurriedly. "The swabs I sent out were full of blood, river water, and the black, gelid substance I found in the wounds. The report came back confirming a little blood, no apparent river water contamination, and puffer fish liver toxin."

"Puffer fish liver toxin? In the upper reaches of a northern river?"

The doctor nodded gravely. "It's ridiculous, but it was instructive. Whoever tampered with the samples told me indirectly that there was a neurotoxin at work. When I saw those wounds on the foreigner, I saved a little of the gelid compound and experimented."

"You used it on yourself."

"Yes, the other day. I didn't dare have the samples tested, not with everyone watching, so I put a little in a pinprick on my arm. Just a little. I felt a tingling in the outside fingers of my right hand, just as expected. My breathing and heart rate slowed, less than two percent each. I didn't feel the euphoria we get from eating puffer fish. As a matter of fact, it was the opposite, a dysphoria like waking from a nightmare, all afternoon. I wanted to die. I sat in the dark until I fell asleep. I had a very small dose."

"Did you hear anything?" Takuda asked.

The doctor frowned. "Hear anything? Like ringing?"

"No, like voices."

"No. Did you?"

"Yes. Yes, I heard voices, Doctor. They told me to ask what you make of all this."

"*Hmmph*. I think someone is using an unknown neurotoxin in gel form. It immobilizes the victim, mostly locally, but if enough poison got into the bloodstream, the victim could suffocate."

"That's how my son died?"

"Both your son and your brother drowned. They died quickly in the water. I'm sure of that. The abdominal wounds were postmortem."

Takuda closed his eyes. His old nightmares of the

boys squirming as the Kappa's beak ripped into them were nightmares, nothing more.

"To that degree, the police report was accurate," Fujimoto said. "The parallel cuts on their legs, however, were not made by the rocks. They were made by some bladed device designed to deliver the neurotoxin."

Mori eased into the room and sat down by the doctor. "Let's let him rest now, Doctor. There will be more time for this talk later." He took the doctor by the elbow. "Come into the other room."

The doctor reached for his bag, but Suzuki already had it. He grasped the doctor's other arm, and Suzuki and Mori hauled the doctor to his feet.

"Where—where are you taking me?"

"I just want to have a little talk with you about the treatment of neurotoxin poisoning. You'll supply me with what I need to make sure this never happens to any of us again. I believe that Reverend Suzuki wants to talk to you about karma and social responsibility."

Suzuki grinned so widely that his gums showed all around. It was not a pleasant sight.

As they walked the doctor out, Takuda called to Suzuki. "When I was lying there dying, cut up and poisoned, you were there with me."

"Oh? What was I doing?"

"Smoking too much, spending too much money. Wearing skimpy clothes. Telling me how Buddhism was a scam."

Suzuki blinked at him. "I remember thinking, day before yesterday, in the afternoon . . ."

"Your voice in my head saved my life. You reminded me that if all we have is this life, we had best not squander it."

Suzuki looked at him with a furrowed brow.

"I'm the weapon, the blunt instrument," Takuda said. "I never wanted it, but there it is. Now, here's your job: You're the light in the darkness. When we get into a jam, you're the one who'll cheer us on and keep us active, keep us useful. You're an awful swordsman, and I'm assuming you're worse than useless as a tactician, so you must become an inspirational leader. Keep our spirits up, Priest."

Suzuki released the doctor's elbow to point a bony finger at Officer Mori. "I told you that was my job. Didn't I tell you?"

The officer made a disgusted face as he yanked the doctor into the kitchen. Suzuki grinned at Takuda and slid the door shut. Takuda drifted off to sleep.

He dreamt of drowning, and he woke several times clutching at the blankets as if clawing his way to the surface. He soaked his bedding with sweat. The poison came out through his pores, and the fish stench permeated the room.

On the third day, Suzuki burned the bedding, and Takuda scrubbed himself with sand, salt, and citron. That got rid of the worst of the smell.

His appetite had returned, so Suzuki made a stew with meatballs, chicken, Chinese cabbage, and fat buckwheat noodles. Takuda ate until his belly hurt, but he still couldn't keep up with Suzuki. Suzuki was a bottomless pit.

Playing with the noodles at the bottom of the bowl, he said to Mori, "You didn't tell me the tunnel would be flooded."

Mori paused with his chopsticks halfway to his mouth. "I didn't know."

"You're sure of that? You're a pretty sharp fellow. How would you not know something like that?"

Mori looked at Suzuki for support. Suzuki glanced up from his bowl as if just joining the conversation.

"I never . . ." Mori said. "I didn't . . ."

Takuda rose to his feet. Mori quickly laid down his chopsticks and stood to face him. Mori seemed to realize that what he said at this moment would be very, very important to their continued cooperation.

Maybe to his continued life, Takuda thought. He hadn't realized till this moment that he was ready to take Mori to pieces if he gave the wrong answer.

"It's usually pretty dry over there," Suzuki said around a mouthful of noodles. "It only floods over that bank in the spring melt. No surprise that it was deep after a dam release."

Takuda bowed in acknowledgment. "Thank you, Reverend Suzuki." He turned to Mori. "I had to ask, Officer. You're full of surprises these days."

Mori sat formally. "I understand why you might doubt me. In the beginning, I didn't tell you the whole truth. I didn't tell you that I fought a mythical water sprite to avenge my sister. Would you have believed me?"

"Not until I saw it, but that begs the question, doesn't it? Was sending me to face the Kappa in that tunnel part of the plan?"

"Not my plan," Mori said. "I started following you around when I found out about your brother Shunsuke and your son Kenji. I knew you would eventually lead me to the monster that killed my sister Yoshiko. But I've followed you for more than simple revenge. We are devoted to a common cause." He bowed properly.

Takuda bowed in return. He sat and resumed the meal. He noticed Mori's fingers shaking slightly as he picked up his chopsticks.

Suzuki gave Takuda the thumbs-up and wiped broth and bits of noodle from his jowls.

A few minutes later, Mori said, "It just means the danger is greater than we imagined. Someone outside the valley is watching us. Watching you, at least. And someone inside the valley is in communication with the Kappa. How else would it have known to wait for you in the tunnel?"

They finished their meal in silence, each lost in his own thoughts.

After another nap, Takuda examined his gear. The fishing equipment had been discarded. The clothing was ruined, stinking. It should have gone into the fire with the bedding. The sword had gotten wet. Takuda could clean a sword even if he could barely stand.

Under the sharkskin wrapping, the sword hilt was

laminated bamboo with brass pins through the tang. He pushed the pins out and removed the hilt and guard, wiping each piece with his handkerchief. As Suzuki had said, the fittings were modern, but they weren't worthless. They fit the blade perfectly.

As he wiped down the tang, Takuda noticed tiny characters etched into the metal. He held it in the sunlight—

Chapter two of the *Lotus Sutra*. The whole second chapter was etched into the metal. He had chanted that chapter as a boy, and it came back to him in a rush. The chanting rang in his head as he reassembled the sword.

Mori and Suzuki were in the garden, drilling with bamboo practice swords. They stood at attention when he called to them. They looked like warriors.

Mori might make a swordsman of that gawky crane.

"I'm going down to Oku Village," he told them.

Mori said, "Not today. I'll drive you tomorrow if you leave the sword. Until your wounds heal, you won't be able to use it correctly anyway."

Takuda slept eleven hours that night. He woke from a dream of a monster slashing at him with poisoned claws, but he was alone. He fell back asleep immediately. His sleep was deep and dreamless, and it lasted till noon.

As they drove beside the river after lunch, Takuda looked for a greenish, misshapen head to break the surface of the water, but he saw nothing.

Mori let him off at a narrow lane running alongside the canal, just north of town. Takuda followed the lane to a bridge that took him to the foot of the mountain, a stone's throw from the bend in the canal behind the old woman's house. From there, it was a five-minute walk to the cemetery.

There, under the cedar canopy, he recited the full sutra at his parents' tomb for the first time since his mother's death.

Then he stood and headed for the police station. He had business with Ogawa.

CHAPTER 30

Takuda entered the village police station by the back door. It was that simple.

He walked into the main room just as Sergeant Kuma turned away. Takuda walked behind Kuma for a few steps, then ducked into the hallway to the interview room and the holding cell. The chief was berating Patrolman Inoue in the hall. They did not notice him, so Takuda quietly opened the door to the old armory.

He let the door close behind him with a soft click. The old mascot suit leered at him from the wall. The large, glassy eyes and the puckered beak seemed too familiar. Takuda ripped the fabric off the wing to reveal a claw. The Kappa's claw, missing one finger.

Takuda moved like a ghost through the interview room. Through the glass in the interview room door, he saw the chief storm out of the hallway. Patrolman

Inoue saw Takuda and almost stopped. He averted his eyes and followed the chief.

Good man.

Takuda waited until the hallway was clear. Then he slipped out of the interview room. The holding cell door opened without a key from the outside; there was no knob on the inside. As he stepped in, Takuda blocked the locking mechanism with Counselor Endo's business card.

The room no longer stank of rotting fish. It stank of sour sweat, old laundry, and nightmarish sleep. Ogawa stood in the center of the cell, listening to nothing.

Takuda called Ogawa's name, and Ogawa turned. He was a changed man. His face was gray, and his skin sagged. He was obviously ill. For a second, his face dropped back into its heavy, loose-lipped grin, the idiot's mask he wore on their first meeting. "I thought the chief ran you off."

"He did. I came back to see you."

Then the grin faltered. Ogawa was tired. He ran his fingers through his hair. "Why? I can't tell you anything. They're just keeping me because they can't find my wife." His face twisted with rage. "That fat little vixen has gotten away, and you helped her. You helped her, didn't you?"

Takuda said, "What makes you think so?"

"My lawyer told me so," Ogawa hissed. "He said you misplaced her paperwork and helped her disappear. I will make you pay for that, and then my lawyer will help me find her." Ogawa grinned. "He has promised."

"I'm not here to talk about your wife," Takuda said. "I'm here because I met an old friend of yours."

Ogawa put his hands in his armpits and hugged himself. "I don't have any friends."

"You have one. It was waiting for me in the tunnel."

"What tunnel?"

"The old railway tunnel from the spur line."

Ogawa blinked. "Railway tunnel? Who are you talking about?"

"Your friend from the canals. The Drowning God."

Ogawa shook his head as he walked away from the door. "He—railway tunnel? That's ridiculous. How did you meet him? Did he start talking to you in your sleep? In your head? Through the water pipes? Through the walls? How did you meet him?"

"I met him years ago." Takuda drew his clawed fingers down his own face, just as Ogawa had done in the examination room during their first meeting.

Ogawa winced at the action as if he were being clawed himself.

"It was waiting for me as if it knew I was coming. Did you tell it anything?"

"Me? He's not talking to me—Did he make sounds at you? Can you repeat the sounds?"

"No, I'm not a linguist like you. I heard the words in my head."

Ogawa's shoulders fell.

"Ogawa, the noises it made had nothing to do with Japanese. What does it speak?"

"Why do you care?"

"The more I know, the closer I am to killing it."

Ogawa snorted.

"Does it speak some sort of mixture of aboriginal speech and ancient Japanese?"

"Aboriginal speech? You know nothing about the old words. You say he found you in the tunnel? I can just see you there in the dark, all your senses straining, waiting for the god to take you, realizing that everything anyone ever told you about the world was a half-truth at best, really just a pack of lies."

"It wasn't quite that bad. I had a flashlight."

Ogawa almost smiled. The laughing boy from their first interview was definitely gone. "He has your scent."

"I can kill it. I can destroy it. I know I can."

Ogawa shook his head. "You should get out of the valley. Head for the bay or head for the mountains, either way, but get out of here. Don't walk too close to the water, especially the canals, but don't think that will keep you safe. Keep away from strangers."

"Girls with beaks and lumpy heads?"

"Girls? Yes. And boys. And monks."

"When the little girl Hanako first spoke to the police, she said she saw a boy behind you. A strange boy with a crooked mouth and a misshapen head."

"That would be him, yes."

"By the end of the day, it had dropped out of the reports. The chief remembered it, for a moment, the next day."

"That's what happens. People forget. They look the

other way. There's a sort of fog that follows him, and it envelops everything it touches. If you stay around here long enough, you inhale the fog too often. It makes you forget he's even here. Unless, of course, you know him. No fog can cover that. You, for example. You'll never forget. You should just go."

"Ogawa, why do you want me to leave? What makes you care what happens to me?"

Ogawa shook his head. "Your bumbling could make him angry. When your bloated corpse washes up in the overflow pond, he'll come for me."

The overflow pond. It was too simple. Ogawa was setting another trap.

"How did it know I was coming through the railway tunnel?"

"Why ask me?" Ogawa flopped down on his bunk.

Takuda pulled the only chair over to the bedside. He might have only a few minutes. "Ogawa, we've met a few times now, and I don't believe you're insane. I don't believe you're a child molester. So, why Hanako Kawaguchi? Why try to snatch a local girl in broad daylight? Deep down, did you want to get caught? Did you want to be in jail, safe from your new master?"

Ogawa snorted. "Are you still angling for a confession, Detective?"

"If I handed the village chief a letter-perfect confession, in triplicate, stamped with your personal seal, he would tear it up because it came from my hand. My boss down in the city would forget to file it because I've somehow ceased to exist. I'm hidden in that fog you're talking about. I'm no longer a threat to your freedom, Ogawa. But if you don't tell me what I want to know, I'll become a threat to your life."

Ogawa pretended to think about it, rolling his eyes at the ceiling and poking the inside of his cheek with his tongue.

"Who pointed her out to you, Ogawa? Someone with the old cult? Someone with a grudge against the Kawaguchi girl's father?"

Ogawa's brow furrowed. "You really don't get it, do you? The cult lost control years ago. The old priest might have been the last special target. No one controls him anymore, and no one controls his hunting."

"Your creature wanted you to snatch the girl. You didn't choose her."

"She walked past every morning," Ogawa said, "and he just couldn't stand it, but he knew he couldn't catch her on land. He knew she would run. He didn't know she would bite, but who could guess?"

"You went along even though you knew what would happen if a little girl disappeared?"

"No one can oppose him and live. The truth is, I thought he knew what he was doing. I thought he would take care of me." Ogawa crossed his arms to pillow his head and whispered toward the ceiling: "I still thought he loved me."

Takuda looked at his own feet, avoiding Ogawa's eyes. If he looked directly at the prisoner, he might lose his own self-control. "And now?"

"Now I know that he has nothing but hatred and

contempt for us, for all living things. If he had power enough, he would murder life itself. If he had appetite enough, he would consume the universe in his black mouth of destruction. If his claws had poison enough, he . . ."

"Okay, okay. What is this thing, Ogawa?"

"He is hunger incarnate, wild bloodlust with no cheer, no innocence, nothing but malice for . . ."

"No, no, no. What is it? Is it really a Kappa? Is it the last of its kind or something?"

"Oh. That. Perhaps he will tell you his story one day, and then you will understand, if you survive the narrative. To answer your question, though, I believe he is unique. He is not the last of his kind. He is the only Kappa who ever existed."

Takuda blinked, and Ogawa smiled.

"You remember Ogawa, the bright boy? The one from your skinny little folder? When he was in school, he wrote a paper about Richard Feynman's one-electron universe. To Feynman, of course, it was just a footnote, a passing mention in his Nobel lecture, but it was intriguing to the young Ogawa."

"Why was it so intriguing?"

"Because it was so simple that no one could disprove it. We could observe only one electron at a time, and it always had the same mass and the same charge. Maybe there was only one electron holding the entire universe together, always there to make an ionic bond or to quantum-leap valences or to zip through the temple electrode in an American electric chair."

"The Kappa is the electron."

"There is only one, and there has ever been only one."

"Then why are there so many stories about him from so many places?"

"He got around in his youth. We know that he traveled all over Japan before we were even a single nation. He made quite an impression, didn't he? The funny thing is that even within the most ridiculous embellishments lie grains of truth. Legend has it that he is a master herbalist who taught the Japanese how to use medicines and set bones. Of course, if you are of no use to him, he's more likely to suck the marrow from your bones than set them, but that's the chance you take."

Takuda rose from his chair. "It's good that you're sharing your knowledge now because the time has come for your Drowning God to die, and you'll tell me how to kill it."

Ogawa smiled and shook his head. "There is no way."

"Someone had some ideas at some point, surely. Someone in this valley must know."

"They may think they know," Ogawa said, "but they are fools. There's no way." He rolled over with his back to Takuda.

Takuda stood over Ogawa as he pretended to sleep. Suddenly, the timeline made sense. It all made sense. It struck him like a thunderbolt.

Takuda knelt and whispered into Ogawa's ear:

"We know things you don't. We know exactly who

was feeding your stinking monster from the time the cult members failed to the day you came along. We know how you were feeding it while you worked at Zenkoku."

Ogawa had gone very still. He wasn't even breathing.

Takuda doubled down on his bluff because it seemed to be working. "We can track missing Zenkoku employees, name by name, to the day you were fired. Then it's just a countdown to the botched kidnapping of the Kawaguchi girl. A countdown to the day you failed the Kappa."

Ogawa burrowed into his covers.

Takuda leaned in closer. "This lawyer you keep on talking about, Counselor Endo, allowed you to be fired so you would have to procure victims outside the plant. So you would be caught. He's ready to give you up at a moment's notice. You know it's true. You're on your own here."

Ogawa tried to pull the pillow over his head. Takuda lifted the corner of the pillow to whisper: "I'll catch that stinking monster again. If I can't kill it, I'll tell it you helped me, and I'll bring it here in irons. I'll feed ten meters of rusty chain into the toilet to keep it from squirming out that way, and then I'll handcuff you together so that it can eat your bowels from the bottom upward in tiny, tiny little bites."

"You've convinced me." Ogawa turned over on the bed, smiling sweetly. "I'll tell you whatever you want to hear."

CHAPTER 31

Takuda was sitting in the darkened apartment when Yumi came home. When she turned on the light, he said, "I'm sorry I didn't call. I lost my phone, and they've cut off phone service at the temple."

She dropped the groceries and sat on the floor.

"You thought I was still in the valley," he said.

"I thought you were dead."

"That doctor from the valley, Fujimoto. He said he called you and Yamada . . ."

"He said he treated you, but I was sure it was a lie. You had to be dead to let him touch you."

He collected strawberries that had spilled from their package. She straightened her skirt and would not look at him.

They ate in their accustomed places. Everything was in its accustomed place. The apartment was spotless. She would not look at him.

"Four days ago, I finally saw it," he said.

She sat still, but she didn't look up from her rice.

"You told about the face in the water, the claw that dragged Kenji under, and the same claw ripping down my face when I almost had our boy safe again."

She put her chopsticks and rice bowl on the table. Finally, he pushed the table aside and sat formally. He placed his palms on the straw matting and bowed his forehead to the back of his hands.

"For not fully believing you, I apologize. I did not know—I did not let myself believe—that Kenji's killer was inhuman. It didn't make sense. I would like to blame my failure on the poison the creature left in my face, but I cannot. I was a coward and a fool, and I beg your forgiveness.

"Further, for failing to—I'm sorry. I caught it, Yumi, and it got away. I had it pinned, but I wasn't careful enough, and it almost killed me. I beg your forgiveness. I swear on our family tomb that I . . ."

He heard her step into her shoes. By the time he looked up, the door latch clicked, and she was gone.

He was already under the covers when she came back. She did her nighttime routine silently, in the dark, and then she crawled in beside him.

"Yumi, I just want to say . . ."

Her husky voice was heavy with sadness. "You thought we could compare notes, as one does in an investigation. Process and discipline."

"I thought it would help."

"You expected a rational conversation about this," she said.

After the fifth breath of silence, she said, "Tell me everything."

He told her everything. She did not cry when he told her what the creature had done to him. He finished with Officer Mori sneaking him out of the valley so he could recuperate at home.

"Again, Yumi, I just want to say . . ."

"Be quiet," she said. "Let me think. Just let me think."

They both lay thinking until the sun rose, and she got up silently. She left for work without a word.

It was only a few minutes' walk to the coffeehouse where Mori and Suzuki were waiting, just far enough to stretch his legs and loosen the kinks in his back and neck. One night on his own pillow didn't make up for days of drugged and unnatural sleep on Suzuki's thin pallets. Still, he was beginning to feel better. Despite the uncertainties with Yumi, he was almost back to normal. The gray curtain of sadness had drawn back bit by bit as the monster's poison left his system. It was a beautiful spring day, and he was on his way to see new friends. He believed on that morning that he was not much more complicated than a houseplant.

Having a monster to kill was a bonus. *A man likes clear objectives.*

Mori and Suzuki seemed amazed by his recovery. When he told them that his wounds had already closed, they made him roll up his sleeves to prove it. Mori moved his tiny table aside and stood to see. They had chosen a coffeehouse near Takuda's apartment, a place so small that each man had taken a tiny table for himself.

"Wow," Suzuki said. "That's fast."

"I'm not taking the stitches out for another week, just to be sure, but they feel pretty good."

Suzuki leaned over to see. "You see? Something is happening to us. He's stronger than ever, and he heals up overnight."

"This is the sixth day," Mori said.

"Well, it's still very fast. Meanwhile, I can't get enough food now. I'm hungry all the time."

Mori sat. "That's not new."

"Yes, it is. After I finish my dinner, I walk back to the temple, and I'm hungry by the time I get home."

"You should get takeout."

"If I did that, I'd have to stop and eat on the way home, and I'd go back for more. I'd never get home at all."

Takuda leaned forward. "How about you, Officer? Is it still like having a strobe light going off in your head?"

"Music helps. I'm not sleeping, though. I stay up all

night reading about monsters and Japanese financial conglomerates. The big ones. Zenkoku, actually."

"Let's put it to work," Takuda said. "Tell me everything you know about Zenkoku."

Mori scratched his head as if polishing his brain. "Well, it's either the largest and oldest corporation in the world, or it barely exists at all."

"What do you mean?"

"Zenkoku was one of the big conglomerates from way before the 1860s. As a matter of fact, it's older than any of the 'big four' conglomerates. Mitsubishi and Mitsui only date back to the seventeenth century, but parts of Zenkoku may date from medieval times. As for what kind of thing it is, it's hard to describe the structure because Zenkoku actually started to dissolve and weave its way deeper into Japanese life while the other conglomerates were getting fat and bossy."

"Dissolve . . ."

"Zenkoku started going underground in the nineteenth century. When the Admiralty attempted to nationalize the corporation's shipping concerns during the first Sino-Japanese War, that part of the firm just evaporated. Disappeared. No forwarding address. Zenkoku General went public, the key industrial concerns stayed private, and the whole company was managed through a series of interlocking directorships that was nearly impossible to trace."

"What about the brain? The family?"

"The Endo clan. They died out."

Takuda and Suzuki looked at each other, alarmed,

but Mori shook his head. "Not the same name as the counselor. Same pronunciation, *en-do*, but it was made up of characters that aren't even in standard use anymore. Losing that family name and becoming Zenkoku allowed the company to shed and reabsorb subsidiaries at will. 'Zenkoku,' meaning 'the whole country,' or 'nationwide,' is such a common phrase that there were—and are—literally hundreds of companies by that name in every city phone book, companies that have nothing whatsoever to do with Zenkoku General. I take my uniform to Zenkoku Cleaners. It's a chain that might have been part of the Zenkoku group at one time. Maybe not. It's impossible to tell."

"So it's not like a normal corporation."

"It's like a kudzu vine. You see one stalk over here, and you see another stalk over there, but there's no way to know if they're connected underground."

They sat for several moments, lost in thought. Finally, Suzuki said, "Why is a gigantic conglomerate like that interested in the Naga River valley? Why did it open a synthetic fiber mill there, of all places?"

Mori blinked rapidly as if awakening from sleep. "Another question is why that plant still operates at all. The fibers it makes there are almost useless. It's an antiquated technology, and Zenkoku must be selling them at a loss. More than once, they've quietly dumped the product into the sea."

"They wanted something else in the valley," Takuda said.

Suzuki nodded. "They wanted to study it."

Mori looked from one to the other. "They wanted to study the valley?"

Suzuki shook his head. "It. *It!*"

"Oh. Oh!" Mori leaned back in his chair. "Well— Why? There's no way to train such a thing. There's no way to use it as a weapon because it's too dangerous to keep in captivity. The toxin would be of limited use and very hard to synthesize, I imagine." Mori looked out the window. "Anyway, why open a whole factory just to study one beast? It doesn't make sense. Perhaps it's not just the creature they wanted to study. Maybe it's the situation, the valley and the creature together."

Suzuki looked horrified. "They wouldn't. They wouldn't do this just as an experiment. They wouldn't let the monster live and bring new workers, new families into the valley just as some sort of insane sociology experiment."

Takuda shook his head. "I think both of you have missed the point."

"What do you mean?" Mori said.

"We'll never know if there ever was a profit motive, or a lesson to be learned, or any tangible interest to be served. It doesn't matter for our purposes."

He tossed Endo's business card on the table. The others looked at the card as if they expected it to burst into flame.

"It's over. Endo and his masters have grown tired of keeping a pet monster hidden in that little valley, and they want someone to clean it up for them." Takuda looked up at them. "I believe we should oblige them."

CHAPTER 32

Takuda sat cross-legged on Okamoto's balcony. She wouldn't expect him, and she would be very jumpy, despite the note he had left her. When she entered her apartment, he rose and bowed, gesturing through the plate glass for her to be silent. He could be seen from apartment buildings across the expressway, but he doubted that her balcony was under visual surveillance.

She stepped out silently and slid the glass door closed behind her.

"There was a note at my desk that I would find a package on my balcony. What kind of nonsense is that? Did you leave the note?"

He bowed in assent.

"Well, this is ridiculous. You followed me all the way to Yamaguchi Prefecture, snuck into my office on a Saturday, and climbed like a monkey—Wait, did you go through my apartment?"

"No, of course not."

"Of course not. Yet here you are. Are you the package?"

"No." He pulled the bulky packet from inside his jacket. "This is the package I wrote about." He presented it with a bow. "Please accept it."

She sighed. "Detective, I appreciate your help, and I followed your advice. I want to leave my former life behind me, so please just let me be."

Takuda stood with his head lowered and the packet extended. "You followed part of my advice, and you didn't even follow that very well. I found you too easily. Be assured that your husband's former employers know where you are. They probably have listening devices in your apartment."

"I thought it might be better to hide in plain sight."

"This is the eleventh day since your husband botched the kidnapping of the Kawaguchi girl, so they must charge him with a crime or release him very soon unless a judge grants an extension. I think they would rather release him quietly."

Her face was immobile. Takuda had learned that this was her reaction to fear. He continued: "The only thing working in your favor is that Ogawa thinks you are still overweight. He doesn't know what the strain has done to you. He might have trouble picking you out of a crowd, but eventually, he will find you, and he will kill you."

She gathered her breath to argue.

"There is a man named Endo," Takuda said, "a

counselor for Zenkoku who has promised to help your husband find you. I don't know if this counselor cares about fulfilling your husband's revenge fantasies, but I think he dislikes leaving loose ends."

He waited. Finally, she took the packet.

"It's a detailed escape plan," he said. "Execute it Monday. That gives you two days to commit as much of it to memory as possible. Carry it with you at all times."

She stared down at the packet.

"Do not tell anyone you are leaving. At noon Monday, withdraw your entire savings in cash and go straight to the station. Use only cash. Your life depends upon it."

"This is insane," Okamoto said.

"At the station, you will stop once to drop your cell phone off at a courier kiosk. The enclosed prepaid mailer is already addressed to your parents in Osaka. The longer the phone works, the longer Zenkoku will think you're on your way home. Make sure it's fully charged and turn off the ringer to save power."

She opened the packet. Takuda watched her eyes twitch across the maps and timetables as if she could absorb this all at once. She would not.

"You will have to memorize this like a dance. The train times, platform switchbacks, shortcuts, and clothing changes leave you little margin for error. The instructions tell how many changes of clothing you'll need, lightweight clothing that will fit easily into trash bins as you discard outfits. You can't miss a beat, but luckily, you'll only have to do it once. Do it correctly, and you will be free."

She blinked at him.

"I didn't have time to write everything down. The travel timetables end on the third day. You'll be at a seaside town called Hikari. Buy a can of lighter fluid at the tobacconist's on the corner opposite the fishmonger's. Walk down to the sand. There are piles of driftwood from last year's typhoons. Build a fire big enough to burn your old ID, credit cards, bankbook, everything. When the coals are hot, throw in your personal seal. Then go to the ward office to start activating your new identity. That's page two."

"Umm—this says Yoshiko Kawamura. You want me to become Yoshiko Kawamura?"

"Yoshiko Kawamura is an amalgam of old ID numbers and medical records. Essentially, you'll be merging bits of three different identities to make a whole."

"You have identities just lying around?"

"They are debris of other lives left behind by murderers in the Naga River valley. A clever coworker of mine showed me how to put them to good use. Once you've activated all the different bits, your new identity will be in synch with an old family register buried in the archives of a town in Shikoku. The text of a letter that will allow you to retrieve that old register is included. The parents of your new identity, unfortunately, will have been missing for decades, presumed deceased."

"Fine by me." She examined her new personal seal, pristine in its plastic case. "Can I get caught?"

"No. Even if something doesn't work the first time, or you take the steps out of order, there's a perfectly reasonable explanation and an alternative method for getting each document reassigned or account reactivated for your new identity. Learn it, and you'll disappear."

"You'll know where I am."

He nodded. "This is the best I can do."

"Why are you doing this?"

"Because you can get away. My son didn't get away, and neither did my brother. Your husband didn't get away, and I won't get away. But you can get away. If I can help salvage a single life, it'll make my own self-destruction seem more worthwhile."

"That's your selfish reason."

He nodded. *I'll sleep better in prison*, he thought.

She resealed the packet. "Monday, huh? Why not today?"

Takuda tried not to smile at her false bravado. "Once you withdraw your savings, it will set off alarms if they're watching you the way I think they are. If you follow the plan, you'll disappear into the Japan Rail timetables. But the plan depends on your leaving work at noon on a weekday."

She folded her arms with the packet to her chest. "This really means freedom, doesn't it?"

"You'll just be a poor orphan girl who's grown up and made a life for herself."

She bowed. "I'm afraid to do this, but I'm deeply indebted."

He returned her bow. "Don't let anyone see that packet. Sleep with it. Carry it with you every minute till Monday." He started climbing the balcony side railing back up to the roof.

"You could go through the door."

"They might be listening inside. Not a word about this, anywhere. Not a word." Before he pulled himself up on the roof, he said, "Good luck."

He hit the street four buildings closer to the train station. Two stations later, he bought a seat on a train headed home but boarded a bullet train headed the other way. He sat in the first unoccupied seat until the train got moving, but then he went to the public telephone.

Yumi answered on the third ring. "Why are you calling me? Don't you think they'll find you?"

"I just wanted to tell you I'm not coming straight home."

"Good. You're ready to go do your duty," she said.

"Umm, I've still got a few days' leave," he said. "If you'll be okay . . ."

"No, do your duty, not your job. Go to the valley."

She wants me dead. He felt a pain like stabbing in his chest. The Kappa hadn't hurt him this badly. He laid his head against the polished steel surrounding the telephone.

"Do you hear me?"

"I hear you."

"Kill it. You and your strange new friends kill it. Then come home to me."

Tears welled in his eyes. "I thought you meant—ah, never mind. Thank you for your forgiveness."

"Don't get soft. Listen to me. There might be people protecting it. If you have to kill them, kill them dead. Wring their necks or cut them in half. Don't leave them half-dead so they can shoot you in the back. And if you get caught, lie down and let them take you. Don't fight. Then pretend to be insane. Just tell them the same story you told me the other night."

"Yumi, I . . ."

"No, no, no. Listen to me. One: Kill it. Two: Kill anyone who stands in your way. Three: Don't get caught. Four: If caught, act insane. But most important, number one: Kill it. Kill the monster that took away my baby. Do you understand?"

"I understand."

"If you kill it, I'll wait for you forever. As long as it takes. Do you understand?"

"I understand."

"And don't hurt Nakamura."

Takuda listened into the tinny silence for a few seconds. "That's it?"

"That's it."

"I thought you hated Nakamura."

"He's stupid. Stupidity isn't a crime."

"I'm innocent, then."

"You're only stupid about women. Now, go kill it and come home to me."

"Yumi, I just need to say a few things. First . . ."

"Shut up. Shut up! You will not die. You will not! Say it."

"I will not die."

"You will kill it, and you will come home to me."

"I will kill it, and I will come home to you."

She let out a ragged breath. "I'll wait for you," she said, and she hung up.

The conductor stopped Takuda to check his ticket. "Passenger, this train is going up to Tokyo. You're headed in the wrong direction."

"Yes, I realized that when I saw the water to our right."

The conductor didn't even blink. He had heard it all. He gave Takuda a transfer that would allow him to take another bullet train back west. "It will still add almost two hours to your trip, but you can get off at the next regular stop. You're lucky you're on the regular bullet train and not the super express bullet train. That would have ruined your day."

CHAPTER 33

Miyoko Gotoh's voice shook. "So, now you know. That's what happened to your brother. And your son. Your father was the last good man in Oku Village, but he was too old to fight them, and he finally broke from the grief."

She sat on her doorstep before him with her broom over her knees as if she would use it to protect herself. Takuda stood very still. If he moved, he might be unable to stop himself from killing her.

"You never told," he said.

"Who would I tell? Half the valley knew, and the other half suspected. Dirty bastards. I'll bet they're in the Hell of Incessant Suffering right now. I can't imagine how many lifetimes you'd have to stay in hell for offenses like those. A lot, I'll bet. I'll be there, too. I'll swim the River of Fire and climb the Mountain of Needles."

He reached past her to open her door. It ground along on its track. Takuda wondered how she managed to slide it open.

As he stepped in, she said, "Don't tell him. Don't tell him how much I know. Don't tell anyone."

He looked down at her. "Don't worry. I doubt I'll ever speak your name again."

She bowed her head as he stepped inside.

The dark house stank of kerosene and incontinence. Takuda kept his shoes on. The ground floor was three rooms of junk and a foul-smelling kitchen. He climbed the narrow wooden stairs. The air was warmer as he climbed, and the stench of sickness was thicker. There was no scent of Kappa, not yet. Gotoh had become careless as he aged, so there might be some Kappa trace in the house. Takuda would follow his nose as long as he could stand it.

The old man lay on a filthy pallet in a dingy bedroom. A newish television squatted on a stand at his feet, and a shiny kerosene heater took up the center of the floor. The remote controllers for both lay on a wooden box at the old man's fingertips. Nothing else in the room looked as if it had been touched in years. An empty rice bowl lay at his side. The straw matting was dark with overlapping stains radiating outward from the edge of his pallet. The stench filled the room.

Gotoh had no words of greeting, and there was no surprise in his face. "You're Tohru Takuda's son."

"The old woman told you I was coming."

"That shark-skinned hag hasn't spoken to me in a month. More than a month."

"You expected me anyway."

"I expected you. When I saw on the news that the idiot police chief arrested an outsider for our crimes, I knew you would come. That was the first slip in fifteen years."

"What was the last slip before that?" He held up the Kappa's severed finger. "Was it when your filthy god lost this?"

The old man squinted at it. He tried and failed to sit up, and then he reached for the Kappa's finger with a spotted, withered hand. His own left forefinger was missing. Takuda knelt to pass the grisly relic to the old man, but he stayed tensed in thigh and shoulder to spring away or to hammer Gotoh where he lay. *Just as Yumi says, even the oldest dog has one more bite.*

Gotoh turned the finger over several times. He held it out to Takuda without any change of expression, but his breath had become sharp and ragged. "Where did you get it?"

"It was one of the treasures of Eagle Peak Temple." Takuda took the finger carefully.

"The old priest kept secrets better than anyone in the Naga River valley. Better than we did."

"He drowned anyway, didn't he?"

The old man pointed at the finger. "You know it has grown back, don't you?"

"I've seen it." Takuda held up his bandaged fore-arms. "I've felt it."

The old man's eyes widened.

Takuda shook his head in disgust. "Didn't you imagine the creature could be fought? Didn't anyone in the Farmers' Co-op ever fight it?"

"Fight him? We didn't want to fight him. He made us rich."

"Made you rich." Takuda wrapped the finger and put it away. His hands were surprisingly steady. He was getting used to talking about murder in terms of profit and loss. "You had your pick of anything good in the valley, didn't you? You could have the best land. You could have the prettiest girls, at least until the next solstice or equinox. You could settle grudges and relieve debts by making whole families disappear. And no one could stand up to you. The Farmers' Co-op used your Kappa to hold this valley hostage for—how long? A hundred years?"

The old man noticed that Takuda had kept his shoes on inside the house, an unforgivable insult, and he laughed until his laughter had him coughing and choking on his pallet.

Takuda sat on the floor, well away from the high-water mark of stains on the straw matting. When the old man recovered, he said, "Come closer. Are you afraid of me?"

Takuda shook his head. "If you had wanted to re-write my family registry, you had your chance."

"You know everything. Everything but the truth."

"I know who was running that Q-35 typewriter in the village office until 1981."

The old man looked at the ceiling. Finally, he said, "The Co-op was just since the war. We made it look like a rural labor movement. The real cult died in the war."

"Not entirely."

"You're talking about the festival? The dance? That was nothing. A drunken after-party. The cult was the main event. The cult was conversation with our Drowning God, with the shaman translating for us. Our Drowning God told us everything. He told us when to plant, when to fish, when to have babies, where to find money in the canals. He was the voice of the wind and the water and the rocks. He's older than anything. He's older than Japan. There hasn't been a shaman who could talk to him since the war. I was just a kid, and I was in a prison camp for a year after it was over. When I got back, he was out."

"From under the shrine."

"He was trapped down there for centuries. There was a time when he was free, but a shaman trapped him down there to protect him from the temple. He got out during the war. No one knew if it was a stray bomb or the river or the last shaman going mad. Maybe he took the shaman's mind and forced him to remove the rocks. He can steal a man's mind, you know. Anyway, it's a mystery, because the shaman was the first one to die. They said they found his skin emptied like a rice sack."

"So your Kappa steals a man's mind to make a new shaman. That's how the little girl was almost kidnapped. The Kappa stole Ogawa's mind."

"It's not that simple. Most of us are too deaf, you see? Anyone can learn the old speech, but a shaman understands the *meaning*. We couldn't talk to him after the war. The best we could do is point out likely sacrifices and try to cover it up, you see? He has no idea about the modern world, how impossible he has become. We kept him penned in till the war, and after the war, we thought we could contain him in the canals."

"So, with a little help and direction, the Kappa killed on his own."

"His name isn't 'Kappa'. It's 'Returned Apprentice of Black Water' when we pray to him and 'Earthly River Spirit-swallower Drowning God' when we speak of his physical presence."

"Did you tie victims to the uprights in the river?"

"The stone pillars? Sometimes, at first. We built a wall to keep him in, and we tried to trap him again. It didn't work. When we tried to trap him, he grabbed old Nakamura, the chief's grandfather, and he waited till the rest of us got down to the water, all of us standing there with our torches. He tore old Nakamura to pieces and ate his liver right in front of us. Right in front of us. Then he laughed and swam toward us. We scattered like rats."

"And you did nothing. You and your wife. You did nothing."

"Don't tell the old woman. If she knew how much I know, she'd leave me for sure."

Takuda opened his mouth to tell him that they needed to get their stories together, but it didn't matter. They would take their horrible secrets to the tomb.

"So you kept the secret for all these years, just waiting for someone to ask you."

"No, no, no. If you had come to me like this ten years ago, you would have been the next one down the hole, and your wife would have followed you three months later. You still have a wife? You don't want to tell me? That's okay. I don't really care. Anyway, that's how I was. I would have told them everything, and then I would have come home and stayed in this room until the phone rang. That's the only time the phone rang, in the end. We don't even have a phone anymore. There's no one to call us."

"So you all got old. When was the last time? When did you last sacrifice?"

"For sure? Seven years ago? Six years ago? I don't know anymore. Probably the same year as the last dance. I don't know."

"Someone helped it. Between the time you cultists got too old and the arrival of Ogawa the patsy, someone helped it. Otherwise, how could the disappearances be covered up?"

"Every day, I've wondered about that. I've watched the calendar and watched the news, just waiting for the Drowning God to be spotted or for someone to find the chamber below the shrine. Then someone finally finds the chamber, and it all gets washed away in a dam release! Who's protecting him now? We're all old men! We wouldn't know how to get an accidental dam release! Anyway, I don't know where the sacrifices have been coming from, but they haven't been coming from the valley unless someone has come up with a better system than I ever could."

"Did you know there was a new shaman? The Zenkoku worker who tried to take the little girl. He understands what it says."

The old man waved it off. "He can't be a shaman. He doesn't know the old rituals. All that is gone. He's just—he's just a procurer. It's not a religion anymore."

"You're right. It's not a religion. It's just murder. But, old man, it was always just murder."

The old man spoke in dead monotone: "The things I did, the things I believed, for all my power, they left me with nothing, worse than nothing. As I've gotten older, I've seen things spin out of control. It's been like being drunk. I feel the darkness and the chaos creeping in from all sides. I have done what I could in the past few months to release my bad karma, but the things I've done—it's terrible. Maybe after a few eons, I'll get out of the Avichi Hell to be reborn as a gutworm or a flea. Show me that finger."

Takuda pulled it out. As he unwrapped it, the old man struggled to sit up. "You know, when he lost that finger, he made us bite off our own fingers for not protecting him. His finger was already growing back, but he made us line up so we could bite off our own fingers. The punishment for failing to protect him. That mean-spirited, dirty creature! I can tell you how to kill him. It seems impossible because he grows back anything you cut off, but there's a way, and I'll tell you because I'm dying, and I'm going straight to Hell. I'm more afraid of dying than I am of the old frog-face himself. If telling you how to kill him can erase a few lines of the library of bad karma I've written during this life, it will be worth it, even if he comes right up those stairs and sucks my liver out through my ass. Now, listen closely . . ."

CHAPTER 34

"It's too dangerous," Officer Mori said. "This time, it will kill you."

They sat on the straw matting of the worship hall. No one had come to evening service for three days. Suzuki had dressed for services just in case, but he expected to chant the sutras by himself.

Mori sat back with his arms folded. Suzuki still bent over the maps and the blueprint Takuda had lain on the floor, but his face was grim. He shook his head as he sat upright.

"This is suicide," Suzuki said. "It's not like the railway tunnel. We didn't have enough information then, and we thought we could go undercover, like spies. Now we know we're being watched."

"Yes, we're being watched," Takuda said. "I'm counting on it."

"Detective," Suzuki said, "there's a lot to be said

for this kind of bravado, but there's nothing to be gained by dying. We'll be stronger if we're all in the fight." Suzuki stood. "Someone just drove up. Stay for the service. Afterward, we can have buckwheat noodles. There's a nice place right on the mountainside, a twenty-minute walk. Why not enjoy the evening, clear our heads?" He pulled his vestments straight and walked toward the entrance pit. "If you'll excuse me, the few congregants who still come are very old, and they need a little help up from the parking lot."

As Suzuki slid into his shoes, Mori turned back to Takuda. "He's right, you know. Your suicidal plan will just leave us to deal with this monster on our own. Not to mention your wife."

"You're reminding me that I'm married?"

"Well, you just don't seem to be thinking clearly. That's all."

"Enough. This is the first time you've mentioned my marriage, ever. You suddenly care about my marriage—when you don't like the plan?"

"No, it's not—look, I just mean . . ."

"She knows I might not come back. You might not come back, either. We might all die. You need to absorb that idea, too. She already has!"

Mori knelt formally. "I *absorbed* that idea when I was nine. I was a foolish little boy who was mad with grief for his sister. You, on the other hand, are a grown man."

Suzuki came back into the entrance pit. "It's the chief. And the sergeant. They're coming up. Let's meet them outside."

Takuda and Mori joined Suzuki halfway down the stairs. Chief Nakamura and Sergeant Kuma made so much noise with their own huffing and puffing that they didn't notice the trio until Nakamura came face-to-face with Takuda. Nakamura's eyes lit with rage.

"You can't be in the Naga River valley. You're not on a case. You've been removed. I'll report you to your supervisor."

"I'm off duty," Takuda said. "I'm consulting the priest on a spiritual matter."

"Spiritual matter? This priest is a joke. He's not even a priest."

Suzuki leaned forward. "Oh, I'm a priest, all right."

"You inherited the post from your father. He ordained you. You don't even know the sutras by heart. You recite them from the book."

"I never said I was a *good* priest," Suzuki said.

Nakamura started berating Mori, and Takuda's attention wandered. He looked out over the valley, already in twilight, then to the reservoir to the south. In the long rays of the afternoon sun, each ripple and each leaf stood clear and sharp as if outlined by an artist's pen. The deep blue reservoir reflected the wild spring sky. The shore glowed with the bright yellow-greens of spring and the last few sprays of plum blossoms. They were in a world of clear water, blue sky, and green trees, a clean world unpolluted by the evil of the valley below.

"Chief Nakamura," he said as the old man shook his finger at Mori's bemused expression. "We're going for a stroll, and then we'll eat some noodles. We would be pleased if you and Sergeant Kuma would join us."

The chief froze. He stood rigid on the stair with his teeth bared.

"That would be good," Suzuki said. "We'll have hot buckwheat noodles and a little cup of something, eh?" He nudged Kuma, who flinched. "You can go off duty, can't you?"

"We can all just relax," said Mori, who looked relaxed himself for the first time since Takuda had met him. "The priest says it's good. While we all have a nice meal, we'll tell you everything we know about the valley."

"And the cause of the water safety question," Suzuki said. "The true cause."

The sergeant covered his mouth with both hands and turned back toward the parking lot.

"Everything in detail back to 1945, plus some sketchy information back to medieval times." Takuda looked down at his own shoes. "I won't tell you if you don't want to hear, but I know how your grandfather died."

The chief's face was pale, and he breathed through his clenched teeth. His cheeks puffed outward, and spittle flew with each ragged breath. Suzuki reached out to steady him, but he shook off Suzuki's hand.

"He drowned," Nakamura said. "They never found him."

Takuda shook his head. "The old town clerk Gotoh told me. He saw it firsthand. He knows everything."

The chief closed his eyes. A wave of grief passed over his face, and he put his hand to his forehead. When he opened his eyes, he looked exhausted and lost. Suzuki reached out again, this time to comfort him.

Again, he shook off Suzuki's hand. "You are all liars!" The chief's eyes lit with hatred, and his face stretched into a mask of rage and disgust. "You make up lies about our valley, and you know nothing! Nothing! I came here for information on the prisoner, Ogawa. He escaped."

"Escaped, huh? That's not surprising," Takuda said.

"Oh, you're not surprised at all, are you?"

"A few days ago, I just walked right in."

"You were in my holding cell?"

"It might not be the last time," Suzuki said.

"That's true," Mori said. He turned to the chief. "We may need to be in your custody someday. Maybe someday soon. If it comes down to that, we won't resist. We don't want anyone to get hurt."

The chief stared at them. He turned to the sergeant, but Kuma was already down in the parking lot, standing beside the car with his back to the temple.

The chief backed down the stairs. "You're all insane," he said. "You'll come to a bad end, and I don't want any part of it."

"Chief Nakamura," Takuda said, "I forgive you for everything you've ever said about my family, and I'll make this promise to you and to everyone in the valley: We're going to solve the water safety question once and for all, or we'll die trying. No one will have to fear the canals or the river. No one will suffer what I have suffered, what you have suffered. Families will finally be safe here. Little girls like Hanako Kawaguchi will finally be safe here."

Chief Nakamura almost spoke. Almost. He turned and walked stiffly down the stairs.

The chief and the sergeant didn't look at each other as they got into the car. As they drove away, Suzuki clapped Takuda on the shoulder. "Well done. He'll start to sleep better. He might even find peace in his old age."

"It's odd that I feel charitable to the chief now that I have nothing left to lose," Takuda said.

"It's not odd. It's not odd at all." Suzuki headed back up the stairs. "I'll change out of my vestments quickly. I really don't want to miss this sunset."

Back in the worship hall, Mori watched in tight-lipped silence as Takuda folded the map and blueprint.

Suzuki led them along the shoreline and up a trail to a country lane. They passed a handful of farmhouses and a small fishing camp. Just as the sun disappeared behind the treetops, they came to a crossroads where the country lane met the prefectural highway threading its way among the mountaintops. The country grocery at the crossroads was overflowing with fresh spring produce, the run-down bait-and-tackle shop was packed with fishermen preparing for the morning, and the parking lot of the old noodle shop was filled with panel trucks that smelled of strawberries and melons.

The noodle shop was crowded with truckers. The

only table open was on an improvised deck built over a sheer drop-off to the neighboring valley. The lights of the villages below were just visible through the trees.

Suzuki was a regular. A grinning waitress brought him noodles with sliced pork. She blushed and ran away when Suzuki teased her about all her "trucker boyfriends."

"Wonderful people up here. Wonderful air. Best in the world. Perhaps I've deserted my congregation, but I do my business up here on the country roads instead of down in the valley."

Mori gestured at Suzuki's noodles. "I'll bet you're glad your sect isn't vegetarian."

"My sect? No, no, it is vegetarian, ideally, but I'm not." He looked down at the lights below. Confused moths began to circle the lamp above their table. "You know, it's very fitting that the last of the old congregants have just quit showing up. My sect really isn't about much except preserving knowledge of the Kappa. If your plan succeeds, then there is no reason to continue."

"What will you do?"

"I don't know. If we're successful, I'll try to sell the temple to one of the Nichiren sects, I think. They're sort of cousins to our sect, anyhow. Selling the temple at a good price will almost settle my bills."

He slurped up half of his noodles at once. They were so steaming hot that Takuda winced just watching Suzuki.

"Priest, almost? You're a whole temple's worth in debt?"

"Oh, yes. Maybe a temple and a half, but I can get a lot of it forgiven, I think." He had to repeat himself when his mouth wasn't so full. "It's expensive to run a temple of old people who don't pay their dues and expect funerals when they die. What else could I do? I've been treading water here for years waiting for you two to show up."

After noodles and beer, Takuda brought out the map and the blueprint.

"You two knew from the start that we were a team. You both knew we would fight this beast together, and you both knew we would become outcasts in the process. But I know one thing you don't: I have to go in alone."

Mori placed both hands on the table. "I can't allow it."

Takuda bowed to hide his expression, but Suzuki laughed out loud.

"Officer, don't be so—oh, now you're turning red. Look, don't be angry. Do you really think any of us can stop the others? Do you think anyone is boss here? You two don't have bosses anymore, right? At least you won't have bosses anymore once you answer your phones."

"They don't fire detectives over the phone," Mori said. "He'll have to go into the office to get fired."

"Ha! That's the spirit," Suzuki said. "See, even a small joke helps."

Takuda looked over at Mori. The young man stared off into the night. *It must be difficult. He had a bright future with the force.*

Takuda said, "Officer Mori, I'll be around to help you find other work. You two will make sure of that."

Mori and Suzuki glanced at each other. "You aren't going to be around. You're committing suicide. You said you would go in alone," Mori said.

"I will." Takuda said. He leaned forward and pointed to the map. "I'll go in the back door. You'll go in the front door." He pointed to the blueprint. "Right here."

Suzuki ran a bony hand over his shaved scalp. Mori stared at the map and the blueprint as if he had never seen such things before.

"We know we're being watched. As I said, I'm counting on it."

CHAPTER 35

Takuda's heart slammed against his ribs as he waded through the drainpipe. His mouth had been dry ever since he lowered himself into the spillway, and his hands had trembled on the hilt of his sword. The adrenaline had gotten stronger with each step. With waterproof LED flashlights strapped to his forehead, his shoulders, and his thighs, Takuda lit the hexagonal drainpipe as bright as day. The skittering light didn't stop the sweat from his palms.

No one can train for this. He watched the water ahead for ripples. He listened in the close, echoing space for any sound not caused by his own motion. *Nothing can prepare a man for this.*

Takuda had run courses to help men and women make better choices when their brains were flooded with adrenaline. The initial session was just like this concrete drainpipe: a search for a dangerous suspect down a narrow corridor. The trainees were jittery, pan-icked, and confused. In their first sessions, they made terrible mistakes, mistakes that could end careers and kill innocent citizens. By the time Takuda was done with them, they could function in the narrow cone of silence where time slows down to the split-second de-cision that must be correct. They told him later that the training had saved lives.

Memories of those sessions flashed before him as he scanned the drainpipe, his sword held above his right shoulder. *My training sessions didn't have monsters. They didn't have grates in the ceiling or runoff pipes in the walls. I should have built in places for monsters to hide.*

Takuda's own adrenaline usually peaked the night before a raid or an arrest, leaving him relaxed and ready when the action came. This time, even though he had all night and a few hours in the morning to prepare, his heart beat faster and faster in his chest. He hadn't known this much adrenaline was possible. He hadn't known he could be so terrified. His fingers twitched on the sword hilt.

He stepped out of the narrow drainpipe into the main underground spillway. It was a smooth-walled, tubular structure almost ten meters in diameter. The floor had been filled to give a flat surface, and the walls rose above him like an underground cathedral. Echoes of his slogging through the shin-deep water were lost in the sounds of water rushing through the cavernous pipe. His lights barely reached the ceiling, but they turned his shadow into a chorus line of insubstantial, spindly-legged puppets curving up the wall behind him. Debris and sandbars had built up on the spillway floor since the peak of the spring melt had passed. He saw movement from the closest island of debris, a man-tall mound of trash and driftwood, and he turned toward it, sword floating by his ear in a tight little circle, ready for a strike at the slightest motion from the . . .

A score of tiny red eyes glared at him from the island.

Lord Buddha protect us. It spawned. He broke into a run, lifting his feet high out of the water. He reached the debris at full speed, ready to slash any little creatures he found there, to deal with each and every one just as Gotoh had told him he should deal with the Kappa. On the last step, his spiked boots skidded on the slime-covered bottom of the pipe. He pulled up his elbows to protect his face as he flew headfirst into the debris. He landed in a net of filth and broken branches, his sword arm pinned uselessly against a bicycle wheel.

Bicycles. He tore himself free, walking backward out of the collected garbage and whipping the muck off his arms and his sword. With each of his backward steps, his flashlights winked in the reflectors of the rusted bicycles and scooters entangled in the branches. He cursed in the darkness, and then he crouched in the water and washed the silty muck away. *Bicycles!* He knelt in the water. *If I don't calm down, I'm going to die down here, just like the poor citizens riding those bicycles when the cult caught them.*

He whispered a verse of sutra until his breathing steadied and his heart slowed. He had time. His lights would last all day if necessary. Mori and Suzuki wouldn't catch up to him for half an hour if they got through. He had time. He chanted and opened his heart and his mind. He let the fear drain away from him.

On the third repetition of the verse, he caught a whiff of rotting fish.

He stood up slowly. He was alone, despite the stench. He was sure of it. If he was correct, the Kappa's lair was upstream on his right, among the old holding tanks. The LEDs projected phantoms on the curving walls as he moved toward Holding Tank One.

Holding Tank One, originally a cooling tank, was used for storage of caustic agents that could not safely be released in any form. Ogawa's office, a cubbyhole off the main wastewater management control room, was the closest point to Holding Tank One. The blueprint showed a service hatch in the floor; Ogawa would have been able to get down into the tank area through the hatch.

This was what Chief Nakamura meant when he said Ogawa's brain had been damaged by fumes in restricted areas. The bay beneath Holding Tank One was the Kappa's new lair. This was where the Kappa had seduced and possessed Ogawa, where Ogawa had become its murderous priest.

The drain that would take Takuda to Holding Tank One was a black oval in the high, curved wall. The bore was smooth rather than hexagonal, and it rose at a forty-five degree angle into absolute darkness. Cool air flowing down through the pipe carried the stench of rotting fish and another stench, the same as in the cavern underneath the old shrine, but stronger, *fresher*. There was something dead up there. Takuda was going into the Kappa's active lair.

He shook out his shoulders and forced his fingers to grip his sword more loosely. *If I'm going to die in here, it's got to kill me. I'm not going to kill myself with stupid mistakes.* His heartbeat had dropped to a steady, manageable thud, and his hands hardly trembled at all. He was still terrified, but he was ready to go. He started up the incline into a foul headwind.

As he passed into the pipe, the sound of rushing water dropped away behind, and all he could hear was his own ragged breathing and the scrape of his spiked boots on concrete. The spiked boots were made for fly-fishing on a sand or gravel streambed. He stopped, then backed down the incline. At the bottom, he pulled off the boots and dug his toes into the cold, silted sand. He walked much more quietly when he started back up the pipe. With his feet bare and his sword drawn, he hardly thought of his pulse rate at all.

The air became denser, fouler, and hotter as Takuda neared the top of the pipe. The drainpipe ended in a concrete basin below the holding tank itself. He stepped up onto the gentler incline. The stench was incredible. Takuda turned in a circle, sword at the ready. The circular floor sloped downward to the drainpipe he had just left. Unseen sluices at the perimeter of the tank, apparently meant to keep the floor clean, supplied the stinking rivulet that ran down the drainpipe.

The whole floor is wet, but they need more water to clean this up, Takuda thought. *They need fire hoses.*

Four massive steel columns held up the holding tank, which loomed in the darkness above. The smooth, curved walls of the tank narrowed to a giant funnel poised to spill caustic poison into the concrete basin where he stood. The spout was shut with a wheeled valve painted bright red. The valve wheel itself was geared to a pulley chain that ran up through the steel-grate gantry circling the tank and upward into deeper shadow. A forest of I-beams supported the gantry. The I-beams were so rusted and blistered that at first, Takuda didn't notice the lumpier, rounder shapes on the floor among them.

He stepped forward, his circle of shaking light a few steps ahead of him. The shapes on the floor were pitiful human remains, all in Zenkoku coveralls. They were ripped halfway from their clothes, exposed to the bone, bloated, blown, and half-consumed. Around the corpses were scores of dead rats. The rats had been broken, twisted, sometimes torn in half. The Kappa had killed its victims, eaten its fill, and left the rest to rot. When rats had come to investigate, the Kappa had killed them for pleasure.

So Ogawa really procured sacrifices from among the Zenkoku workers. He must have had a lot of inside help to cover that up. I wonder if it was as easy to cover up for miss-

ing *corporate employees as it was to make whole families disappear.*

Takuda hefted his sword as he turned, scanning the rest of the room. He was not alone. He heard a shoe scraping the serrated bar grate far above, but closer, down below, he saw a shifting shadow among the gantry supports.

Anyone lurking above could wait. He moved slowly toward the shadow, sliding his feet silently over the inclined concrete. The darkened shadow among the pillars stopped moving. Takuda raised his sword, ready to cut the Kappa in two. It would appear as a woman, of course, or maybe a little boy, maybe even as his son, but he wouldn't be fooled.

The shadow gurgled deep in its throat.

His lights would blind the creature long enough for him to get the first blow. Once he started, nothing could stop him. Takuda stepped sideways, swinging his lights around to shine full in the creature's face—

It was Ogawa, blinking in the glare. His eyes were wide as saucers. "Detective! What are you doing here?"

Takuda did not lower his sword. "Me? What are you doing here? How did you get out of jail?"

"I was given a chance. If I can clean this up, clean up this room, there was never a crime! None of it ever happened!" He brandished a fistful of household garbage bags. "You can't stop this. It comes from very high up. Very high! You can't ruin this for me."

Takuda lowered his sword and grabbed Ogawa by the collar. "Where's your monster? I'm here to kill it."

"Kill him? You? Kill him? Heh heee!" Ogawa's heavy, loose-lipped grin widened. "You're lucky he's not here! He's hunting!"

Takuda released him and sheathed his sword. "Ogawa, you're a fool. They may let you clean up the mess for them, but if you think they're going to let you go, you really are brain-damaged."

Ogawa stared past Takuda's shoulder. He dropped the garbage bags as he slipped backward into shadow.

Takuda grasped his sword hilt as he turned. He felt the Kappa before he heard it, and then it was too late. It was on his back before he could face it, hissing with pleasure as it wrapped slimy fingers around his throat.

CHAPTER 36

Takuda couldn't even unsheathe his sword. He reeled, breathless, as the Kappa strangled him from behind, cutting the oxygen to his brain so that he saw bright blue-and-orange dots in the darkness. The Kappa's beak snapped at his ear as their joined shadow danced and twisted among the I-beams. The LED lantern from Takuda's forehead fell to the concrete.

Takuda was suddenly too weak to stand, and his vision was narrowing to a dark tunnel. The Kappa was pumping poison into his neck. He dropped the sheathed sword and fell to one knee on the inclined concrete. He stretched his head back to peel the Kappa's fingers from his throat, and he spotted Ogawa shinning his way up a rusted I-beam.

"Ogawa, help me," he whispered hoarsely.

"Help yourself, Detective," Ogawa shouted down. "He hates the metal, he does. Grind him off against a girder there, then climb up here with me." He climbed another meter. "Of course, that leaves him down there and us up here. We'll cling to these girders, and that's as long as our lives will be, heh-heh!"

"Angah khu, tan hrag!" I'll eat you next, coward.

Ogawa clambered upward into darkness.

Takuda gathered the strength left in his trembling legs. He pushed upright and ran backward, hoping he would hit a girder before he tripped over a corpse.

"Shuu hun. Ha-raa, ha-raa—" Enough, the Kappa whispered as Takuda picked up speed. *Sleep, sleep—*

They hit an I-beam so hard that Takuda felt the squared edge right through the Kappa's rubbery flesh. It squealed and released him. Takuda stumbled forward as the Kappa hit the concrete. He scooped up his sword by the hilt and whipped off the scabbard in one motion, almost losing the sword in the process. To stop his headlong fall, he hit another I-beam with his outstretched arm and spun around the beam to face the Kappa, slashing wildly as he spun just in case it had followed him.

The Kappa was nowhere in sight.

It's not weakened. It's not weakened at all. There was enough water on the floor for the Kappa to regain its strength. It could do this all day. Takuda couldn't.

Takuda's lights swayed with him as he stood panting, trying to regain breath that would not come. Shadows sawed against each other in the bright, white light. Each girder left a greenish trail as Takuda swayed, and each shadow left a purplish trail. The poison had hit his brain, and he didn't have long. He gripped the hilt with both hands, but his fingertips were so numb he could barely feel the sharkskin wrapping.

"Detective," Ogawa hissed from the shadows above, "are you alive?"

Takuda didn't answer. He strained all his senses searching for the Kappa among the I-beams. He felt drunk. His breath was slow and shallow, and he couldn't quite fill his lungs. He hoped he died of heart failure before he suffocated.

All I need is seven cuts. Seven. Lord Buddha, allow me seven cuts to cleanse this valley.

"Detective, there's someone up here on the gantry."

Takuda moved forward slowly, one foot before the other. His bare feet slid on the slimed concrete, past the dead rats and defiled corpses. He was ready to cut in any direction. He was as good as dead, but he still had strength enough to wield the massive sword. *That's why this blade is so heavy and tempered so hard.* He finally understood. It was made to be wielded by a man so near death he could only swing it in the right direction such that the sword itself would cut down the enemy by its own mass.

"Detective, someone is coming down!" Ogawa hissed. "Coming down the stairs! Just let them come. While he's killing them, I'll slide down and get help! I can save you!"

He tried to smile at Ogawa's lies, but his lips were

oddly frozen. He heard feet clattering on steel. *If they're human, I can deal with them.* He walked toward the stairs, sword at the ready.

As if in slow motion, one of the corpses exploded to Takuda's left. Blood-slimed ribs and strips of purplish flesh twisted in the air in front of Takuda as the Kappa burst from its hiding place inside a human torso. Takuda swung the sword, but his loins twisted slowly, so slowly, and his arms lagged behind his body like streamers in the wind. The Kappa ducked under the blade, its eyes locked on his. As the ribs and gobbets of flesh started to hit the ground at Takuda's feet, the Kappa stood erect and drew back its long, bony paw. Takuda tried to bring the sword back, but it was too heavy. Its mass continued to twist him sideways, exposing his chest to the Kappa. The Kappa shrieked in triumph as it drove its claws in under his sternum.

That's it, then. The thought was simple and clear. His life was over. The sword dropped to the concrete. His hands dropped to his sides.

"Heh ho zhe hyah khu kho." I won't eat you quickly. It looked him in the eyes. *"Kho to heh ha-raa."* You will sleep with me.

Takuda swayed, looking down at the claws digging into his chest. A vision flashed before him: He was lying on the concrete, eyes wide open, awake but paralyzed. The Kappa sat beside him, chewing the flesh from his hip bone.

He looked at the Kappa. It nodded, grinning. *"Zhaaaa—"*

It was still grinning as he grabbed the fingers protruding from his chest. It tried to pull away, but he held its hand against his body and clapped the handcuff on its bony wrist.

"*Iyaaaahhhh!*" The Kappa shrieked, dragging Takuda on his belly through the rats and corpses, banging him against the I-beams as it tried to escape the burning steel cuff. The lights were stripped from Takuda's biceps and thighs, lying behind him like a short trail of fallen stars. He still held the cuff with both hands. The Kappa turned on him, giving Takuda just enough slack to snap the other cuff on his own wrist. He laid his cheek on the filthy concrete. He had done his best.

The Kappa was enraged. It lifted Takuda by the cuffed hand. Now that he was so weak, the Kappa seemed fearsomely strong. It put its long, skinny foot against his bleeding chest and pulled. The cuff would not budge. The Kappa grasped the chain between the cuffs, placed both feet on Takuda's chest, and *pulled*. Takuda tensed with the strength left in him as his shoulder began to dislocate. The Kappa snarled with pleasure as it prepared to rip his arm off.

Instead, there was a bright flash, and the Kappa's own arm fell. The paw gripped the chain for an instant, and then the severed arm rolled into the Kappa's lap, leaving the one-armed Kappa cuffed to Takuda.

Takuda and the Kappa stared at the stump as the blackish blood gushed. Then they both noticed the point of a dripping blade, a thin and streamlined blade arcing up into the darkness. Suzuki stood at the other end, his bony face barely lit by Takuda's fallen torches.

From behind the Kappa shone a sudden, blinding light. A figure moved inside it. The Kappa, confused, half turned toward the light, and then its head jerked oddly, sliding forward on its shoulders before it also fell. Twin spouts of black blood arced from the stump of the Kappa's neck into the blinding light, then thinned and wavered as the dying heart slowed. Mori, lit bright as day with the lantern hung round his neck, flicked the blood from his blade and sheathed it. As the blood ceased, the Kappa's torso fell backward. Mori stepped backward as if to keep it from soiling his boots.

Takuda pulled the poisoned claws farther from his chest. "Step clear of that head, Priest." His voice sounded thick and distant, even to himself. "It's killed me, and now you have to kill it."

"You're not dead yet," Mori said. He knelt and tore open Takuda's coveralls. Five livid wounds stood out in a tight semicircle on Takuda's chest.

"Most of this is right over the sternum," Mori said. "It didn't even penetrate the bone."

"It didn't even try," Takuda said. "It wanted me alive and paralyzed." He flinched as Mori squirted saline into the wounds. "What are you doing there?"

"Dr. Fujimoto's orders. He said 'irrigate, irrigate, irrigate.' "

"It feels worse than the original wound." He was just beginning to realize that he would live. "You might have to carry me out, but let's not carry the corpse. I want this filthy thing off me. Hey, Priest, get the cuff key out of my belt, will you? It's on the leather loop at the back—Reverend Suzuki, stand down. Sheathe that ridiculous blade."

Suzuki stood with his forearms knotted, fingers clenched on the hilt of his sword. He stared in horror at the Kappa's head at his feet. "What have we done?"

Takuda tried to push Mori away. "Secure the priest. It's gotten to him."

Mori brushed his hand away. "You've got to talk him through it." He continued to squirt stinging water into Takuda's wounds.

Suzuki's face was ashen in the bright glow of Mori's lantern. His face was lined with grief. "No, no, no. What have we done?"

"Priest, look at me. You know it can appear in different shapes, right? What do you see?"

Suzuki continued to stare at the head.

"Priest! Look at me!"

Suzuki looked up mournfully. Tears streamed down his cheeks.

"What did you see? Don't look at it! Just tell me what you saw. A pretty girl? A little boy? An apprentice priest? What did you see?"

"A little b-boy—Shunsuke."

Mori pushed Takuda onto his back and sat on his belly. "I'm sorry, Detective, but this just can't wait." He placed a plastic cylinder like a large marking pen to the left of Takuda's sternum. "You may feel a slight pressure." He held the cylinder over Takuda's heart with both hands and leaned forward to put his weight on it. When he depressed the button, white gas shot out a vent at the side, and burning cold blasted into Takuda's chest.

Takuda roared and tossed Mori off. Even in the dim light, he saw a new wound in his chest, a circular welt leaking blood and clear fluid. He swore, holding his hand to his chest.

"We murdered a little boy," Suzuki whispered.

Takuda dragged the Kappa's headless, twitching corpse toward Suzuki before he realized he was back on his feet. He moved aside so Mori's lantern would illuminate the Kappa's head.

Mori stood, brushing off his coveralls. "I need to dress those wounds."

Takuda bowed to him in gratitude, but he motioned him to stand back. The laundry-pole sword trembled in Suzuki's fevered grip.

"Priest, this boy you see, there's something wrong with its mouth, isn't there? And the shape of the head is all wrong. And if you really look at the eyes, right in the eyes, you'll see that it isn't a boy at all. It's the monster that killed your father."

Suzuki looked down at it. The creature's eyes were open, staring. The cracked and leathery beak twitched in a rhythm like speech: the Kappa speaking to Suzuki's mind.

"Oh, you filthy thing," Suzuki said to the Kappa's head. "To make me think we killed an innocent boy! Oh!" Suzuki kicked the head, and it sailed toward Mori.

"Hey!" Mori dodged the head. "Watch it!"

The head bounced off an I-beam and began to roll down the concrete toward the drainpipe. If it started down that slope, it would be in the shin-deep water of the spillway before they could stop it. They would search, but it would be lost to them. Then it would lie quietly in the muck until it found another priest to bring it victims. It would feed off innocents as it slowly grew another body. Then it would hunt, unstoppable again.

Takuda lunged, but he was too weak, and the rolling head was picking up speed. The squirming, child-sized corpse handcuffed to his arm dragged Takuda down like lead. He would never catch it.

The Kappa's head hissed with glee as it rolled toward the drainpipe.

CHAPTER 37

Suzuki, sword flailing, leapt for the Kappa's head. Takuda and Mori pulled up short, reflexively dodging the arc of Suzuki's spastic blade.

Suzuki caught up to the head just before it reached the drainpipe. He tried to spear it with his sword, almost stabbing himself in the shin on the second try. His bungled attempt at stabbing the head diverted it from the drain until he could stop it with his foot. He kicked it back up the slope, where it stopped at Takuda's feet. It hissed and spat, rolling its yellow eyes at Takuda and Mori.

Suzuki's sword hung from his fingers. He was breathing more heavily than Takuda was. "I'm sorry. I'm sorry."

Takuda pointed at him. "Sheathe your blade. Now!"

When Suzuki's blade was secured, Mori released the hilt of his own. He stepped toward them. He let out his breath. "Okay," he said, looking from Takuda to Suzuki. "Okay."

They stood looked down at the head in the brilliance of Mori's lantern. Mori sighed. "It's still dangerous, isn't it?"

It stared back at them, one after another, pouring out pure hatred through its eyes. But it also poured out visions of its long, hideous life.

Takuda saw it as a young man, a monk traveling to the darkest reaches of China. He saw it dragged down into a pool under a secret temple, black water and black prayers entering its mouth and its heart and its eyes. He saw it change to something less than human as the black goddess of the temple made it one of her children. He saw it learn to snap with its new beak and pull the unwitting innocent down to the depths to feast on their soft, sweet entrails. Takuda saw himself, as if in a mirror, as if in a film, bending down and taking the Kappa's head to his chest, holding it safe, feeding it until it could feed itself again . . .

He blinked. He stepped back as if pulling himself free of the Kappa's eyes. Mori was staring at the Kappa's head, entranced. Suzuki was staring too, the corners of his mouth drawn into a frown of concentration

That's your best trick, filth. In a second, you'll see my best trick. He bent for his sword.

"Mori, uncuff me. The key is in the back of—"

Then Suzuki stepped back and drew his long, long blade.

"Mori! The priest!"

Mori stepped back into a deep stance as he drew his own blade, ready to dispatch the maddened priest.

Suzuki raised his sword above his head and brought the blade down between the Kappa's eyes. The thin blade sprang sideways off the Kappa's rubbery face. It dug a divot out of the Kappa's slick brow and split its beak, but the head remained intact. Lightning and scenes of green, cloudy water shot through Takuda's head.

Suzuki frowned at Takuda and sheathed his sword.

Takuda scanned the concrete for his own sword—now was the time. He retrieved his blade and lopped off the Kappa's cuffed arm at the wrist, just below the handcuff, and the severed claw slid out as well. Takuda let the empty cuff dangle as he gripped the sword for close work and settled into an easy front stance. He let out slack on the hilt as he raised the sword above his head, and then he stepped forward into a "four-point" stance, bringing the blade straight down into the Kappa's face with all his might.

For my son Kenji.

The impact was tremendous, but even so, the Kappa's head spread and flattened for an instant before splitting in half. It lay open slowly as coiled cartilage and black, gelatinous blood spilled onto the concrete. The eye facing Takuda winked furiously, focused on him for a second, and then rolled back in its shallow socket.

Takuda saw a vision of a primitive farmhouse and a gray-haired woman drawing water from a stream.

As it dies, it thinks of its mother? Ridiculous. It's much too late for that.

Takuda addressed the left side of the head. It was harder to split, but it split. *For my brother Shunsuke.*

The Kappa's last coherent vision: returning to the village of its birth while it still resembled a man in some ways, walking down the dirt path to that primitive farmhouse to see its gray-haired mother. Then looking into her eyes as it strangled her.

As the right half of the cranium split, the blade struck sparks off the concrete below. *For your poor mother.*

For my wife Yumi. A shard of the blade whizzed past Mori's head.

For my parents, for all the parents of the Naga River valley. The blade shattered, leaving him with a cleaver as long as his forearm. It would do.

For Mori's sister Yoshiko. With the final blow, the tang separated from the blade, leaving him with a bladeless hilt. He let it roll off his fingers onto the concrete.

The Kappa's head lay cut into seven pieces. They eyes were dead, spilled onto the concrete, and the rubbery skull was empty.

Suzuki poked a dead eye with the toe of his boot. "Just as it's written on the great mandala of the Nichiren sects, '*Those who trouble the practitioners of Buddhist Law will have their heads split into seven pieces.*' Who told you to do this?"

"Gotoh, the old village clerk."

"Gotoh? Really? That old rascal." Suzuki chuckled

as he dropped to his knees. He unzipped his coveralls to reveal the priestly robe and sash.

Mori aimed the lantern at him. "What are you doing, Priest?"

"Well, I'm praying for this creature. It was a man once, but it must be reborn in the depths of hell. Imagine how many lifetimes—" Suzuki's voice died away as Mori stepped up and unzipped his coveralls as well. "Ah, Officer . . ."

"I'm not a policeman anymore, and this piece of filth murdered my sister." Mori's urine chattered among the fragments of the Kappa's head, jostling its loosened eyeballs and sending a rivulet of steaming muck down the concrete. Suzuki closed his eyes and began chanting the sutras low in his throat.

When Mori finished pissing, he grinned at Takuda and tossed his chin at the trickle of filth heading for the drainpipe. "See that? That's all the Kappa that will ever get back to the river."

Takuda laughed more out of surprise and embarrassment than actual amusement. Mori was a young man acting out a tough-guy routine. He would probably cry when it was all over.

Mori leaned over to spit precisely in the center of the seven fragments.

Then again, maybe he won't cry after all.

The trickling sound hadn't stopped with Mori's stream. It seemed to be getting louder, and more streams of liquid were joining Mori's urine on the floor. They looked behind them. Slowly, the valve wheel was turning, and greenish, soapy water trickled out of the spout.

"Ogawa? Ogawa, are you up there?"

The pulley chain jerked, and the valve opened all the way. A torrent as thick as Takuda's thigh hit the concrete.

Suzuki jumped up just before the torrent hit his knees. It was up to Takuda's ankles in a second, and it burned.

"What is this stuff, Mori?"

"I don't know," Mori said. He coughed and gagged, pointing up to the bar grate above. "Did you hear the door? I just heard the door." He bent over, gagging and heaving.

"Chloramine," Suzuki said. "It's chloramine. The fumes will fill the room and choke us out before we make it to the door."

"Door . . . locked . . . Ogawa" Mori vomited explosively.

Suzuki pulled them by the sleeves. "Come with me. Quickly!" He led them to the drain where the greenish wastewater swirled downward. Fresher air shot up from the funnel. "Cover your eyes and your mouth and your nose and just slide down. When you hit the bottom, go—which way is upstream, Detective?"

"Right."

"Go right. Do not swallow it, and do not get it in your eyes. When you get down there, roll in the water and strip off your clothes."

Mori retched uncontrollably.

"Okay, he goes first," Takuda said.

They sat him in the swirling liquid and pushed him down the incline. He slid a meter down the concrete and stopped, the caustic flow buffeting his back. Suzuki sighed and pushed Takuda down after him. Their combined mass sent them rocketing down the drainpipe. They hit the spillway sputtering and coughing. Takuda was so weak and jittery, it took all his strength to drag Mori upstream and roll him in the water.

"Don't get the water in your wounds," Mori gasped.

Takuda sat. They had lucked into a sandy spot. "Too late for that." In the light of Mori's lantern, Takuda's feet were red and puffy. He wondered if his fishing boots might still be near the foot of the drainpipe, but a glance over his shoulder told him they had been swept away in the greenish froth from the holding tank.

Suzuki hit the spillway with his legs straight out, his arms folded on his chest. He seemed to skip across the water and out of the glow of Mori's torch. Then he floundered upstream toward them, his face streaked with blackish muck.

They sat panting, Mori's lantern a bright spot in the cavernous dark.

"It's dead," Suzuki said, wonder in his voice. "It's dead, and we're alive."

"I need help," Mori said. His lips were purplish, and there were deep purple bags under his eyes. The rest of his face was a frightening pale green.

"Let's get you out of here. There's a—breeze,"

Suzuki said as he washed the mud off his face. "We're upwind—from the spill. That's—the best medicine. You're sick, but you—won't die."

"I lost my sword."

Suzuki knee-walked in the sand and presented Mori his sword. Sick as he was, Mori bowed from the waist. "Hey, Priest, you're not sick at all."

"Oh, I suppose it's because I'm taller." He helped Mori to his feet. "Also, I started shallow breathing as soon as I smelled it. Maybe shallow breathing is why Detective Takuda isn't sick either. Dr. Fujimoto's epinephrine kept him moving, but his lungs are still half-paralyzed. No deep breaths from him. Always lucky."

"Always lucky," Takuda said. "How did you know it was chloramine?"

"The temple is so poor that I clean the bathrooms myself. I've learned that ammonia and chlorine don't mix. You never forget that smell."

"We don't have time for chemistry class," Mori said.

Behind them, flashlight beams danced in the cavernous spillway.

"Well, here they come," Takuda said. As he stood, they heard the first voices echoing off the concrete. "It's probably the village police. Zenkoku won't do its own dirty work down here. Stash your swords up under that ledge. We'll probably be going from jail to hospital to jail before we can get back here."

"No, no," Mori said. His skin wasn't pink yet, but he was already a little less green. "Priest, keep your sword. There's an entrance to the spillways right there. We can double back through the spillways to go out the way the detective came in. Come on."

Takuda and Suzuki helped him along. They stepped into the spillway pipe just as the lights came around the bend.

CHAPTER 38

Over the next three days, Takuda relaxed for the first time he could remember. He spoiled Yumi. He read frivolous magazines and watched nonsensical game shows.

He also realized that no matter how strange and fantastical the last two weeks had been, no one around him seemed to notice. Takuda's world had been turned upside down, but everyone else just went about their business.

The first time he went to a public bath after the Kappa's death, he soaped and scrubbed self-consciously. He was sure the men and boys around him were staring at his bruises, his scrapes, the stitched lacerations on his forearms, and the five-pointed wound on his chest. He resigned himself to being mute and mysterious and suspicious. He eased into the water, resting his arms on the tiled edge to keep the last of stitches dry.

After nods of greeting, no one seemed interested in him at all. The old men took turns complaining that foreigners had dominated the March sumo tournament in Osaka. Out of politeness, they called on younger men to agree with them. They included Takuda in turn, but otherwise, they didn't seem to notice him at all. He enjoyed it so that he stayed in the water too long. It helped sweat the poison out.

Later in the day, he went to prefectural police headquarters to quit. His resignation waited for him in a plastic folder at the front desk. Sitting in reception, he filled out the forms, dated them, stamped them, and then he handed them over along with his handcuffs, his badge, his black leather notebook and his ID. He hadn't checked out a firearm since his most recent training, so he just had to sign a statement that he possessed no ammunition and that he agreed to a search of his apartment, a search that would probably never occur. He asked to see his supervisor, but his supervisor was not available. He left a note of thanks, and he walked out a free man.

That afternoon, he lay on the floor with Yumi. She made noises of disgust as he took out his stitches, but she watched carefully, and she dabbed with alcohol just in case.

"You can be a security guard," she said. "If you really don't have a black mark from the prefecture, you might open your own practice hall someday."

"I was thinking the same thing," he said. "As long

as I don't make trouble on the way out, they don't seem to care what I do."

She traced his strange new scars with a cotton swab. The alcohol dried in seconds, leaving behind the unreadable characters written in human flesh. "I doubt you'll go long without making trouble," she said.

Later, he found her sobbing quietly at the kitchen sink. "I don't know what I expected," she said. "I think I expected that everything would be different if we found out what really happened. I hoped I wouldn't feel the grief anymore."

He slid to the kitchen floor with his back to the cabinet doors, holding her calf.

"I think I expected that Kenji would come back," she said. "I almost thought that once you killed it, our boy would pop out of its stomach. Like a fairy tale."

He rubbed her leg as she cried. He didn't tell her that everything was going to be all right. He was tired of lying to her and to himself.

They brooded the rest of the day. After dinner, he pretended to read the newspaper and enjoy his beer, but he wasn't fooling either of them. When the news came on, she slapped him excitedly as she turned up the volume. "Look, there's your priest!"

Village patrolmen Kikuchi and Inoue led Suzuki from his temple. The newsreader said Suzuki was being evicted for simple nonpayment of taxes and utilities, but that he was under arrest for fiscal malfeasance and "squatting," a term Takuda hadn't heard in official use in years. Suzuki was leaving with only what he could carry: scrolls in cardboard cylinders, a vase, and an old cardboard accordion folder bursting at the seams. He carried one cardboard cylinder for an extra-wide scroll, a cylinder just about the right length to conceal a laundry-pole sword.

Clever priest.

"How did you know that was him?" Takuda asked.

"He's so tall! Look at that! That patrolman barely comes to his shoulder."

The newsreader said there was an ongoing investigation into Suzuki's responsibility for the destruction of a shrine and of historically significant human remains. He was also under investigation for the recent chemical discharge into the spillway running under the Zenkoku Fiber plant, but police had been unable to prove that he had ever entered the plant itself.

"Your friend is in trouble there. Will they hold him?"

Takuda laughed. "They just want him out of the Naga River valley. That's the only reason it's on TV. They want us to see him. We'll go get him tomorrow."

"Where will he go? Will his congregants take him in?"

"I don't think there are any."

"Well, for now, I'll stitch up some extra-long bedding for the second bedroom. He can sleep in there if he can stretch out diagonally."

"Are you sure? He's clumsy and impractical. He eats like a horse."

"He saved your life and avenged Kenji. He can eat what he likes."

The next day, Mori and Takuda went to Naga River valley to pick up Suzuki. The skin around Mori's nose and mouth was still peeling from the gas and the subsequent treatment. He wore jeans, flip-flops, a United Future Organization tee shirt, and the beginnings of a goatee.

"I didn't have you pegged as a jazz fan, Mori."

"It makes the girls think I'm smart."

Mori's ancient, rust-red Suzuki Fronte screeched up the inclines toward the Naga River valley while the tinny alarm announced that they were straining the three-cylinder, two-stroke engine. Mori and Takuda kept the windows open and shouted over the racket.

"We're going to have to find work," Mori said. "I can do whatever I need to. The priest can probably teach at a cram school."

"Probably not," Takuda said. "The other night, he said he would try to make a living as a priest. At least there's no one left in his own order to excommunicate him."

Takuda was glad he had relaxed for a few days. All he had to do was get into the car with Mori, and a whole new set of questions came up. He was still wrestling with the answers to the old questions.

"You know we were set up," Takuda said. "That's how you two got into the holding tank so easily."

"There was no one there. No one," Mori said. "We

walked right through at the front desk, and there was no one at reception. We walked down to Ogawa's floor. The wastewater management office was empty. The hatch to the holding tank gantry was propped open with a cinder block."

"A cinder block? That's a restricted area. Didn't it strike you as odd?"

"My sense of what is odd has shifted a great deal lately. Really, it makes sense if Zenkoku used us." Mori tugged at the goatee. It didn't suit him, Takuda thought. It just gave focus to his nervous energy.

"It makes sense because Zenkoku used us to clean up the valley." Takuda closed his eyes in the spring sunshine. "I can't wait to see this valley we've cleaned up."

In Oku Village, the storefronts were still empty, but the shopping street seemed brighter, more welcoming. Old women in spring kimonos stumped along in pairs. Children in school uniforms wandered idly as if surprised to find themselves on the street at all. The florist swept the sidewalk in front of his store. The greengrocer sat on a crate, sunning himself.

"It's better," Takuda said. "Can you tell?"

Mori nodded, looking back and forth as they approached the village police station.

Chief Nakamura and Sergeant Kuma stood at the station door. They stepped forward as Mori's tiny car pulled up, and then they stepped back as they recognized Mori and Takuda. The chief turned and went back into the station, and the sergeant pointed down the shopping street toward the Gotohs' dead end. His face was expressionless. Takuda was about to speak to him when Mori nudged him. Even a hundred meters away, they could make out Reverend Suzuki's white robes against the blackened ruin of the Gotoh house.

The police station door had slammed shut by the time Takuda looked back. The sergeant had probably locked it for good measure.

Suzuki was kneeling before the ashes of the Gotoh house when Mori and Takuda pulled up. His belongings were piled beside him.

"They just let me out about ten minutes ago," he said. "Good timing."

"Good timing is one word for it," Takuda said. "Somebody was watching. They were just waiting for us to come down the straightaway in Mori's car before they let you out. They want us all gone."

Mori kicked a chunk of heat-shattered pavement past the police barrier and into the charred shell of the house. "Was this arson or suicide?"

"I don't know. I watched from the holding cell window. There was an explosion, and flames were shooting through the eaves before the first siren. The fire must have started upstairs."

Takuda imagined old Gotoh pulling his withered body toward the kerosene heater. "We'll probably never know," he said.

Suzuki's silk sash was gray with silt from the spillway, but he draped it over himself anyway. "The sash is the only thing that doesn't stink," he said. "It's a kind of miracle. Everything else went into the trash."

"You two will have to get new scabbards and fittings for your swords," Takuda said. "Everything will stink, everything but the steel itself."

"Maybe even the steel," Mori said.

"Stay here," Takuda said. "I'll pray for the Gotohs at their tomb after I pray for my family."

"The Gotohs have a tomb here? Miyoko Gotoh never mentioned it. I assumed they would have a shrine burial somewhere. I'll join you and pray at their tomb, as well."

"You two know what they did," Mori said. "They're responsible for hundreds of murders. Hundreds. Including your father, Priest."

Suzuki wrapped his beads around his fingers. "I know that. I'll chant now. Are you going to piss again? I'm downhill from you. Warn me if you're going to piss again."

Takuda left them to it. The gravel path leading past Gotoh's house was sodden from the fire hoses and blackened with soot. At the end of the path, the cemetery lay still beneath the towering cedars. The few remaining tombs stood like sentinels. To his right, stacks of toppled stones squatted like toads.

Takuda walked past the Gotoh tomb. The tombstone lay toppled in a trench dug by its own weight. The base held a stump of shattered granite. The stump was rotten with moss and slick with veins of black fungus as if moisture and decay had seeped into the stone for generations.

A solitary figure stepped out onto the cleared path. Takuda walked under the silent trees to meet whoever awaited him at his family tomb.

CHAPTER 39

Endo, the Zenkoku corporate lawyer, stood between Takuda and his family tomb. He was larger and squarer than Takuda remembered, and his suit was even finer. Even in this twilight under the trees, it shone as sleek and iridescent as a crow's feathers.

"An immaculate tomb, standing in the place of honor," Endo said. "The contrast of the polished black granite and the gold leaf is very striking."

"You might have an abstract appreciation of Buddhist tombs, but you are clearly not familiar with the rites," Takuda said. "You're burning the wrong kind of incense. You might as well burn a mosquito coil for my family."

Endo smiled and bowed. "I beg your pardon. I wanted a word with you, Detective, and I simply wanted to show my respects in the meantime."

"I'm not a detective anymore."

"We shall have to come up with a title for you." He produced a thick envelope from inside his jacket. "Please accept this as an initial token of our appreciation."

The whole right side of Takuda's body tensed to strike the envelope from Endo's hands, but he didn't move. Endo was in a perfectly polite pose, offering the envelope with just the right angle of bow, arms outstretched just so.

Takuda returned the bow. "I must decline, but I would like to know what this payment is for."

"This is a nontaxable reparation for moving your family tomb to a similar plot on the grounds of Shofuku Temple, a very tranquil spot on your wife's way home from work. This reparation is separate from all other expenses, of course. It's all taken care of."

"We refuse."

"Acceptance is irrelevant. The trucks are on their way. You would need an injunction to stop the move. You see, you're the last living relative of any family represented here."

Takuda looked around. The plot was only large enough for a dozen houses, even if anyone wanted to build in the Naga River valley. "Why do you want the cemetery? Why does Zenkoku care?"

"Thanks to you, Zenkoku is free to diversify its interests in this little valley. We'll rebuild the Shrine of the Returning Apprentice right here. Call it a thank-you gift."

"Are you closing the plant?"

"Closing? Of course not. The people of the Naga River valley have been very cooperative for generations. No, Zenkoku General can make itself quite at home here. Of course, we need to upgrade and expand operations in this valley. Initially, we will scale back to monitoring and mothballing the current plant, but even that will require staffing increases."

"Mothballing is a good idea. You kept losing employees down in that holding tank."

"No one is reported missing."

"How did you cover that up? Transfers? Relocations in the middle of the night?"

"Any discussion of personnel allocations would require a formal query to Human Resources. Human Resources in the Tokyo office, actually. Special Requests Section. I believe there's an array of specialized request forms from which petitioners may choose. In person. Good luck with all that."

"Chief Nakamura doesn't know you're expanding operations in the valley, does he?"

"I cannot speculate as to what Chief Nakamura knows. He seems preoccupied with keeping his job after the escape of the suspected pedophile and kidnapper Ogawa though everyone else seems to have forgotten it."

"Ah. How is Ogawa, anyway?"

"I wouldn't know. I suppose he's trying to find his wife. She seems to have eluded him altogether. Once that romantic entanglement is resolved, I hope he comes back to me. He is a very resilient and resourceful man, a highly integrated individual."

"You knew all along that he was feeding the Kappa. How did you make that happen?"

"Make that happen? It would be difficult to overstate his enthusiasm for the project."

Takuda nodded. "But your enthusiasm waned."

"The creature was of very limited usefulness. It couldn't even tell us how to find its mother."

"You had Ogawa fired so the Kappa would have to hunt outside the plant. So Ogawa would be caught. So someone would come to eliminate the Kappa."

Endo beamed. "We are grateful beyond words that you answered the call of duty."

"You couldn't do it yourself."

"There are certain rules that must be observed." Endo laid the envelope on the base of Takuda's family tomb. When Takuda lunged forward and slapped it onto the ground, Endo didn't flinch or waver. He retrieved the envelope and bowed so low that Takuda had to step back.

"Again, acceptance is irrelevant. That sum will find its way into your hands. That sum and much more. By the way, this was in the depths of the plant," Endo said. He held out a plastic bag.

Takuda stepped back from the plastic bag, from the greenish disc within, from the fingers that encircled it. He was suddenly unwilling to touch the counselor, or to allow the counselor to touch him.

Two figures blocked the small spot of sunlight at the cemetery entrance. Mori and Suzuki stepped into the cemetery and started down the path. When they saw Takuda, they paused for a step. When Mori spotted Endo, he began to run. Even Suzuki's long legs didn't let him catch up.

"Here they come," Endo said. "You know they'll only hurt themselves, don't you?"

"You make your own choices. You can choose to leave them alone."

Endo smiled. He turned his back on Mori and Suzuki as they ran up. "So nice to see all three of you together again."

Mori looked from Takuda to Endo. "Is there a problem here?" He flashed a look of anger when Suzuki grasped his forearm and pulled him farther from Endo.

"No need to pull the man's arm off, Reverend Suzuki." Endo had been looking the other way. He stepped away from the tomb, and they fanned out to form a triangle around him. He tossed the plastic bag at Takuda's feet. "Really, no reason to be afraid. I'm just a lawyer with a souvenir of your adventures. Isn't that right, Reverend Suzuki?"

"I thought you were a land speculator."

Endo smiled as if to himself. "I'm honored to represent the Zenkoku group in the purchase of your debts from the bank and the revocation of your heretical sect's lease on Zenkoku Development property. It will make a fine management retreat. Scenic reservoir location, plenty of floor space. Perhaps I will dedicate it to my mother."

"You don't have a mother," Suzuki said. "What are you?"

"I would ask in return what you are." He turned to include Takuda. "What are any of you?"

They looked at each other. Endo laughed. "Whatever you are, we will all meet again when your services are needed."

Mori fell back to stand beside Suzuki as Endo walked toward the entrance.

"We might see you sooner than that," Suzuki said.

Endo cocked his head at Suzuki.

"There's not a sword for you, is there? What's the object for you? A sutra to nail to your forehead? A clay jar to bury you in? An iron pot to boil you in? What sort of object will we need for you?"

Endo said quietly, "The object for me right now is a big, shiny automobile, and it's going take me away from this stinking little valley. If you're such an expert on objects, explain that." He nodded toward the plastic bag in the dirt. "Explain that to these other two, if you can. I'll find you when I need you." He sauntered out of the cemetery, apparently enjoying the spring air.

They crowded around the plastic bag lying in the cedar needles. Within the bag lay an oval hilt guard from a Japanese sword. It was bright green with corrosion.

"That's your hilt guard," Mori said to Takuda. "Why is it green?"

"Chloramine and something else," Suzuki said. He knelt beside the bag. "Something ate away the lacquer that covered up the design. Look."

The hilt guard was cast with an intricate pattern of overlapping concentric rings, like ripples in still water. "That was the water sword, the one made for the water monster. The Drowning God." Suzuki handed the plastic bag to Takuda. "The designs on the other swords are probably different, but the lacquer is so thick I never noticed."

Takuda slipped the guard out of the plastic and laid it carefully on the base of his family tomb. Mori and Suzuki paid their respects at the tomb. Takuda was afraid Suzuki would turn it into a big production, but he just recited a single section of the sutra, as he did at the ruined Gotoh tomb.

"We're done here," Takuda said. He let out a sigh, breathing easily for the first time in what felt like years.

As if they had been waiting for the sigh, an earth-mover crashed through the bamboo and cedar near the entrance of the cemetery. A pickup truck squeezed between the entrance pillars, a small phalanx of work-men walking in its wake.

"What are they doing?" Mori said.

"They're going to move my family tomb down to the city," Takuda answered. "I won't stop them."

"Well, then, we really are done here," said Suzuki. He strode down the gravel path toward the workers.

He called over his shoulder, "Let's get my things and load up your car. I think I'll have to sit sideways all the way. It's not really built for my height."

"Let's get some noodles before we start," Takuda said, as he and Mori started after Suzuki. "We don't want to be trapped in your car with the hungry priest."

Mori forgot himself and grinned a broad, boyish, grin. He, Takuda, and Suzuki made their way out of the cemetery. They left the village and the valley for the very last time.

CHAPTER 40

Hanako Kawaguchi stepped out of dark water. She
hadn't been anywhere near the canal since the rotten-
fish man had tried to take her, but the water had com-
pelled her to enter. She climbed up the bank toward
the fence. Beside the fence was a claw hammer. She
could use it to tear down the fence so she could get to
the shopping street. When she picked it up, though, it
would not keep its shape. It was not a hammer at all. It
was something like an eel pretending to be a hammer.
She hated eels. She dropped it.

At the fence stood a man who was not a man. He
was made of eels squirming all over each other in the
shape of a man. His shiny black suit held him together.
He lifted the chain link easily, like a volleyball net, and
she stepped through. She walked quickly because he
wanted her to hurry. She didn't look back at him. He

wanted her to pretend he was really a man, and that's what she would tell everyone on the shopping street.

The fingers that touched the eel-hammer were eels now, even though they didn't look like eels. The eel-man wanted that hand for himself, and now it was his, but if she was a good girl and let that eel-hand do what he wanted, he would leave the rest of her alone.

Secretly, she was going to go home and tell her mother about the eel-man. Maybe her mother could change the hand back.

When she got to the shopping street, there was no one. The buildings were all flat and gray like cardboard. When she turned to go home, the eel-man was in front of her. He pointed to her hand, and it shot up to her mouth. The eel-fingers were swimming into her nose and up into her head, and she couldn't breathe. She gagged on the eels, and then there were more, and then some turned around to come out her ears and eyes . . .

Hanako woke choking and coughing, and her dream of the canal and the abandoned shopping street faded in her own little room. She had the special room, the little four-and-a-half-mat room, and it was very, very cute. Even waking from a nightmare to a nasty coughing fit was okay in her cute room.

She heard her parents' door slide open.

"Mama?"

Her mother knelt by her side. "It's late, little one. Do you need more special tea?"

Hanako shook her head. The medicine was worse than the cold.

Her mother sat cross-legged, like a man. "Well, come here, then. Sit with me."

She crawled up into her mother's lap.

"Hanako," her mother said, "why did you go into the canal? What were you thinking of? Everyone knows the canals are dangerous."

"Everyone knows they aren't so dangerous anymore," Hanako said, but she admitted, "I really don't know why I went in. I don't remember anything about it. It's like a dream. I just dreamed I went in again . . ."

"A fever dream," her mother said. She felt Hanako's forehead. "At least you're not as hot. You were burning up this afternoon! I hope that teaches you about going into freezing water like that."

Hanako was tired of being scolded about going into the water. She tried to change the subject. "Who was here earlier, Mama? I heard voices."

"It was a man from Papa's work," her mother said. "He came here to give us some good news. We're leaving this valley."

"Are we going back to the beach house? Will we live close to Grandma again?"

"No, it's not near anyone we know. We're moving away into another company house . . ."

"I liked the beach house!"

" . . . and you'll go to a very special school with very special teachers. The man from the company said you will have wonderful work someday, too."

Hanako looked at her hand. It was not squirming. It was a normal hand.

Her mother drew her close. She hugged her mother's neck, but over her mother's shoulder, she watched her own hand very carefully.

"I know you want to go back to the beach house, but we'll be even happier in our new house. It won't be in the mountain shadow, and it will be nice and dry and sunny. It will all be okay. Yes, it will."

Hanako's forefinger twitched, all on its own, then stayed raised a little, separate from the rest. *Yes, it will.*

"Don't you believe me, Hanako?"

The finger waited.

"Yes, I do," she said. She decided not to tell her mother about the eel-man in her dream. Ever. "I do believe you."

The finger relaxed. *Good girl.*

"Yes," Hanako said.

She would cut the finger off, but she would have to surprise it. Not tomorrow, not the next day, but someday. Maybe when slicing pickled radishes for dinner.

"I do believe it will all be okay," she said. "Yes, I do."

ACKNOWLEDGMENTS

Thanks to Thao Le of the Sandra Dijkstra Literary Agency for her energy and enthusiasm, and thanks to Kelly O'Connor of Harper Voyager for bringing out the best in this story.

Special thanks to Gordon Gaar, Zakariah Johnson, Elizabeth Kendley, George D. Kendley, Alison Schemmer, Leslie Sperry, and Tate Reece.

ABOUT THE AUTHOR

JAMES KENDLEY is the author of *The Drowning God* and has written and edited professionally for more than thirty years, first as a newspaper reporter and editor, then as a copy editor and translator in Japan (where he taught for eight years at private colleges and universities), and currently as an educational software content wrangler living in northern Virginia.

www.kendley.com

Discover great authors, exclusive offers, and more at hc.com.